Praise for the first Gilded Age Mystery
Still Life with Murder

"What a thoroughly charming book! A beautiful combination of entertaining characters, minute historical research, and a powerful evocation of time and place. I'm very glad there will be more to come."
—*New York Times* bestselling author Barbara Hambly

"Utterly absorbing. Vividly alive characters in a setting so clearly portrayed that one could step right into it. I look forward to many more."
—Roberta Gellis

"*Still Life with Murder* is a skillfully written story of intrigue and murder. Nell Sweeney is a winning heroine gifted with common sense, grit and an underlying poignancy. Readers will speed through this tale and be clamoring for more."
—Earlene Fowler,
bestselling author of *Broken Dishes*

"P. B. Ryan captures an authentic flavor of post Civil War Boston as she explores that city's dark underbelly and the lingering after-effects of the war. The atmosphere is that of *The Alienist,* but feisty Irish nursemaid Nell Sweeney is a more likeable protagonist. I look forward to seeing her in action again."
—Rhys Bowen, author of *Evan's Gate*

"P. B. Ryan makes a stunning debut with *Still Life with Murder* bringing nineteenth-century Boston alive, and populating it with a vivid and memorable cast of characters. The fascinating heroine, Nell Sweeney, immediately engages the reader and I couldn't put the book down until I discovered the truth along with her. I can't wait for the next installment."
—Victoria Thompson,
author of *Murder On Mulberry Street*

"Spunky . . . Readers will admire [Nell] and won't be able to resist her many charms. *Still Life with Murder* is a well-constructed and fascinating mystery in what looks to be a great series."
—*Midwest Book Review*

DEATH ON
BEACON HILL

P. B. RYAN

BERKLEY PRIME CRIME, NEW YORK

THE BERKLEY PUBLISHING GROUP
Published by the Penguin Group
Penguin Group (USA) Inc.
375 Hudson Street, New York, New York 10014, USA
Penguin Group (Canada), 10 Alcorn Avenue, Toronto, Ontario M4V 3B2, Canada
(a division of Pearson Penguin Canada Inc.)
Penguin Books Ltd., 80 Strand, London WC2R 0RL, England
Penguin Group Ireland, 25 St. Stephen's Green, Dublin 2, Ireland
(a division of Penguin Books Ltd.)
Penguin Group (Australia), 250 Camberwell Road, Camberwell, Victoria 3124, Australia
(a division of Pearson Australia Group Pty. Ltd.)
Penguin Books India Pvt. Ltd., 11 Community Centre, Panchsheel Park, New Delhi—110 017, India
Penguin Group (NZ), Cnr. Airborne and Rosedale Roads, Albany, Auckland 1310, New Zealand
(a division of Pearson New Zealand Ltd.)
Penguin Books (South Africa) (Pty.) Ltd., 24 Sturdee Avenue, Rosebank, Johannesburg 2196,
South Africa

Penguin Books Ltd., Registered Offices: 80 Strand, London WC2R 0RL, England

This is a work of fiction. Names, characters, places, and incidents either are the product of the author's imagination or are used fictitiously, and any resemblance to actual persons, living or dead, business establishments, events, or locales is entirely coincidental.

DEATH ON BEACON HILL

A Berkley Prime Crime Book / published by arrangement with the author

PRINTING HISTORY
Berkley Prime Crime mass-market edition / March 2005

Copyright © 2005 by Patricia Ryan.
Cover design by Rita Frangie.
Cover art by Mary Ann Lasher.
Interior text design by Kristin del Rosario.

ISBN: 0-425-20157-0

BERKLEY PRIME CRIME®
Berkley Prime Crime Books are published by The Berkley Publishing Group,
a division of Penguin Group (USA) Inc.,
375 Hudson Street, New York, New York 10014.
BERKLEY PRIME CRIME is a registered trademark of Penguin Group (USA) Inc.
The Berkley Prime Crime design is a trademark belonging to Penguin Group (USA) Inc.

PRINTED IN THE UNITED STATES OF AMERICA

10 9 8 7 6 5 4 3 2 1

For Morgan,
who's everything a mother could ever want in a daughter.
It's been awesome sharing the past two decades with you.

In tremendous extremities human souls
are like drowning men; well enough they
know they are in peril; well enough
they know the causes of that peril;
nevertheless, the sea is the sea, and
these drowning men do drown.

HERMAN MELVILLE

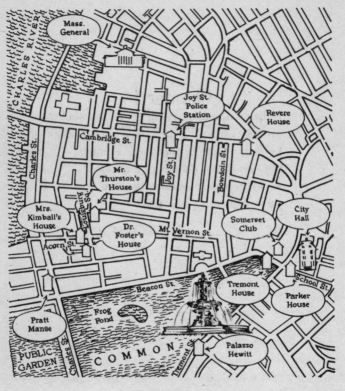

Beacon Hill

& Vicinity

N.S. 1869

Chapter 1

June 1869: Boston

THE first thing that struck Nell Sweeney about that morning's *Daily Advertiser,* even before the front page headline in inch-high type, was the illustration that accompanied it. It was a portrait in three-quarter profile, deftly inked, of a lady of dark and arresting beauty: feral eyes, audacious cheekbones, and rouged lips slightly parted to bare the edges of her teeth. Diamonds encircled her throat and her great, gleaming torrent of loose hair. She gripped a dagger the size of a butcher knife with both hands.

The caption read THE LATE MRS. KIMBALL AS LADY MACBETH.

Late? Taking a seat at the kitchen table—a slab of age-scarred pine that, when required, could seat all twenty of the Hewitt family's servants at once—Nell set down her coffee cup and unfolded the newspaper.

FOUL MURDER ON BEACON HILL

'Life's Drama' Draws to a Tragic Close

FOR

MRS. VIRGINIA KIMBALL

Actress Found Shot to Death in Her Home

A THRILL OF HORROR RUNS
THROUGH BOSTON

"You reading about that actress that got killed?" Peter, one of the Hewitts' two young blue-liveried footmen, looked up from across the table, where he was working his way through a breakfast of cold ham, creamed chicken hash, and scones.

Nell held a finger to her lips and shot a glance toward the huge cookstove across the room, where little Gracie Hewitt stood on a step stool to stir a pot of porridge under the supervision of Mrs. Waters, the Hewitts' cook. The old bird had pitched a fit the first time Nell brought the child down to the kitchen before dawn to see how the breakfasts that were delivered to her nursery every morning were actually prepared. Family members didn't mix with the household staff, and they certainly didn't partake in household chores. It was only when Viola Hewitt herself intervened, decreeing that Gracie should be taught whatever Nell, as her governess, deemed appropriate, that Mrs. Waters had grudgingly relented.

"That child is having far too much fun to pay us any mind." Peter nodded toward the picture of Virginia Kimball. "You ever see her onstage?"

Nell shook her head as she contemplated the little line drawing. "I think she's . . . I think she *was* retired."

"I saw her in *Romeo and Juliet* when I was just a kid—not a regular performance, just a rehearsal, but they were wearing their costumes. Me and my cousin Liam, we sneaked into the Boston Theatre one afternoon and hid up in the dress circle, just to catch a glimpse of her in the flesh. We used to see her picture on playbills and the like. She was even more beautiful in person, if you can believe it, and she wasn't any young chickabiddy back then. She must have been . . . Let's see, this was the summer I turned eleven, so it was back in fifty-six, and the paper said she was forty-eight when she died, so . . ." His brow furrowed as he chewed over the math.

"She would have been thirty-five." The artist who'd drawn Mrs. Kimball had captured a snap of electricity in her eyes . . . half madwoman, half seductress.

"About halfway through the rehearsal," Peter continued, "I saw a little flicker of light in one of the boxes, like a match being struck. They've got these real fancy boxes with red velvet curtains, three levels of them, right there on the front part of the stage."

"Proscenium boxes," Nell said. They were the most luxurious boxes in the largest and most opulent theater in the city, maybe even in the whole country. The top box on stage right was under subscription by the Hewitts.

"He'd lit a cigarette, the fella sitting in the box," Peter said. "It was dark in there, but I could see his face every time he took a puff." He grinned as he dunked a chunk of scone into his milky tea, a great shock of sandy hair falling into his eyes. "You'll never guess who it was."

"William Hewitt," Nell said.

Peter looked up at her. "How'd you know?"

"Someone once told me Will had had a—"

" 'Will,' is it?" Peter asked with a quizzical little quirk of his eyebrows.

" 'Dr. Hewitt,' I meant. His mother calls him Will, so . . ." Nell hoped the warmth rising up her throat wouldn't ignite into one of those scalding, telltale blushes, the bane of her existence. Thankfully, Peter was one of the few Hewitt retainers who actually considered her a friend; she mustn't let herself slip like that in front of the others.

She said, "Someone once told me that Dr. Hewitt had had a brief . . . flirtation with Mrs. Kimball." The eldest of the Hewitts' four sons, Will had indulged in a weakness for actresses during his visits home from England, where he'd been brought up and educated.

Peter chuckled as he cut a stack of ham slices into a pile of bite-sized pieces. "Looked like more than a 'flirtation' to me—on his part, at least. Looked to me like he was smitten but good. He had a bunch of white roses on the seat next to him—biggest bouquet I ever saw, a mountain of flowers. And the look on his face while he watched her down there on that stage—you could tell he had it bad."

"You knew who he was?" Nell asked. "You were just a boy. This was long before you came to work for the Hewitts, and back before the war, Dr. Hewitt only spent a few weeks out of every year in Boston. There were acquaintances of his parents who didn't even know he existed." Bizarre, considering the family's position in Boston society, but Will had always nurtured a contempt for that world, and avoided it during his school holidays. And he also had been at odds with the family patriarch, the venerable August Hewitt, since early childhood, hence his exile to England, where relatives had shunted the young firebrand from boarding school to boarding school, and finally to Oxford. It wasn't until he took his fate in his own hands, defying his father to study medicine at the University of Edinburgh, that he began to feel as if he had a place in the world, a role, a purpose. Then came the war, and all that changed.

"Oh, I didn't recognize him at the time," Peter said, "but he stuck in my memory, what with that shiny black hair and those fine clothes, and . . . I don't know. He had an air about him, the air of an older gentleman, a gentleman of the world, even though he couldn't have been much more than"—Peter shrugged as he forked up some hash—"mid-twenties?"

"He would have been twenty-one."

"I remember thinking he looked like a young prince, except for the cigarette. I'd only ever seen ruffians and laborers smoke them—men like my pa and his mates. So, between his looks and the cigarette—oh, and that limey accent—I didn't have any trouble recognizing him when I came to work here a few years later, even with him in his uniform."

Will had returned to the States when war was declared to offer his medical services to the Union Army. Of the other three Hewitt sons, the next eldest, Robbie, was the only one to volunteer. Harry, the third son and as selfish a lout as ever drew a breath, had made excuses to stay home, and Martin was simply too young.

Viola Hewitt had once shown Nell a photograph taken of her two eldest sons after their enlistment in the Fortieth

Massachusetts Mounted Infantry. Will and Robbie had
struck dashing figures in their blue, brass-buttoned frock
coats and slouch hats—especially the tall, angular Will,
who wore an officer's saber belted over a maroon sash, his
status as a battle surgeon having earned him the rank of
major. Robbie, who'd mustered in as a sergeant, had
achieved a captaincy by February of '64, when both brothers were captured at the Battle of Olustee and condemned
to the Confederacy's notorious Andersonville prison
camp—a hell on earth that claimed Robbie's life and left
Will grievously wounded, both in body and in soul.

"Miseeney, look!" Gracie clambered down from her
stool with a bowl in her chubby little hands, feet tangling
in her adult-sized apron as she scurried across the room.
"I made it. It has waisins and honey in it. Twy it!"

Nell ate the offered spoonful with a great show of relish. "Oh, that's really good, sweetie. That's some of the
best porridge I've ever had. You're turning into quite the
cook." She reinforced the compliment with a hug, whereupon the child returned to her stool by the stove and Nell
to her conversation.

"You noticed Dr. Hewitt's accent?" she said. "Did he
speak to you?"

Peter shook his head as he chewed. "Not to me—to
her, after the rehearsal was over and they were practicing
their curtain calls. He stood up and applauded and called
out to her. 'Brava, Mrs. Kimball, well done,' something
like that. Then he tossed the flowers down, and they
landed right at her feet. I thought she'd pick them up, but
she just smiled and said, 'I prefer orchids, Doc. A clever
boy like you might have found that out.'"

Nell winced, recalling what she'd been told about

Will's futile pursuit of Virginia Kimball—how there was an Italian count who'd bought her a house on Beacon Hill and the skeins of diamond necklaces that were her trademark. That hadn't stopped her from teasing and tormenting Will until the count was due for a visit, whereupon she'd told the smitten young surgeon to "run off like a good boy and quit pestering me."

Peter said, "The thing that surprised us, Liam and me, was that she had a little bit of a southern accent. When she was acting, she sounded real, you know, hoity-toity. Almost English, like. Anyway, she just left the roses where they were lying and swept offstage with her costume billowing and folks scrambling after her like a litter of puppies. And I thought, that fella might be a prince, but she's a queen—and she knows it."

"Yes, I imagine she did," Nell murmured as she turned her attention to the newspaper article.

> Mrs. Virginia Kimball, first lady of the Boston stage, has been wrenched from the world by an act of unspeakable violence. Yesterday at approximately 4 o'clock in the afternoon, Mr. Maximilian Thurston, a playwright of some note in this city, arrived at the Mt. Vernon St. home of Mrs. Kimball, his neighbor and longtime acquaintance, for the pot of tea which it was their daily custom to share at that hour. Upon knocking twice and receiving no answer, Mr. Thurston opened the door and called out, "Virginia! Are you home?" The fretful visitor searched the ground floor of the townhouse, and upon finding no one about, proceeded upstairs,

only to encounter a scene of the most gruesome and lamentable nature.

Mrs. Kimball lay in the open doorway of her bedroom, the bodice of her walking dress soaked with blood. On the floor nearby rested a Remington pocket pistol, which Mr. Thurston recognized as belonging to the actress. Although mortally wounded, she yet retained the spark of life, enough so to clasp Mr. Thurston's hand before expiring in his arms. He was to receive a second shock upon discovering, on the floor at the foot of Mrs. Kimball's bed, the lifeless body of her young maid, Fiona Gannon, who had been shot in the head.

Already there are many rumors afloat relative to this tragic affair, which is perhaps to be expected, given the notoriety of the deceased and the circumstances of her demise. One such rumor, the veracity of which has yet to be determined, is that Miss Gannon was found clutching a number of her late mistress's famous diamond necklaces. Parties have been dispatched by the authorities to the scene of the murder, and a coroner's inquest will be held this afternoon, which will doubtless shed further light upon this sad affair.

Mrs. Kimball had no known next of kin, the details of her life prior to her arrival in this city some twenty years past being shrouded in mystery. For this reason, her personal attorney, Mr. Orville Pratt of Pratt and Thorpe, has taken on the melancholic duty of making his late client's

final arrangements. Mrs. Kimball is to be in-
terred in Roxbury's Forest Hills Cemetery following private funeral services at the Arlington
Street Church tomorrow, the third of June, at 10
o'clock in the morning, the Reverend Dr. Ezra
Gannett to officiate. It is Mr. Pratt's intention to
mark the grave with a handsome tombstone. He
believes Mrs. Kimball to have been forty-eight
years old at the time of her passing, although
her precise age, like so many other details of
her life, will doubtless remain a matter of spec-
ulation for some time.

"They're burying her tomorrow?" Nell pushed the paper away from her, as if that would make it all less real,
less horrible. "A bit hasty, isn't it?"

"Maybe it's a Unitarian thing," Peter said as he wiped
up the last of his hash with a chunk of scone. "That's a
Unitarian church they're holding her funeral at."

All Nell knew about Unitarianism was that staunchly
devout August Hewitt was in the habit of accusing his
youngest son, Martin, a Harvard divinity student, of lean-
ings in that direction. So opposed was Mr. Hewitt to any
whiff of liberality in his Sunday services that he'd recently severed his relationship with King's Chapel,
which he and Viola had attended for some thirty-two
years, in favor of the resolutely Congregationalist Park
Street Church. His wife's continued allegiance to the
nominally Episcopalian King's Chapel, which he considered "secretly Unitarian," rankled him—it didn't look
right, he said, for a couple of their standing to attend different churches—but Viola Hewitt had always made her

own decisions, and that wasn't about to change any time soon. For Nell, who'd never been able to sort out the differences between the various Protestant denominations, the rift was perplexing at best.

"It just strikes me as a little unseemly to hold a funeral two days after the death," she said. "There's hardly any time to notify the people who knew her, let them know what happened and when the funeral will be held so they can pay their last respects."

A grunt of laughter drew Nell's attention to the service stairs, which Peter's fellow footman, the darker, heavier Dennis, was descending. "You really think anyone in this town would want to be seen paying their last respects to the likes of her?"

Following Dennis down the stairs was the parlormaid, Mary Agnes Dolan, busily tucking her great froth of red hair, wild as spun copper, into her white ruffled maid's cap. She and Dennis grabbed plates and set about filling them up at the cookstove.

Peter said, "Hey, Denny, weren't you finishing up your breakfast when I came down here half an hour ago?"

"I worked up an appetite between then and now." Dennis caught the eye of Mary Agnes, who smirked and nudged him with her shoulder.

Peter looked at Nell and then quickly lifted his teacup, ears reddening.

Dennis scooped up the newspaper and handed it to Mary Agnes as they sat side by side at the other end of the table. "That's the one I was telling you about," he said, pointing to the picture of Virginia Kimball as he speared a slice of ham with his knife and lifted it to his mouth.

"What did you mean about people not wanting to be seen at her funeral?" Nell asked.

Dennis chuckled as he tore off half the slice with his teeth. Chewing with a wide-open mouth, he said, "Let's just say I've heard some things that'd make a prissy little miss like you keel over in a dead faint."

"Rumors," Peter said.

Dennis rolled his eyes. "She was an *actress,* Pete. You know as well as I do what that means. A whore's a whore, and all the diamond necklaces in the world won't—"

"Watch your mouth in front of the lady," Peter warned.

Denny said, "The *lady* shouldn't ask a question if she can't handle the answer."

"You might at least mind what you say in front of Gracie," Nell said.

"What about *me*?" Mary Agnes demanded through a mouthful of hash, scowling petulantly when no one responded.

Dennis frowned at Gracie, still stirring her porridge with her back to them, blessedly oblivious to the conversation. "You ask me," he said, "the little by-blow's got no business being in this house, much less—"

"Denny!" Peter looked around anxiously. "What are you thinking, man?"

Nell leaned toward Dennis and said, in a voice strained with fury, "If Mrs. Hewitt were to find out what you just called that child, she would sack you on the spot, and without references." When Viola adopted the newborn Gracie five years ago, she made it clear to her household staff that the child was to be treated exactly as if she'd been born into the family. Any reference to her being the illegitimate child of a former chambermaid would be punished with dismissal.

"You gonna tattle on him?" Mary Agnes sneered.

"*I* will," Peter said, "next time it happens—so help me God, I will. You're pushing your luck, Denny."

"And you're wasting your time, Petey-boy, trying to impress that one." Dennis cocked his head toward Nell. "The likes of us ain't good enough for the high-reaching Miss Nell Sweeney, never mind we was all spawned out of the same slimy Irish bogs."

High-reaching. Highfalutin. Lace-curtain. Priggish. Stiff-rumped. Nell had heard them all, and then some.

Being a governess—that is to say, neither servant nor gentlewoman, but that most exotic of species, an independent working woman—was complicated enough, inasmuch as one never quite fit in, either with the household staff or the family. But being a governess who'd sprung from such humble roots, most having been born into the upper classes, meant that not only was she unique, she was uniquely reviled. The rank and file servants, most of them, anyway, resented the special treatment they felt she'd somehow finagled for herself. As for the nobs, well, there were exceptions, like Viola and Will, but the majority neither understood nor trusted her; some, such as August Hewitt and his son Harry, viewed her with outright suspicion, if not loathing.

In the Hewitts' household—indeed, in their entire world of Brahmin pomp and privilege—there was literally no one quite like Nell, no established niche for her in the caste system, no recognized rules of comportment, no *place*. On the one hand, it could be, and often was, a somewhat lonely existence. On the other, the lack of ready-made parameters left her free to establish her own, within certain limits, which she'd gotten awfully adept at stretching.

"Denny's right, Pete. You're wastin' your time." Mary Agnes darted a sly little glance in Nell's direction. "Her Highness has got her sights set on bigger game than you. You know who she's been makin' time with in the Public Garden every afternoon, don't you?"

Peter came to Nell's rescue while she was groping for a response. "You shouldn't be listening to idle talk, Mary Agnes—either of you, whether it's about Nell or Mrs. Kimball or anyone."

"Especially Mrs. Kimball," Nell said. "The lady was murdered, for pity's sake, and all you can do is gossip about her. Anyone's death should be greeted with respect, if not sadness. We all deserve that much."

"Brady sure seems to think so," Dennis said with a snicker.

"What do you mean?" Nell asked. Brady, the Hewitts' driver, had become, during Nell's five years with the family, almost like a father to her.

Dennis grinned as he stuffed half a scone into his mouth. "He was in here before, when I was having my breakfast—my other breakfast. I was trying to make conversation, but all he wanted to do was read the paper, which is how he is. All of a sudden, his mouth drops open and he kind of . . ." Dennis gasped and covered his mouth in illustration. "I asked him what was wrong, but he never pays me no mind. He just finished his reading. When he looked up, I swear to God he had tears in his eyes. A grown man—old as my pa, older maybe—and he's blubbering like a little girl. Never knew he was such a cow-baby."

"Where is he now?" Nell asked.

Dennis shrugged. "He left right after that. Said he had to go wash the brougham."

Nell looked from Dennis to Gracie—still stirring away industriously—to Peter. "Peter, do you think you could keep an eye on her for a few minutes while I—"

"Go," Peter said, shooing her up from the table and out the back door.

Chapter 2

NELL stepped outside to find the half-risen sun casting a sanguine luminescence over the backyard. It
was a small yard, absurdly so considering the size
and grandeur of "Palazzo Hewitt," as Will had dubbed the
Italianate mansion overlooking Boston Common. Viola
had planted a charmingly frowsy English-style garden on
the tiny patch of land. It was framed on either side by ivy-
covered trellises and in back by a sizable red-roofed Tus-
can cottage, which served as a carriage house or, more
accurately, a combination stable and carriage house. Half
of the ground floor was fitted out with horse stalls, while
the other half housed the Hewitts' fleet of coaches and
buggies. The sprawling second floor provided living quarters for Brady and most of the other male servants.

Nell hesitated before the iron-hinged double carriage
door, thinking it was unlike Brady to close it while he was

working inside, especially on a mild summer morning like this. She knocked, waited, and, receiving no response, knocked again. "Brady?"

Once, shortly after she'd first come to work for the Hewitts, Nell had addressed the amiable Irishman as "Mr. Brady." He'd laughed and said, "It's just Brady, miss— plain old Brady." She had no idea whether that was his first or last name. To this day, despite their close friendship, he insisted on addressing Nell as Miss Sweeney in deference to her station within the household.

She creaked open the door and entered the long, stone-walled carriage bay, which was utterly silent save for the rustling of her skirts. It was cool inside, and dim, the windows being few and small. Through the arched doorway to the right came muffled whinnies and the scents of horseflesh and hay. To the left stretched a shadowy double row of vehicles, with a corona of light at the very end. Squinting, Nell made out a lantern hanging from one of the far back rafters.

She walked toward the light, passing Mr. Hewitt's one-seat bachelor coupe, Viola's elegant little Victoria, Martin's Coal Box buggy, the pony wagonette that had been Gracie's Christmas present from Viola last year, a four-passenger bobsleigh for winter traveling, two nondescript gigs and a cart for the servants' use, and finally the gem of the collection, the family brougham.

The stately coach shone like black glass through a constellation of droplets, except for the oilcloth-draped driver's seat. Water dripped from its body and wheels, dissolving into the floor of packed earth; a bucket with a washrag slung over it stood on a bench in the corner. Brady, in shirtsleeves and a damp canvas apron, his back to Nell, stroked a chamois methodically over the vehicle, coaxing it to a high gloss as he dried it off.

Nell was about to say his name again when he stilled and wiped his eyes with his sleeve. Without turning around, he said, in a damply gruff, Irish-accented voice, "Go away, miss. I'm fine."

"Did you know her?" Nell asked softly.

He expelled a long, tremulous sigh. "She was my niece."

Stunned, Nell almost said, "Virginia Kimball was your niece?" when she realized her mistake. "The maid, you mean?"

"Fee Gannon. Fiona, but we called her Fee. My little sister's girl." He sniffed, straightened up, and resumed his polishing.

"Oh, Brady, I'm sorry." She came closer, rested a hand on his broad back.

He just kept on rubbing the chamois over the brougham, taking care to obliterate every trace of moisture from its surface.

Shot in the head, that was bad enough, Nell thought. But *Miss Gannon was found clutching a number of her late mistress's famous diamond necklaces.*

"Brady . . ." she began.

"She didn't do it." He met Nell's gaze over his shoulder, his customary good humor replaced by a rheumy-eyed anguish that made her heart contract in her chest. "She's a good lass." He turned back around and continued his work. "Was. She would never . . . She could never . . ." He banged his fist on the side window, muttered something under his breath, and squeaked the chamois over the glass to wipe away the mark. "They got it all wrong. It's *all wrong*. They didn't know her like I did. They don't know."

"I know."

"No you don't," Brady said as he spun to face her. It was the first time he'd ever raised his voice to her, and it stabbed something deep inside her, something that made her feel alarmed, uprooted. "You *can't* know because you didn't *know* her." His chin quivered, and tears spilled from his eyes. "You didn't—" The words died on a choking sob. He slumped against the brougham, the chamois fluttering to the floor, his big, work-roughened hands shielding his face.

Nell drew him into her arms, led him to the bench. "Sit. Sit, Brady."

He was crying in earnest now, amid muttered imprecations that she couldn't quite make out. She handed him her handkerchief. He covered his face with it and doubled over, great, hoarse sobs heaving out of him while she patted his back and made comforting noises.

The carriage bay grew brighter during the several minutes it took Brady to pull himself together. Sunlight streamed through the east-facing windows, gleaming off the brougham.

"I'll have to wash it again," Brady said in a shaky, sandy-wet voice as he wiped his nose with Nell's handkerchief. "It'll have spotted where I didn't wipe it down."

"That can wait." Nell tightened her arm around this man who'd been her bedrock, her salvation, so many times over the past five years. "Are you all right?"

Brady sighed, his elbows resting heavily on his knees. "She was my only kin, Fee was. My only kin over here.

The rest of 'em, they're still in the old country." He wadded up the sodden handkerchief, dabbed his eyes, then flattened it out, frowning at the elaborately embroidered monogram in the corner. "Oh, look what I've done to your pretty handkerchief. I remember when Mrs. Hewitt gave you these."

"Don't worry about it."

"I'll have it cleaned," he said as he folded it up into a neat square.

"I don't care about the handkerchief, Brady," Nell said. "I care about you. I feel so . . ." Helpless. Frightened. He *was* like her father—more of a father, certainly, than her real father had been. He'd always been there for her, rock-solid, cheerful, reliable. Every Sunday morning, before dawn, he drove her up to St. Stephen's in the North End for early mass. They'd take one of the little gigs so that they could sit next to each other and talk. He'd offer advice, tell her jokes . . . Sometimes he even sang to her—hymns or drinking songs, depending on his mood. To see him undone like this . . . It felt as if the very earth were sliding out from beneath her feet.

Nell said, "I remember you mentioning her." Brady rarely talked about himself, but he'd spoken with affection of "Fee," for whom he'd found a position in service when she was orphaned in her teens.

"I thought she worked for the Pratts," Nell said. Orville Pratt, one of the wealthiest and most powerful men in Boston, had a law practice with August Hewitt's closest friend, Leo Thorpe.

Brady nodded. "She started off with them. I got her hired on as a chambermaid when her parents passed on, back in sixty-three. Or rather, Mrs. Hewitt did, as a favor to me. She's a very great lady, Mrs. Hewitt, with a good heart. You don't find many like her up in them lofty ranks."

"That's for sure."

Brady drew in a shaky breath and let it out slowly. "Fee never did take to the Pratts. Said they demanded too much of her."

"In terms of the workload, or . . . ?"

"That, and how they expected her to conduct herself, even on her off hours."

"There's nothing unusual about that," Nell said, "especially for a family as prominent as that one."

Frowning at the floor, Brady scrubbed a hand over his jaw. "Aye, but it rankled Fee somethin' fierce. See, my sister and her husband, they had a more or less free and easy way about 'em. Fee didn't ever really learn to toe the mark. She wasn't a bad kid, mind you, she just didn't like havin' to pretend she was somethin' she wasn't."

Nell nodded noncommittally, all too aware of how it felt to play a role, and chagrined that this man to whom she'd grown so close had no idea who and what she'd really been in her earlier years. The only person who knew everything—the only person in Boston—was Will Hewitt.

"Fee hated service," Brady said. "She wanted to open a notions shop."

"Really?"

"Yeah, she was savin' her money for it, what little she made. They paid her a buck and a half a week. God knows how long it would have taken her, but she was real keen on the idea. She'd always loved fripperies and trifles and such. Ribbons and laces . . . gloves, parasols, bonnets . . . She aimed to sell yard goods, too, I think, and writing paper and the like. She used to go on and on about it, but I can't remember it all. I reckon I wasn't really listening, on account of I didn't think anything would ever come of it." He closed his eyes, rubbed his face.

"When did she start working for Virginia Kimball?" Nell asked.

Brady turned the damp handkerchief over and over in his hands. "Just three weeks ago. I met her sometimes at Pearson's on Sunday afternoons for a spot of tea. It was the first Sunday in May that she told me Mrs. Kimball had hired her away from the Pratts."

"As a chambermaid?" Nell asked.

"A maid of all work. There weren't no other servants, just her."

"Oh, dear."

"Yeah, I warned her what she was in for. I said if she thought the Pratts overworked her, just wait till she had to do it all. But she said it was worth it, on account of she'd get to do the work of a lady's maid, which was good experience for her notions shop, and also 'cause Mrs. Kimball was gonna pay her two dollars a week, so she figured she'd be gettin' the shop that much sooner. Oh, and she'd get her own bedroom. She'd always hated havin' to bunk in the Pratts' attic with all them other girls. I told her it wasn't worth it in the long run. I begged her to go back to the Pratts, if they'd have her. One of the daughters had helped her get the job with Mrs. Kimball, and—"

"One of the Pratt girls?" Nell asked. "Cecilia?"

"Nah, the other one, the one that spent all that time in Europe."

"Emily."

"Emily, that's right. I said maybe Miss Emily could put in a good word with her parents, and if that didn't work, I'd try to get Mrs. Hewitt to help, but Fee wouldn't hear of it." He shook his head, looking weary, grayish.

"It was that important to you?" Nell asked.

"It wasn't just the work she'd have to do, it was . . . who she'd be workin' for."

"An actress."

"It didn't sit well with me, Fee associatin' with that sort. I felt an obligation, don't you know, to my sister, to look after Fee and make sure she stayed on the straight and narrow. And now look what's happened." His voice started faltering. "She gets a bullet in the—" He pressed the handkerchief to his mouth, his eyes welling. "And they think she . . . they think she was a thief and a murderess. Forevermore, that's how she's gonna be known. Mother of God, how did things ever come to such a pass?"

Banding an arm around Brady again, Nell said, "There's going to be an inquest today. I'm sure if your niece is innocent of—"

"She *is* innocent. I told you she could never have done such a thing."

"Yes, I know. I misspoke." Trying, despite her doubts, to sound reassuring, she said, "The inquest jury will sort through the facts, and when they realize it wasn't an attempted robbery, they'll clear Fee's name."

"It's already been sullied right there on page one, underneath a headline a blind man could read. How are they ever gonna clear it? And why should they? To them, she was just some no-account Irish serving girl. You know what they think of us. You know the names they call us. We're vermin to them, foreign riffraff. It won't even occur to them to question Fee's guilt. You mark my words."

Nell didn't know how to respond to that, given that he was probably right.

Shaking his head, a truculent thrust to his jaw, Brady said, "In the twenty-some odd years I've lived in this city, nothing has changed for our kind. Seems like the more of us that come over, the worse it gets for us. The Board of Aldermen, the City Council, the constables, they're all out to keep us down. Sometimes I wonder why I didn't just stay in the old country."

"Because there was nothing to eat," she reminded him with a gentle pat on the back. "And you're wrong, actually. There are a few councilmen with Irish names, and at least one police detective that I know of."

"An Irish copper? Now I've heard everything."

"His name is Colin Cook," she said. "They hired him to police Fort Hill."

"Got a mick to keep the other micks in line, eh?"

"Exactly. He's been promoted, though. He works in the new Detectives' Bureau at City Hall now. He handles cases all over the city."

"A detective, no less." Brady turned toward her, a glimmer in his eye that made him look, for the first time that morning, almost like his old self. "How well do you know this fella?"

"Well enough to consider him a friend."

"A detective, that's not like a regular constable. They're the ones to look into robberies and killings and such."

"Yes, but Cook is only one of eight or ten detectives in that bureau. I'll be happy to speak to him for you—I gather that's what you're getting at—but he may not know much more than you or I. And there's no reason to think he could clear your niece's name."

"I'll clear it myself, but first I need to find out what really happened. This Cook, he'll have to know *something*."

Nell offered Brady as comforting a smile as she could muster. "I'll go to City Hall tonight and talk to him."

Brady's face fell. "You've got to wait till tonight?"

"I've got Gracie to take care of. Anyway, Detective Cook isn't there in the daytime. He works from four to midnight." She patted Brady's hand. "A few hours won't make any difference. In the meantime, try not to dwell on it too much."

He squeezed her hand, his eyes damp. "She looked a little like you. Not quite as pretty, I reckon, but pretty enough, with the same rusty-brown hair. You're a fine young lady, Miss Sweeney, an angel. You're doin' the good Lord's work, clearin' my Fee's name."

If she *could* clear it. How would Brady take it, Nell wondered, if it turned out Fiona Gannon was just as guilty as the *Daily Advertiser* had made her out to be?

Chapter 3

"WISH I could help you, Miss Sweeney, I surely
do," said Detective Cook that evening after
Nell had filled him in on the reason for her
visit. "But Chief Kurtz assigned that case to Charlie Skinner. I got nothin' to do with it."

Cook, leaning back in his chair with his feet on his
desk, held his palms up to underscore his point. He had gigantic hands, in perfect proportion to the rest of his hulk-
ing frame. He was a black Irishman who, like so many
others, had come to this country during The Hunger back
in the late forties. Colin Cook had a deep-chested voice
seasoned with just a hint of a brogue. Brady's accent was
much stronger, probably because he'd been an adult when
he left Ireland; Cook would have been but a youth. As for
Nell, she'd been only a year old, right before the famine.
Her speech bore no trace of the old country, and over the

past few years, it had acquired the cultivated intonations of the class in which she'd found her home.

Nell said, "I don't suppose you attended the inquest this afternoon."

"It was before my shift started, and if you think they pay me enough to come in during my off hours for cases that aren't mine . . ."

"Surely you must have heard something after you came to work this evening." Nell sat forward in her chair, gloved hands gripping the edge of his big, cluttered desk. "Isn't there some overlap in the shifts? This is an important case—the whole city's talking about it. You must have heard *something*."

"What I heard was that it was an open and shut case of robbery and murder by the maid." Grunting, the detective lowered his big feet to the floor and straightened his rumpled sack coat. "I know it's not what you want to hear, but that's how the inquest shook out."

Trying to master her disappointment, Nell asked, "Did Detective Skinner happen to share any of the details with you?"

Cook snorted as he reached for his teacup. "All Charlie Skinner ever shares with me is how he can't stand the sight of us uppity micks that steal good jobs from real Americans by playing the bootkisser to Chief Kurtz."

It was pretty much what the Hewitts' servants thought of her, Nell mused—that she'd somehow tricked Viola into hiring her for a position ludicrously far above her station. "Try as I might," Nell told the detective, "I can't imagine the likes of you puckering up to anybody's shoe-leather, even that of the chief of police."

Cook chuckled as he sipped his tea. "Sure you won't have some of this?"

She shook her head. "It would keep me from sleeping tonight." Though she'd probably lie awake, anyway, trying to figure out how to tell Brady that his dead niece had been officially branded a thief and murderess.

Cook said, "Skinner and his pals, which is to say just about every detective here, they won't so much as give me the time of day. Same goes for the rest of 'em in this office—the deputy chief, clerk, truant officers, superintendents . . . No, that's not true. The Superintendent of Pawnbrokers is all right—fella by the name of Ebenezer Shute. Him and me used to share a pint now and then, before I married Mrs. Cook and went off the drink. But I hardly ever see him anymore 'cause he works days."

"Chief Kurtz must think well of you," Nell said, "or you wouldn't be here."

"Sure, but don't you know that only makes the rest of 'em hate me more. Ah, the devil take 'em," he said as he lifted his teacup. "They'll get their comeuppance in the next life."

"Was Detective Skinner still here when you came to work this afternoon?" she asked.

"Yeah, for about an hour. His office is that one right next door." Cook nodded toward the wall to Nell's left, which was thoroughly papered over, even the door in the middle, by a patchwork of photographs, marked-up maps, leaflets, yellowed newspaper articles, and Wanted posters. "The walls here aren't as thick as they look," he said, "so voices travel through, which makes it hard to concentrate when Skinner's in there with somebody."

She sat up straighter. "You mean you can hear what's said in there?"

"Only if they're talking real loud, havin' a row, something like that. Otherwise it's too muffled to make out, but it's still damnably distracting."

"Did you notice if anyone came to see him this afternoon?" Nell asked.

"Sure. His office door's got a window on it, just like mine. When I first got here, he was in there with that law sharp that represented Mrs. Kimball."

"Orville Pratt?"

"Yeah, and when Skinner saw me pass by the door, he got up and shut the blinds, like he thought maybe I would have stood there and tried to read his lips. Rat-faced little mutt."

"Could you hear anything through the wall?"

"Nah, they were talkin' real low. For all I know, it was a perfectly legitimate meeting. Pratt *was* the victim's lawyer. But it did make me wonder, the way Skinner rushed to shut them blinds. If it was any other lawyer, maybe I wouldn't feel that way, but Orville Pratt always did rub me wrong. He's one of the richest men in Boston—in the whole country, probably—so you got to wonder why he chooses to practice law. You ask me, it's so he's got a good excuse to throw his weight around. God knows he loves doin' that."

"I know Mr. Pratt," Nell said. "He's a good friend of August Hewitt's. So is his law partner, Leo Thorpe."

"The alderman whose son . . . ?"

"That's right," Nell said gravely. She still couldn't think of Jack Thorpe without a stab of grief. "Jack was engaged to marry Mr. Pratt's daughter Cecilia when he died, you know."

"Oh, yeah, I remember now. It was supposed to be some sort of grand dynastic merger."

"Something like that. Poor Jack, he would have been miserable with her. She's the quintessential spoiled little Brahmin princess, and he was . . . well, he had his flaws, but he was a thoughtful person. He cared about things, about people." If he hadn't, he might still be alive. "He would have been better off with the older daughter, Emily. She's much more his type, but she was touring Europe at the time."

Cook said, "I heard something about Pratt's daughter and some German nobleman. That would be Emily, then?"

"No, that was Cecilia, and he's Austrian. Jack wasn't even cold when she took up with him. He has some sort of title, and about seven names—I can never remember any of them. He gave her the biggest, gaudiest sapphires you've ever seen when they first started keeping company. They announced their engagement at the Pratts' annual ball this past April"—she paused for effect—"exactly one year to the day from Jack's funeral."

Cook grimaced and shook his head. "Don't surprise me, knowing the father."

"The only people who declined the invitation were Mr. and Mrs. Thorpe. The Pratts' ball is always the highlight of the spring social season. Funny thing was, Cecilia called off the engagement the very next day. And guess who started courting her almost immediately?" Nell smiled in anticipation of Cook's reaction.

He cocked his head as if to ask, Who?

"Harry Hewitt."

"Good Lord," he exclaimed through incredulous laughter. "That spoiled, insufferable—"

"The same. It's a match made in heaven. The only thing they might ever argue about is who's prettier."

Cook chuckled and drained his tea, pondered the empty cup for a moment as if studying his tea leaves, then hauled himself out of his chair. "You sure I can't pour you some?" he asked as he circled his desk. "There's plenty in the pot, and it's good. I made it myself."

"No, I'm fine, thank you."

When the detective returned to his office from the reception area, he shut the door and, to Nell's bemusement, closed the blinds.

"Don't tell me there's a lip-reader out there," she said.

Cook's chair creaked as he settled his bulk into it. He took a thoughtful sip of tea and set down his cup. Raising his gaze to Nell, he said, "After Pratt left, Chief Kurtz went in there, and this time I could hear almost everything, 'cause Kurtz tends to roar when he's on the warpath."

"On the warpath? Against Skinner?"

"What I'm about to tell you," Cook said evenly, "you didn't hear none of it from me."

Nell raised her right hand as if taking an oath. "I'll swear on a Bible if it'll help," she said, appreciating Cook's willingness to talk. No doubt he was also motivated to some extent by Skinner's contempt for him and the miserable working conditions this created.

Leaning forward, elbows on his desk, Cook said, "Kurtz was all het up about some book of Virginia Kimball's that no one seems to be able to find."

"A book? What kind of book?"

Cook twitched his shoulders as he sat back and lifted his teacup. "They called it 'the Red Book.' It was somewhere in her house, or should have been. From what I could gather, Skinner had torn the place apart looking for it, or claimed he did. Kurtz seemed to think Skinner might have it and be holding on to it for some reason, but he swore it wasn't so. Kurtz asked him if the Red Book had anything to do with all the rich la-di-dahs that had been paradin' in and out of his office all morning."

"Did he mention any names?"

"A few. One was Maximilian Thurston, the playwright."

"He was a friend of hers," Nell said, recalling that morning's newspaper article. "He found the bodies, correct?"

"Yeah, Thurston was apparently waiting for Skinner when he showed up at work this morning. Then there was Horace Bacon . . ."

"The criminal court judge? I've met him." Nell had hand-delivered a sizable bribe to Judge Bacon a year and a half ago, on Viola's behalf, to encourage him to overturn another judge's denial of bail after Will was arrested for murder. The judge had accepted the fat envelope as if it were a routine part of his job. "Who else?" she asked.

"Weyland Swann, the banker. And Isaac Foster, Dr Isaac Foster—Harvard big shot." Cook rubbed his great boulder of a jaw. "I reckon that was it."

"And Chief Kurtz thought they were all coming to see Skinner about the Red Book?"

"Either that, or they were paying him off to wrap up the case all quick and tidy, with nobody calling them in and asking them any uncomfortable questions."

"Which implies some measure of guilt on their parts," she said. "Four men? All guilty? And then there was Orville Pratt this afternoon—he makes five."

"Like I said, Pratt may have been here on legal business," Cook said. "But as for them others, one thing you learn in this job is almost everybody's got *something* to hide."

Too true, thought Nell, who'd been no more forthcoming about her past with Cook than with Brady.

"Kurtz said he assumed Skinner's wallet was a good deal fatter after them fellas visited him than it'd been when he came to work this morning," Cook continued, "but that he should remember he's on the city's payroll, too."

"Did Skinner deny taking payoffs from those men?"

"Nah," Cook said. "He wouldn't have insulted Kurtz's intelligence—not to his face, anyway."

Nell bit back her opinion of police department graft. After all, Colin Cook held his hand out every now and again; it was the way of things.

"Kurtz told Skinner to find that book, and fast," Cook said. "Said he didn't want it falling into the wrong hands and complicating things. Ordered him to go back to Mrs. Kimball's house after work and search it again. Skinner said that wouldn't be possible, on account of Orville Pratt had hired a crew of day laborers to go over there tonight and get the place in shape—clean it up, haul out the bloody carpeting, scrub the viscera off the walls . . ."

"But it's a crime scene!"

"That's what Kurtz said, or yelled. I tell you, he was in a regular lather. Skinner said it didn't matter no more 'cause the case was solved, but Kurtz said it was too soon, and it didn't look right, and the department had a bad enough reputation already, and Skinner had no business allowing such a thing, especially with such a notorious case, and . . . well, he was pretty much ranting at the top of his lungs. He wanted to know why Pratt had ordered the cleanup in the first place."

"I wouldn't mind knowing that myself," Nell said.

"Skinner said Pratt told him he's the executor of Mrs. Kimball's estate, and he needs to sell the house as soon as possible so as to pay off her debts. Said he could hardly put it on the market like it is now, with all the blood and whatnot. Kurtz said Skinner seemed awfully eager to accommodate Pratt."

"What did Skinner say to that?"

"Said he thought Kurtz would have wanted the same thing, given that he and Pratt belong to the same club and move in the same circles."

Nell said, "All those silk stocking types belong to the same club and move in the same circles." It was a small and tight-knit world, that of Boston's elite. The men talked business and politics over roast beef and whiskey at the Somerset Club. The ladies supported such noble causes as the Massachusetts Historical Society and the Perkins Institution for the Blind. Their children courted, married, and produced new generations of elite Bostonians, almost always among their own kind.

"The argument seemed to impress Chief Kurtz," Cook said. "It was quiet in there for a minute, then Kurtz says, 'Ah hell, let him . . .' Beg your pardon."

"It's all right."

"He says to let Pratt go ahead and fix the place up, but he should wait a few days, just for appearances. And he said he still wanted Skinner to search the place one last time for that book. Told him to do it tonight, that Pratt would just have to reschedule his cleaning crew. And now"—Cook spread his hands wide—"I reckon you know as much as I do."

"I know that justice can be bought and sold in this city virtually right out in the open, and everyone just winks and goes about their business. I'm surprised they even went through the motions of holding an inquest."

"Didn't have any choice. It's required any time there's a violent or suspicious death. You can read all about it in tomorrow's paper. Reporters from the *Daily Advertiser* and the *Massachusetts Spy* sit in on all the inquests, and they're usually given duplicates of the clerk's transcript."

"Could I see the transcript for myself? I'd rather read what was really said rather than some reporter's interpretation of it."

"I don't have it," Cook said. "It's in Skinner's office, and I can't be seen letting you in there."

Glancing toward the door in the wall to the left, barely discernible beneath the clippings and maps tacked onto it, she said, "Can't we get in that way?"

Cook stared at the door for a moment. "I'd nearly forgotten that was there. I've never once used it. For all I know, it may be locked."

Nell rose and crossed to the door. She turned the knob, pushed it open, then smiled over her shoulder at Cook. "What do you know?"

The detective chuckled through his groan as he heaved himself up from his chair. "If anybody finds out you've been in there, I didn't have nothin' to do with it."

Skinner's office was unlit, but the window shades were raised, so there was enough moonlight to see by. The venetian blinds on the main door of Skinner's office were still closed, which was fortunate. Two large paste-board cartons, one marked V. KIMBALL and the other F. GANNON, sat on the floor against the wall that separated the two offices. A leather folder labeled V. KIMBALL HOMI-CIDE lay on top of the unnaturally neat desk, alongside a smallish, nickel-plated pistol and something tiny wrapped up in brown paper.

Nell unfolded the little paper packet and slid its contents—a spent lead ball—into the palm of her hand. It was hard to believe the squished little blob of lead, which felt much heavier than it looked, had once been a perfect sphere. She refolded the paper carefully around the slug and replaced it on the desk exactly where it had been.

Cook opened the folder and handed Nell the document on top—three pages inked with obvious haste by some poor fellow whose job it had been to record the gist of that afternoon's proceedings. She brought it over to Cook's office doorway so she could read it without straining her eyes.

CORONER'S INQUEST

A jury was impaneled 1:00 Wednesday afternoon, June 2, 1869, and witnesses were examined for the purpose of inquiring into the causes and circumstances attending the death of Mrs. Virginia Kimball.

Maximilian Thurston, sworn:

Was "intimate friend" of deceased w/whom he shared aft. tea daily. Knocked on her door at 4:00;

*entered house; found her just inside doorway of her
2nd floor bedroom, new hatbox and parasol next to
her, blood on chest, her own Remington pistol
inches from her right hand; pistol smelled of gunpowder; deceased kept it under pillow for protection, always fully loaded because she was a poor
shot. Blood bubbled in and out of wound as she
struggled to breathe. Mr. Thurston comforted deceased until she passed. In bedroom found body of
Fiona Gannon shot in head, lying on left side in
roughly east–west orientation; necklaces in hands;
open jewelry boxes on bed bench. Diamonds were
actually paste.* ~~Mrs. Kimball was visited the day before the murder by~~ *Mr. Thurston appeared greatly
distressed.*

Det. Charles Skinner, sworn:

*Summoned to home of deceased about half past
4:00. Two dead bodies, "a gruesome scene" much
as Mr. Thurston described it; bedroom window broken, otherwise nothing out of place except jewelry.
Thoroughly inspected the premises. Mrs. Kimball's
Remington, recently fired and missing three rounds,
was the only weapon in the house. Spent ball recovered from window frame; presumably a shot that
missed its mark. "Clear enough what happened."
Fiona Gannon shot Mrs. Kimball in the chest, after
which Mrs. Kimball, using the same gun, fired one
stray shot into the window and a second into Miss
Gannon's head.*

Samuel Watts, sworn:

Master gunsmith with 17 years' service as firearms expert to the Boston Police Department. Matched the spent ball "with utter certainty" to Mrs. Kimball's 5-shot .31 caliber Remington pocket pistol after test firing the 2 remaining rounds into wood and cotton wool. (Gun, recovered ball, and test balls displayed to jury.)

Orville Pratt, Esq., sworn:

Was att'y for deceased approx. 3 yrs. Her character above suspicion; she retired from the stage some 6 or 8 years ago. Fiona Gannon employed in his (Mr. Pratt's) home from Feb. 1863 until April now last past, when she went to work for deceased. Mr. Pratt "relieved to see her go" due to cheekiness and lack of steady habits; for same reasons was dismayed his client hired her.

Erastus W. Baldwin, Suffolk County Coroner, testified that post mortem examinations by a surgeon would yield no useful results, as cause of death in both instances "should be amply obvious even to a layman."

In the case of Virginia Kimball: Entry puncture wound consistent with gunshot in upper left quadrant of chest between 4th & 5th ribs, ball remaining inside deceased.

Opinion: This is a fatal injury.

As to Fiona Gannon: Gunshot wound to the head, the ball entering the right temple and remaining inside.

Opinion: This is a fatal injury.

At the conclusion of the evidence given by the last witness, and after a full and patient hearing, the jury terminated their labors by rendering the following verdict:

Boston, Massachusetts

County of Suffolk, June 2, 1869

"We, the undersigned, a Jury of Inquest summoned by the Suffolk County Coroner to inquire into the death of Mrs. Virginia Kimball, after hearing such testimony as has been submitted to us, find that said Virginia Kimball came to her death about 4:00 on the afternoon of Tuesday, June 1, 1869, at her home on Mt. Vernon Street, Boston, from the effect of a gunshot wound to the chest.

"The jury does further find that said gunshot wound was inflicted at the hands of Fiona Gannon, a maid. It is our conclusion that Mrs. Kimball arrived home to find Miss Gannon in her bedroom, engaged in an act of theft. Upon being challenged by Mrs. Kimball, Miss Gannon took Mrs. Kimball's .31 caliber Remington pocket pistol from beneath the pillow where she knew it to be kept, shot her employer once in the chest, and thinking her dead, set the gun down and continued about her business. Having not yet

*expired, Mrs. Kimball gained possession of the
weapon and fired twice at Miss Gannon, the first
shot lodging in the window frame, the second striking Miss Gannon in the left temple, thus killing her
instantly."*

*Cornelius Bingham, Phineas Ladd, Edward Acker-
man, Philip Sheridan, Davis Cavanaugh, Silas
Mead, and Lawrence Burke.*

Nell skimmed the coroner's testimony a second time.
"Autopsies weren't performed?"

Cook, reading over her shoulder, said, "It's the deci-
sion of whichever coroner's been assigned to that particular case. He can choose to call in a surgeon, or he can
just examine the body, or bodies, himself, and render his
own opinion. Even if he does order an autopsy, he might
not agree with the findings—it's his prerogative."

"But aren't the coroners all laymen?"

"That they are."

"A surgeon might have found something significant."

"Well . . ." Cook took the transcript from her and
leafed through it. "Perhaps in some cases. Much as I hate
to agree with a lout like Skinner, I'd have to say it's fairly
clear them two died from tradin' bullets. And the testimony of the witnesses seems to support that."

"Only because they were questioned on so few points.
It's absurd. They barely scratched the surface. I would
have tried to find out who Mrs. Kimball's friends and associates were, other than Mr. Thurston and Mr. Pratt. Did she
have lovers, enemies . . . ? Then there's the fact that she
hadn't acted in years, and her diamonds were imitation, so

presumably she sold the originals. Did she owe someone money? Did she have expensive habits? Opium, perhaps, or cards? Was she secretly destitute?"

"I hardly think that's likely," Cook said as he returned the transcript to the folder, "given that she'd gone shopping for hats and whatnot the very afternoon she died."

"Destitution never kept a female from buying hats," Nell said. "Not that kind of female." Pointing to the crossed-out bit from Maximilian Thurston's testimony— *Mrs. Kimball was visited the day before the murder by*— Nell asked, "Why do you suppose this was stricken?"

"Couldn't really say, seein' as how I wasn't there." Cook lifted the top off the v. KIMBALL box, peered inside, and withdrew a lady's ivory kid glove, which he sniffed. "Mrs. Kimball fired that gun, all right."

Nell approached him and took the glove, the palm of which was bloodstained. She sniffed, inhaling, along with leather and blood, the smoky tang of burned gunpowder. Even in the watery moonlight, she could detect a faint, grayish smudge on the back of the glove, emanating from between the thumb and index finger. She handed the glove back to Cook, who returned it to the box.

"That doesn't prove anything," she said. "If you ask me, that transcript is evidence of an appallingly slapdash inquest. I wouldn't be surprised if the coroner—what's his name, Baldwin?—if he'd been bribed to steer the jury toward the conclusion they reached. They're probably all in on the take—Baldwin, Detective Skinner, that firearms expert—"

"Sam Watts?" Cook shook his head resolutely. "I know Sam. He's a good sort, and honest to a fault. And there's not a soul on God's green earth who knows more about guns. If he says that slug was from Mrs. Kimball's Remington, it was from Mrs. Kimball's Remington."

"That's good enough for me," Nell said. "But as for Baldwin and Skinner, my guess is they orchestrated the whole thing together, in exchange for God knows how much money. Someone, or several someones, don't want this case investigated."

"It's not impossible," Cook conceded with a sigh as he rooted around in the box, "but I wouldn't jump to any conclusions. Could just be the inquest was slapdash 'cause that's how most of 'em are around here. Could be this case wouldn't have been properly investigated even if no one got paid off 'cause there's not a single detective on the Boston Police Force who really knows his way around a murder, and that includes yours truly."

Nell gaped at him, astounded that a police detective, especially one whom she respected so thoroughly, would confess to any measure of professional incompetence.

He reached into the box and lifted out a smart little blue bandeau hat trimmed with feathers, bows, silk orchids, and a dotted veil. "I bought something like this for Mrs. Cook for her birthday last year, but she said it was too fancy. Made me take it back and get a plainer one. I told her pretty ladies should wear pretty bonnets. She said it wasn't so much pretty as flashy."

"It sounds as if she's afflicted with good taste." Five years ago, when Nell had first started working for the Hewitts, she'd been both thrilled and disappointed by the wardrobe of custom-made frocks that Viola had bought for her. Thrilled because until then Nell had worn nothing but threadbare castoffs, disappointed because the dresses were so plain. Over the years, she'd come to appreciate their sleek elegance, but it had been an acquired appreciation.

"I do my best, Miss Sweeney," said Cook as he nestled the hat back in the carton, "I surely do. But the truth is us detectives all earned this job on account of how well we deal with thefts. When I was young, you heard about maybe one homicide a year in Boston, sometimes none. I came on the force in January of eighteen-sixty. You know how many people have been murdered in this city since then?"

Nell thought about it, but she couldn't begin to guess.

"Seventy." He pushed the lid back onto the carton and turned to face her, hands on hips. "Seventy homicides in the past nine years."

"My God!"

"Seventy-one counting Mrs. Kimball. When somebody gets killed in this city, it better be plain as day who done it, or it's probably gonna go unsolved. Investigating homicides is a complicated business, and there's nobody I know of who's got any real experience in it. What we do, what most big city cops do, is we offer rewards to the citizenry for providing information or turning in the guilty parties."

"Does that work?"

"Not often enough to suit me. I've been trying to convince Chief Kurtz that we need to get out there and dig and scratch, not just rely on snitches, most of whom are no better than the slamtrash they're ratting on. We need to figure out how to catch these murderin' scum, and then we need to hang 'em by the neck and let the good Lord worry about what to do with 'em after that."

"Do you think the Chief will take your advice?" she asked.

"Nah, the rest of 'em keep tellin' him I'm daft. Skinner, especially. He just thinks all we need to do is offer bigger rewards. Lazy muttonhead just doesn't want to have to do his job." Cook gestured her toward his office. "Looks like we're all done here."

Nell hesitated, eyeing the two cartons on the floor. "Those contain the clothes Mrs. Kimball and Miss Gannon were wearing when they died?"

"And whatever other personal effects they had on 'em." The detective crossed his arms and gave her a look that said he knew precisely what she was getting at. "And how do you suppose Skinner would take it if he found out I let some little miss—some little *Irish* miss—root about in his evidence?"

"He won't find out. I'll put everything back the way it was. Plus, it seems to me it's only evidence if it's going to be used in prosecuting a case, which it clearly isn't, since this case is considered solved and will never go to trial. And doesn't Skinner himself think the police should rely on citizens to solve the city's murders?" She spread her arms. "I'm a citizen, and I'm more than happy to help."

Cook carried the cartons into his own well lit office, setting them on the only section of floor not heaped with books, folders, and old newspapers. She knelt and uncovered the box marked V. KIMBALL, set aside the gloves and hat, and withdrew a small mesh reticule. It contained a folded handkerchief, a silver powder compact, a tiny enameled compact for rouge, a mother-of-pearl card case with several calling cards in it, and an embossed leather change purse, which was empty.

"Looks as if Skinner helped himself to whatever money was in here," she said.

"Maybe she'd spent it all on her shopping trip," suggested Cook as he sat perched on the edge of his desk, watching her. "Or maybe she didn't have any, and she'd been running up bills."

"Detective Skinner has her house key, I assume."

Cook nodded. "It's on this fancy silver key ring. I seen it sticking out of his vest pocket."

Next came two white lisle stockings, a pair of garters, lace-edged drawers, two petticoats, and a crumpled-up spring-steel crinoline. Nell drew in a steadying breath when she came upon the rest of Mrs. Kimball's wadded-up underpinnings—chemise, stays, and corset cover—all stiff with dried blood and punctured with one neat hole on the left side of the chest. The bodice of the fashionable blue-striped silk walking dress was in the same condition. At the bottom of the box, Nell found a fringed silk parasol, a pair of black satin boots with silver heels and appliquéd stars, and a tangle of diamond necklaces.

She lifted the necklaces, squinting at the glittering little stones. "These are paste?"

"Must be," Cook said. "I wouldn't know the difference, myself."

"Neither would I."

"Neither, I imagine, would Fiona Gannon."

Ignoring that observation, Nell opened the box labeled F. GANNON, which held a plain dress of black worsted, a white cotton apron speckled with blood, a rather shabby assortment of underpinnings, scuffed black lace-up boots, and, at the very bottom, the shredded and bloodied remains of a maid's ruffled mobcap. Nell lifted it gingerly by the bit that was still white and undamaged, the greater part of it being black with soot.

"Powder burns," Nell murmured as she studied it. "Very heavy powder burns. And it's been blown to ribbons."

Cook reached out to take it from her.

"You know what this means," she said.

He sighed as he inspected the ravaged cap.

"It means," Nell said, "that the muzzle of the gun that killed Fiona Gannon must have been—"

"Pressed right up against her head," Cook finished. "And where would a nice young lady like yourself have learned a thing like that?"

"From books," she lied, not wanting him to guess how familiar she'd once been with guns and knives—and the damage they could do. "Tell me I'm wrong," she challenged. "Tell me this shot could have been fired from a distance."

Cook glowered as he examined the cap.

"Baldwin didn't mention these powder burns in his statement at the inquest," Nell said. "If he had, it would have called the official theory into question."

Cook looked as if he was going to say something, but changed his mind. He crouched down next to Nell, returned the cap to the box, and started gathering up the other items. "Let's get this stuff packed back up just like it was, so Skinner won't know we were rummaging through it."

"You agree with me, don't you?" she persisted. "The inquest's conclusion is flawed."

"Even if it is, that doesn't mean Fiona Gannon was some innocent scapegoat. You want to think that because she was Irish and you're fond of her uncle, but in my experience, them that meet with bloody ends usually had it comin'."

"Her being Irish made it easier for Skinner and Baldwin to sell their version of events to the inquest jury," Nell said as she arranged the clothes in the carton the way she'd found them. "Fiona Gannon was just another thieving little Mulligan. A murderess, too, but at least Virginia Kimball saved the Commonwealth of Massachusetts the trouble of hanging her."

"If you're wantin' me to investigate this case," Cook said, "you can just drop that idea right now. It's Charlie Skinner's homicide, and as far as he and everybody else in this bureau is concerned, it's been solved. Never in a million years would Chief Kurtz let me conduct some sort of after-the-fact investigation, knowing how it would set Skinner off. And if you knew what my caseload was like right now, you'd know I don't have the time for the kind of work it'd take to set this business straight."

"If you did have the time," she asked as she replaced the lid on the carton, "what would you do?"

Cook stood, joints popping, and handed Nell to her feet. "I'd start off by goin' to Mrs. Kimball's funeral tomorrow. Murderers sometimes like to see their victim bein' sent off—not always, by any means. Not even most of the time. But it's a place to start."

"But it's a private funeral," she said. "Doesn't that mean only family and friends are welcome?"

"No one would question you if you just walked in like you belonged. Not that I'm suggesting it," he added with a wink, "you bein' a civilian and all."

"Oh, wait," she said. "I can't. Tomorrow's Thursday. I'll need to take care of Gracie."

"Didn't you once tell me they have a nanny to share the load?"

"Nurse Parrish is a million years old. She sleeps most of the afternoon."

"The funeral is in the morning."

"Will Detective Skinner be there?" she asked.

"He wasn't plannin' to go, but Kurtz is making him, just for show, on account of Mrs. Kimball being so famous and all."

Nell chuckled through a sigh. "I'll see what I can do."

"Interrogate the mourners, see if anything tickles your whiskers."

"Interrogate? At a funeral?"

"They won't know they're being interrogated if you do it right. Let them think they're making small talk. Ask a leading question, then keep your mouth shut. You'd be surprised what folks'll tell you just to fill in the gaps in a conversation."

Chapter 4

NELL'S first thought when she entered the Arlington Street Church shortly before ten the following morning was that she must have gotten the time of Virginia Kimball's funeral wrong. There weren't enough people here. No more than two dozen heads rose from the sea of pews stretching before her—hardly what one would expect at the funeral of such a notable person.

Then she noticed the sarcophagus in front of the altar. That was what it looked like from Nell's vantage point at the very rear of the huge sanctuary—a big, elaborately decorated burial chest such as she'd only ever seen in books about ancient Egypt. Adding to its peculiarity was the fact that it was painted white, a color normally reserved for the coffins of children.

A group of five, a gentleman and four ladies, brushed past her and proceeded up the long center aisle toward the front of the church. They all wore mourning black, as did Nell, whose simple dress with its modish, crinoline-inflated princess skirt was similar to those of three of the ladies. The fourth had on a garment that, viewed from behind, looked for all the world like the kind of loose, sash-tied wrapper that a lady might wear in the privacy of her bedroom. Nell had never seen anything like it in a public situation.

The group paused before the bizarre coffin and, one by one, stood with heads bowed. Nell recognized them when they turned to seat themselves in the very first pew: Orville Pratt with his stout little wife, his two pretty, fair-haired daughters, and an older lady Nell couldn't place. The oddly dressed one was Emily, recently home from her extended European tour. It stood to reason such a prominent attorney would attend the funeral of his late client, family in tow, if only for appearances. How would it look if he didn't, after extolling her character during yesterday's inquest, praise that had made its way into that morning's *Daily Advertiser*?

The front page article had summarized the inquest in terms that left no doubt as to the guilt of the "cunning and shiftless" Fiona Gannon, who had "schemed with an in-born craftiness" to gain possession of Virginia Kimball's celebrated diamond necklaces.

Brady had been more distraught than ever when Nell sought him out in his carriage house that morning. "She was framed," he insisted, "and everybody believes it 'cause she was Irish. 'Inborn,' that means we're all that way—you, me, all of us from the old country. I won't rest till it's put right."

He'd had Fiona's body transported to an undertaker

on Pearl Street, where he viewed it yesterday evening. "Worst thing I ever seen," he told Nell, his eyes welling with tears. "She'd been such a pretty little thing. Twenty-one years old. To see her like that, with her head all . . ." His words had died in his chest; his shoulders shook. "I wished to God it was me instead."

Wanting to confirm that Fiona had been shot at point-blank range, Nell had coaxed Brady into describing his niece's head wound. The entry wound on the right temple was small, he said, and surrounded by a mottled black stain that spread over the side of Fiona's face. The exit wound was a terrible crater, the left side of her head having been blown entirely away.

Solemn music blossomed forth from the most spectacular organ Nell had ever seen, its pipes soaring toward the lofty, barrel-vaulted ceiling. It was a handsome church with two rows of tall white columns separating the nave from the side aisles and upper galleries. A gentleman of about sixty in clerical robes—the Reverend Dr. Gannett, she presumed—sat in a tall-backed chair on the altar, leafing through his notes. Having never before set foot in a Protestant church, Nell felt glaringly out of place and, although she knew it was absurd, conspicuously Irish Catholic.

A man strolled past her and down the length of the center aisle before pausing at the coffin, one hand stuffed in a trouser pocket, the other tapping a bowler against his leg. After a moment, he turned and surveyed the church, his gaze lighting one at a time on the assembled mourners. He was slightly built, with close-cropped gray hair—prematurely so, Nell could tell, given the smoothness of his sharp-featured little face. In contrast to the other gentlemen, all in identical black frock coats, he wore a charcoal gray sack suit buttoned over a plaid vest, his feet clad in humble brown brogans.

Nell had no doubt whatsoever that this was Detective Charlie Skinner. She smiled to herself. *I can still pick out the coppers.*

Her smile waned when Skinner fixed his pale-eyed gaze on her for a brief but penetrating assessment. To be stared at by a cop, even fleetingly and from such a distance, made her want to turn and dart out the front door.

That impulse grew stronger as the detective strode toward her with an air of purpose, but when he was about twenty feet away, he turned and slid into one of the rear pews. Stiffening her spine, Nell walked toward the front of the church, her pace slowing as she approached the strange coffin and saw that its closed lid was one thick sheet of plate glass, offering a head-to-toe view of the deceased. It called to mind the glass box in which Snow White was laid to rest after eating the poisoned apple. The casket itself appeared to be white-painted cast iron crafted to look as if it were draped with fabric.

Of all the many dead bodies Nell had encountered in her twenty-six years, Virginia Kimball's was by far the most remarkable. Her unbound hair, so black it had to be either a wig or the product of dye, lay in sinuous ripples over the white satin pillow that cradled her head. Even in death, she was striking to look at, with her dramatically arched eyebrows, elegant cheekbones and powder-pale complexion. She'd been painted with stage makeup, Nell realized, right down to the kohl blackening her eyelids. The initial effect was of a lady who looked much younger than her forty-eight years—until one noticed the furrowed throat and slack jowls, the lines radiating from her eyes, the creases bracketing her crimsoned lips.

Not only were her cosmetics theatrical; her attire was, too. The dead actress wore a slim gown of silvery white satin with trailing sleeves and an ornate golden girdle, a medieval costume that echoed the fairy-tale imagery. Garlands of daisies and wildflowers were strewn over her, and lotus blossoms all around her, giving the impression that she was floating on water.

Nell hitched in a breath when it came to her. She wasn't Snow White at all. She was Ophelia.

Even death couldn't keep Virginia Kimball from playing what had evidently been a favorite role, that of the young woman whose love for Hamlet had driven her to drown herself in madness and despair. Nell couldn't imagine an undertaker doing this of his own volition, nor was it likely to have been stodgy old Orville Pratt's idea. Mrs. Kimball must have made her own arrangements ahead of time.

"Jesus," Nell whispered, then sketched a hasty sign of the cross, appalled to have blasphemed, and in a church, no less! Her cheeks stung when she noticed Dr. Gannett watching her from his seat on the altar; Protestants didn't make the sign of the cross. He offered her a reassuring smile before returning his attention to his notes.

There was no kneeler in front of the coffin, so Nell merely clasped her gloved hands and murmured a prayer for the departed soul of Virginia Kimball. Unwilling, despite her discomfiture, to abandon the customs of her faith, she crossed herself again, to the accompaniment of a glassy little giggle from behind. Turning, she saw Cecilia Pratt eyeing her while whispering into her mother's ear.

Nell chose an aisle seat on the left side about ten pews from the front, which afforded her a good view from behind of everyone except Detective Skinner, sitting in back. She withdrew her little tortoiseshell fan from her chatelaine and flicked it open, wondering why it had to be so blasted hot on a morning when she was obliged to wear black wool head to toe. The choir rose and sang "Nearer, My God, to Thee," after which Reverend Gannett stood and crossed to the podium.

"Infinite Father," the minister intoned, "God of light and love, we bless Thy name for this beautiful world Thou hast given us—for the love of our families, the peace of our communities, and, even in our tears, for that angel of death whom Thou dost send to each of us in turn . . ."

Much as Nell missed the traditional Latin funeral mass, she found it rather refreshing—heretically so, no doubt—to be able to grasp the substance of what was being said. The lengthy prayer was concluded with a paltry chorus of "Amen." One deep male voice, emanating not from the first few pews but from overhead, stood out among the others. Looking up and to the left, Nell saw a handsome black-haired gentleman sitting in the front row of the gallery above her, his forearms resting on the balustrade, his gaze directed not at Reverend Gannett, but at her. Nell's fan stilled.

Will.

Her breath snagged in her throat. How long had he

been gone this time? Weeks. No, over a month. It had been April the last time she'd seen him.

Will inclined his head to her, not quite smiling but almost. He looked pleased to see her, if slightly baffled by her presence. She nodded back, wondering if he'd purposely seated himself directly above her.

She might have guessed that William Hewitt would want to pay his last respects to the actress with whom he'd once been so besotted, even if he hadn't seen her in some thirteen years. He was like that. He didn't put parts of himself, of the man he'd been and the people he'd known, in a box to be stored away and forgotten. For better or for worse, he didn't—couldn't—just forget and move on. It was a trait that had earned him more than his share of anguish, although Nell was hopeful that he'd learned how to live with his past without letting it consume him.

Wresting her gaze from Will, Nell studied the mourners in front of her as Dr. Gannett launched into the comfortingly familiar 23rd Psalm. Orville Pratt consulted his pocket watch as his wife batted the air with her fan. Cecilia fussed with the angle of her hat, a stylish little mound of black satin bows and ostrich feathers. The older lady couldn't seem to tear her gaze away from the bizarre coffin. The only Pratt who seemed to be paying any attention at all to the proceedings was Emily, in an oddly appealing chapeau *chinois* of unadorned black straw.

On the other side of the central aisle and a few rows up from Nell sat a lean gentleman of perhaps sixty with sleekly pomaded gray hair and a salt-and-pepper goatee. He had his head turned toward Dr. Gannett, revealing a high brow and aristocratically aquiline nose. It was the kind of profile that cried out to be sketched in ink with a good, supple steel nib. A walking stick lay across his lap, its handle—a curved length of deer antler—resting on the arm of the pew.

Resisting the urge to glance back up at the gallery, Nell surveyed the rest of the meager audience. Three were clearly newspapermen, given the industry with which they were taking notes. Judging by the appearance of most of the others—the ladies' chic frocks and unapologetic face paint, the gentlemen's dandyish attire—Nell guessed them to be theater people, or hangers-on thereof.

Dr. Gannett transitioned from the 23rd Psalm to the 84th—one of Nell's favorites, which he recited beautifully, without a single glance at the notes in front of him. "How amiable are thy tabernacles, O Lord of hosts. . . ."

The third verse always filled Nell with a melancholic yearning. "Yea, the sparrow hath found an house, and the swallow a nest for herself, where she may lay her young. . . ."

As grateful as Nell was for the life she'd been blessed with these past five years, the fact remained that her house wasn't her house at all; it was the Hewitts' house. And her child, the only child who would ever be hers to rear and love, had been sired on a pretty little chambermaid by William Hewitt one night during the war when they were both alone and desolate and needful of comfort.

Gracie had cried when Nell left her in Edna Parrish's care this morning. She'd begged to come along, and had argued relentlessly when Nell tried to explain that a fu-

neral was no place for such a young child. Gracie had
made it clear that she didn't like the doddering old Nurse
Parrish, and she definitely didn't like being abandoned by
Nell on a weekday. That was how Nell felt, at least part of
her, that she'd abandoned her child to go on a wild goose
chase for Brady.

Was Will still watching her? A woozy self-awareness
washed over Nell, exacerbated, no doubt, by the heat. She
saw herself from the eyes of someone looking down upon
her—from Will's eyes—as she sat in her stark black
mourning dress and spoon bonnet, cheeks flushed despite
her continual fanning.

It was very much like Will to materialize, ghostlike, at
the edge of her vision just when she'd begun to wonder if
she'd ever lay eyes on him again. They'd been in close
contact last autumn, while they were trying to figure out
what had happened to Bridie Sullivan, but since then
she'd seen him only sporadically. From time to time, during her post-luncheon outings with Gracie in the Common
and Public Garden, he would appear without warning,
keep them company for the afternoon, and then vanish
for anywhere from two days to two months.

Nell never asked him about his longer absences. She
didn't want to hear about the cities he visited, the games
of faro and poker and *vingt-et-un* that he won and lost. Although he kept a room here in Boston at the Revere
House, where he also stabled his horses and buggy, he still
made his living through cards rather than medicine, and
that meant he still had to travel to wherever the high-
stakes games were being played.

A man with William Hewitt's looks and charisma was
certain to attract women wherever he went—exotic beau-

ties, nocturnal and a little dangerous, like Will himself. That was the part Nell especially didn't want to hear about, although it shamed her that she even gave it a moment's thought.

Whenever Will strolled back into her world again, it was with an air of peculiarly British nonchalance, as if he'd been expected all along. Gracie would squeal with glee and throw herself into the outstretched arms of her "Uncle Will," whom she had no idea was actually her father. Will would smile at Nell as he hugged his child, who was more or less Nell's child, too, and for an all too fleeting interlude, they would be like a real family, the happy little family she'd never had.

After the hug would come the gift. Will never showed up without something for Gracie: a paper doll book, a pair of hair combs, a sack of marbles, a wooden top . . . Sometimes Nell wondered where he'd acquired these trinkets, as when, following his longest absence, he gave her a miniature porcelain tea set illustrated with scenes from "Little Red Riding Hood," with captions in French. Had he been back to his old haunts overseas? Nell knew how treacherous those places were—the unlit back alleys, the opium dens, the cheapness with which life was regarded in certain quarters. Will hadn't told her much, but he'd told her enough. She knew she shouldn't worry about him.

But how could she not? Her friendship with William Hewitt, although hardly the illicit relationship that Mary Agnes liked to insinuate, had grown, over the past year and a half, remarkably deep. They shared a rapport of the mind that she would have thought impossible when she'd first met him, bloodied and filthy and in the throes of opium withdrawal. She couldn't help but care what became of him.

The psalms were followed by passages from Matthew and John and another hymn from the choir, after which Dr. Gannett returned to the podium. "We are met here today to pay the offices of respect to Mrs. Virginia Evelyn Kimball. Her tenure on Earth has come to an end, as it must, in due course, for each of us. No more roles will she play, be they penned by man or by the Heavenly Father. No more trials shall she face, nor temptations, nor discord. The play that was her life has run its course; the curtains have been drawn shut . . ."

At the conclusion of the sermon, Dr. Gannett introduced "Mrs. Kimball's oldest and dearest friend, Mr. Maximilian Thurston."

The gentleman with the goatee rose and stepped up onto the altar with the assistance of his cane, which he leaned against the podium. He withdrew a folded sheaf of paper from inside his coat—an impeccably tailored double-breasted black frock coat with satin-piped velvet lapels, to which a little cluster of violets had been affixed. It was unbuttoned, revealing a waistcoat of black and purple brocade, colors reflected in both his pocket handkerchief and the paisley scarf tied in a lavish bow around his winged shirt collar. Not quite proper mourning attire, but not necessarily a sign of disrespect; Mr. Thurston was a playwright, after all, and artistic types tended to flout convention.

He lifted the gold monocle hanging from a chain around his neck, fitted it to his right eye, smoothed out his notes, and cleared his throat. " 'Doubt thou the stars are fire,' " he read in a pseudo-British accent commonplace among Boston's cultural elite. " 'Doubt that the sun doth move. Doubt truth to be a liar . . . But never doubt I love.' "

Looking up, he said, "So Hamlet wrote to his fair Ophelia. As he revered his lady love, so I revered my dear . . ." Thurston's voice faltered. He paused, eyes shimmering, and drew in a tremulous breath. "My dear, dear Virginia. I daresay she captivated me from the moment I first laid eyes upon her, some twenty-one years ago.

"It was at the Howard Athenaeum, shortly after it had been rebuilt, when it was still quite luxurious, you know. We were casting my play *Merry Misadventure,* which some of you may recall, and an unknown young actress, new to Boston, had come out to audition for the ingenue role. At first, I was loath to even let her read, having been told that she was dark-haired, for I'd written the character as very fair. But no sooner did Virginia Kimball walk onto the stage that afternoon than I knew I had my Gwendolyn. . . ."

Mr. Thurston continued in that vein for quite some time, delivering what amounted to a résumé of Virginia Kimball's acting career, with particular emphasis on plays authored by him, supplemented with personal observations and anecdotes. Some years ago, he said, having grown weary of the footlights and the ceaseless public attention, Mrs. Kimball retired from the stage to devote herself to gardening and good works.

"For that benign, peaceable life to have been cut short in such a manner . . ." Mr. Thurston shook his head. "I shan't ever understand it. My only consolation is that the First Lady of the Boston Stage played her final scene in the manner of a tragic heroine. Somehow I suspect she would have found a certain measure of satisfaction in that. I shall try to do the same. As the grieving Laertes said of his late, beloved sister, 'Too much of water hast thou, poor Ophelia, and therefore I forbid my tears.' "

Mr. Thurston folded up his notes and slid them back into his coat, removed his monocle, lifted his cane, and descended the altar. But instead of returning immediately to his seat, he paused by the coffin, kissed his fingertips, and touched them to the glass over Virginia Kimball's face.

"Lay her in the earth," he said in a horse, shaky voice, "and from her fair and unpolluted flesh may violets spring."

Slipping the violets out of his lapel, he placed them on the spot he'd touched. "Sweets to the sweet. Farewell, Virginia."

He looked up and scanned the mourners until his gaze lit on Orville Pratt. His eyes, bright with unshed tears, iced over with a naked virulence that sucked the air out of Nell's lungs. Winifred Pratt turned to look at her husband, who appeared to be staring not at Mr. Thurston, but straight ahead. Something like contempt crept into Thurston's expression before he finally turned away and walked slowly back to his seat.

The entire episode had lasted two, perhaps three seconds. It had felt like an hour.

I T was about ten minutes later, while the choir was plodding through a particularly long and lugubrious hymn, that Nell noticed movement in the gallery overhead. She looked up to see Will walking toward the back of the church.

His gait was slightly rigid, thanks to the old bullet wound in his leg, but much improved from the terrible limp that had plagued him last autumn and winter, after he'd stopped injecting morphine. Perhaps his body was finally accustoming itself to the lack of opiates, or perhaps it was simply a function of the warmer weather. Pray God he hadn't gone back to the needle.

Nell waited a few moments after he ducked into the stairwell, and then she turned and looked down the center aisle to the front door of the church. Will was standing there, a tall, spectral figure backlit by the glaring morning sun. He lit a cigarette and flicked out the match. His hand seemed to move in a beckoning gesture, or was that just a trick of the light?

Detective Skinner twisted around in his pew to see what had captured her attention. He looked from Will to her, a policeman's speculative glint in his eye. Will vanished into the sunlight.

Nell turned and faced the front of the church. She plucked her handkerchief from the chatelaine on her waistband, intending to blot her sweat-dampened face, but thought better of it. Tucking her fan back into the little bag, which she left unlatched, she rose and started walking up the aisle toward the front door. She paused once to dab her forehead, gripping the back of the pew next to her. Skinner was watching her.

She continued on, one hand pressed to her stomach, the other grasping the handkerchief, her steps slow and unsteady.

"Miss?" Skinner said as she neared. "Are you . . .?"

She looked toward him, swaying ever so slightly on her feet. "I'm . . . I'm . . ."

She reached for the nearest pew, her hands fumbling for purchase as she collapsed.

Chapter 5

SKINNER sprang out of his seat, catching Nell before she hit the floor. "Steady, there, miss."

She clutched at his coat as he pulled her to her feet. "I'm sorry, I . . . I just need some air." His clothing smelled of cheap tobacco, his breath of rum and licorice.

"This way," he said as he steered her awkwardly out onto the front steps. "Here, sit," he urged, easing her down onto the top step, which was sheltered from the bright sun by the church's shadow. His hands lingered on her a bit longer than was strictly necessary, Nell thought.

Coaches, buggies, and a number of hacks were lined up at the curb. Between the hearse and an elegant Dress Landau with the top folded down, the latter doubtless belonging to the Pratts, she saw Will, across the street in the Public Garden, hurl his cigarette aside and sprint toward her.

"Nell!" Will whipped off his hat and sank onto the step below her. "What happened?"

"Must be the heat," Skinner said. "She was pretty shaky there for a minute. I was sure she was fixin' to faint dead away."

"I'm fine, really," she protested.

"Lower your head," Will said, reinforcing that command by pressing gently on the back of her neck.

"You know this lady?" Skinner asked.

"Yes, and I'm in your debt, sir." From the corner of her eye, with her face half-buried in black wool, Nell saw Will extend his hand. "William Hewitt."

"Detective Charles Skinner, Boston Police. Hewitt, did you say? You aren't any relation to Mr. August Hewitt of Colonnade Row?"

"I'm the son no one talks about." Will stroked Nell's upper back, making her skin prickle beneath her stays. "And this rather obstinate young lady is Miss Cornelia Sweeney."

Skinner hesitated for a moment, probably to grasp the fact that Nell was Irish, before saying, with careful formality, "Pleased to make your acquaintance, Miss Sweeney."

"And I yours," Nell mumbled into her skirts.

"No offense, Hewitt," Skinner said, "but if you're August Hewitt's son, how come you talk like a limey?"

"He sent me to England as a child," Will said. "I found my way back home, though, so the joke's on him."

"I'm much better," Nell said. "I can sit up now."

"I'm the physician," Will said. "I'll tell you when you're feeling better."

"A physician, huh?" Skinner said. "So, uh, you got this in hand, then."

"Entirely," Will said. "Thank you for your help."

Nell turned her head to watch Skinner retreat into the church. Through the open door she heard the choir wind up that dreary hymn, and then came the barely audible voice of Dr. Gannett inviting the mourners to join him in the Lord's Prayer.

Will said, "You seem to have an awfully delicate constitution for a lady who claims she's not prone to fainting."

"I'm not."

"What's this all about, then?"

Still bent over double, Nell rummaged in her open chatelaine for the little prize she'd gone to such trouble to attain.

"What's this?" Will asked as she handed it to him.

"Virginia Kimball's key ring. I just pinched it off Detective Skinner."

Will released her neck; she sat up. He gaped at the ornate silver ring in his hand, from which three or four brass keys dangled, amusement warring with astonishment in his eyes, "You *are* joking."

She shook her head, gratified to have drawn such a reaction from the unflappable William Hewitt, although, in truth, she was almost as shocked as he at her audacity appalled, even, but also perversely proud. After all these years of honest living, "Cornelia Cutpurse" still had the touch.

"You picked the pocket of a police detective?" he asked.

"Not so loud," she whispered, darting a glance toward the church. "It was the only way I could get my hands on Mrs. Kimball's house key."

"One hardly knows where to begin," Will muttered as

he rubbed the bridge of his nose. "All right, leaving aside for the moment the question of . . . well, all the many questions that come to mind, aren't you at all concerned about Skinner's reaction when he discovers you stole this?"

"He'll never suspect it was me," she said as she took it from Will's hand. "It was in his vest pocket, and I rebuttoned his coat after I snagged it. When he finally discovers it's gone, he probably won't even realize it was stolen, and certainly not by—"

"Whoa, whoa, whoa." Will cocked his head as if he hadn't heard quite right. "You rebuttoned his coat."

"Yes, of course."

"Which suggests that you first *un*buttoned it, after which you swiped the key ring and stowed it in your chatelaine. Then you buttoned him back up, all while feigning a swooning attack."

She smiled. "I was very good once." Will was the only person in Boston who knew about the life she'd once led, the things she'd once done—the person she'd been. If anyone else were to find out, it would ruin her.

"It would appear," he said as he fetched a tin of Turkish Orientals from inside his coat, "that you're still . . . well, I'm not sure *good* is quite the word. *Talented.* Rather unnervingly brilliant, actually. Do you mind?" he asked as he flipped the tin open and withdrew a cigarette.

"No, go ahead. You must be wondering what I want with this," she said as she held up the key ring.

He struck a match. "You're obviously poking about . . . *once again,*" he interjected gravely, "in very sticky matters that are none of your affair."

Nell filled him in on her efforts, on Brady's behalf, to clear his late niece's name—briefly, because she could hear Dr. Gannett pronouncing the closing benediction. She emphasized the "Red Book," possibly a diary or notebook of some sort, and the gunpowder burns on the mobcap and Fiona Gannon's face, critical evidence never presented to the inquest jury. "They're saying Fiona shot Virginia Kimball, who fell to the ground, apparently dead, but who then managed to grab the gun and shoot Fiona in the head. She presumably got off a shot from where she was lying in the doorway, but then how could Fiona's cap and face have ended up in that condition?"

"That hardly proves Fiona Gannon was innocent of all wrongdoing," Will said, echoing Detective Cook's reservations.

"It *does* prove that it couldn't have happened the way they say it did. I want to have a look around Mrs. Kimball's house, see for myself the room where those two women died. I doubt it was ever thoroughly examined. Skinner didn't care what really happened. He just wanted to pin it on Fiona Gannon and collect his payoffs."

Will crushed out his cigarette and closed a hand over Nell's arm. "Look . . . Nell. I know how much you care for Brady, but are you sure you should be stirring things up like this? It could get a bit dicey. After all, there are several very powerful men who obviously want this whole business brushed neatly under the rug."

Soberly, quietly, she said, "Will, why did you come here today?"

He frowned and lifted his shoulders, as if the answer were obvious. "I knew Virginia Kimball. At one time, well, I was quite taken with her. In my mind, she was this icon of feminine glamour and romance. And she *was* a remarkably gifted actress—I really admired that about her.

Of course, to her, I was just a passing amusement. She never so much as let me kiss her cheek. Still, I've never forgotten her."

"Given all that," Nell said, "doesn't it trouble you even a little, knowing her murder will never really be solved?"

Will shot her an eloquently baleful look to show that he wasn't so easily manipulated. Still, she detected a hint of genuine interest when he asked, "If Fiona Gannon didn't kill her, who did?"

"I don't know," she said. "But I do know that the inquest was a sham. Nobody asked the hard questions because nobody wanted to hear the answers. I'd like to ask those questions."

"Of whom?"

Nell shrugged. "Orville Pratt, Maximilian Thurston . . . I'd like to know what Mrs. Kimball was really like, whom she associated with, what her circumstances were. I'd love to find out more about Fiona Gannon. And then there are the men who paid off Detective Skinner. I'd like to know what they thought they were buying."

"Nell, Nell, Nell . . ." Will groaned as he rubbed the back of his neck. "These are not the kind of men who will tolerate your prying. You'll be a threat to them, and they will deal with you as such."

"You don't think I'm capable of discretion?"

"Of course you are. But men like these have ways of knowing when someone is snooping into their business."

Organ music floated out from the church, accompanied by a bustle of activity. Nell turned to see Mrs. Kimball's heavy iron coffin being borne down the aisle by eight pallbearers. Will rose and helped Nell to her feet.

As she dusted off her skirt, she murmured, "Rumors are starting about us."

"Excellent," he said as he replaced his low-crowned top hat on his head. "Life would be so dull without rumors."

"That's easy for you to say. In my profession, any whiff of scandal would be disastrous. You shouldn't . . ." Nell hated this. She looked down, rubbed her thumb over the big silver key ring. "You shouldn't meet Gracie and me in the park anymore."

Will looked at her, really looked at her, for the first time that morning. His eyes, shaded by that prominent brow of his, were grim; his jaw had that surly thrust it sometimes got. The sharply carved features that looked so engagingly patrician when he was relaxed could turn wolfish in a heartbeat. "You would force such a sacrifice on us just to disarm a few idle gossips?"

"Will . . ."

"More of a sacrifice for me than for you, I suppose. It means a great deal to me, seeing Gracie and spending time with . . ." He looked away, shook his head. When he looked back and saw that the procession from within the church was nearly upon them, he lowered his voice to an earnest whisper. "Would you take that away from me?"

"Would you take Gracie away from *me*?" she asked desperately. "That's what will happen if I lose my job because of these rumors you find so amusing." Gentling her voice, she said, "Will, I'm sorry. I . . . I value those afternoons, too, more than you know, but . . ." She shrugged helplessly.

Will took Nell's elbow and steered her aside as the coffin was carried out of the church, the pallbearers squinting against the sunshine, except for towering, silver-haired Orville Pratt, who stared grimly ahead with eyes like glacial lakes. *His face is dirty,* Nell thought, until she realized, with a start, that he had a shiner. The contusion had stained his left eyelid and cheekbone a dull, mottled purple, meaning it was about two or three days old. On another gentleman, it might have imparted an aura of vulnerability; in Orville Pratt's case, it only made him look more formidable.

The Pratt ladies emerged from the church, Winifred still briskly fanning herself, her face a moist white dumpling nestled in a shirred bonnet, while Cecilia laughingly prattled away to her sister and the older lady. The latter, very thin and with a face pale as bone, appeared lost in thought as she watched the men lug the big iron box down the church steps.

"Aunt Vera!" Cecilia snapped. "You aren't even listening!"

"I'm sorry, dear. You were saying . . . ?"

Nell tried not to stare at Emily's dress. An understated garment gathered at the waist, it was reminiscent of Mrs. Kimball's medieval-inspired grave clothes, albeit more voluminous, and of a fluid black twill. It was clear that there was no crinoline shaping its skirt and, given the blousy bodice and natural silhouette, no evidence of a corset, either. Cecilia, on the other hand, had the kind of cinched-in waist a man could wrap his hands around with a fair expectation that his fingers would touch. She wore a ruby brooch and matching ear bobs, a violation not just of funerary protocol, but of the injunction against faceted gems for daytime wear.

Cecilia, Emily, and their aunt Vera descended the front

steps to watch the coffin being heaved into the hearse. Their mother was about to follow them when she glanced to the side and noticed Will. "William? William Hewitt?" She touched her fan to her great pigeon's breast of a bosom as she stared up at the much taller Will.

"Guilty." Will lifted his hat and inclined his head. "Good to see you again, Mrs. Pratt."

"Good heavens!" she exclaimed in her twittery little voice. "Oh, my word. I can't remember the last time I saw you."

"I believe it was Christmas Eve, sixty-three," he said.

"Quite right," she said. "Yes, quite. Your parents had us over to the house, along with the Thorpes. You were home on furlough, you and . . . Robbie." Her smile faded; that was to be Robbie's last visit home, Nell knew.

If Will was saddened by the mention of his late brother, his expression betrayed no hint of it. Looking from Mrs. Pratt to Nell, he asked, "Do you ladies know each other?"

Winifred Pratt regarded Nell with a sort of vague, puzzled recognition. "Were you at that lovely dinner party on the Cabots' yacht last month?"

"No, ma'am," Nell said. "We did dine together once, you and I, but it was about a year and a half ago, at the Hewitts'. I'm their governess."

"Ah." The older lady blinked at Nell. "You don't say. Ah, yes. Yes, of course. Now I remember. Miss . . .?"

"Sweeney. Nell Sweeney."

"Miss Sweeney. Of course. Of course. How silly of me to forget. I've got the brain of a peahen, that's what Mr. Pratt says. Yes, indeed." Mrs. Pratt's gaze lit on Will's hand, still curled around Nell's arm. Her smile was inert, her eyes knowing. "Well. A pleasure to see you again, both of you, even under such melancholy circumstances. I take it you, er, knew Mrs. Kimball?" she asked, looking back and forth between them.

"I did, some years ago," Will said.

"Yes?" Winifred Pratt's smile was very close to a smirk. As a friend of the Hewitts, she would have known all about Will's penchant for actresses. Schooling her expression, she said, "Terrible thing, just terrible, to happen right on Beacon Hill. One has come to expect this sort of thing in . . . certain quarters, but *Beacon Hill*?"

"Yes, indeed," Will said diplomatically.

"It's not the same neighborhood it used to be," she said. "And not just because of what happened to Mrs. Kimball. My own husband was accosted the other night just a few doors down from our house on Beacon Street by some gutter-crawler from . . . well, I can only assume the North End, or perhaps Fort Hill. Mr. Pratt wouldn't give up his wallet, so this ruffian took a bludgeon to him. Did you see his eye? Did you?"

"I did," Will said. "Gives him a rather dashing air, I think."

"Oh, my dear William," she giggled. "You were always such a card. Dare I hope you've returned to Boston for good? It would so please your dear mamá."

He hesitated, his fingers tightening reflexively on Nell's arm. "We shall see what the future brings."

"Oh! I've a splendid idea." Mrs. Pratt smacked Will on the chest with her fan. "You must join us for dinner tomorrow evening. Yes, indeed. Mr. Pratt's gone and invited some client he ran into yesterday, so I don't see why I might not ask you, especially since your parents and Harry will be coming."

"You don't say."

"Yes, and Martin, too, if he doesn't have too much studying—you know how he is. I do hope he can come. He and Emily used to get along so well when they were young. Don't you think they'd be just perfect for each other?"

"Er . . ."

"Oh, do come. It would smashing to see all the Hewitts together again at one table. I shall die if you refuse."

"Mustn't have that." To Nell's utter shock, considering his estrangement from his family, he added, "I say, you don't mind if I bring Miss Sweeney?"

Nell and Winifred Pratt both stared at Will for a long, excruciating moment. "Why . . . no, not at all," said Mrs. Pratt, her smile riveted in place. "Of course not. Lovely idea. Lovely. Shall we say seven o'clock?"

"We shall be there," Will said.

"Well, then, very good. I, er, I shall save my good-byes until later. You *are* going to the graveside service?"

"I'm afraid not," Will said before Nell could answer in the affirmative. "Miss Sweeney is unwell. The heat, you know."

"Oh, dear, yes," said Mrs. Pratt, her fan fluttering to life again. "My, yes. This blasted heat. Well, then. Lovely running into you. Absolutely lovely. I shall see you tomorrow, then."

Will bowed as she turned away. "Looking forward to it."

"I'll thank you not to speak for me," Nell told Will when Mrs. Pratt was out of earshot. "I had every intention of going to the cemetery. I haven't had a chance to talk to Mr. Pratt yet, or Maximilian Thurston. Or—"

"It shouldn't be much trouble to arrange an interview with Mr. Thurston, given the extent to which he appears to relish the art of discourse. As for Orville Pratt, you'll be a guest in his home tomorrow evening. You can talk to him then."

Watching the Pratts' driver delicately wedge his rotund mistress into the landau, Nell said, "What were you thinking, asking her if I could come?"

"Can't Nurse Parrish put Gracie to bed tomorrow night?"

"I don't mean that. Don't you realize what they'll think?" she asked. "They'll think I'm your . . . that we're . . ."

Will shook his head, smiling. "Poor, conventional Cornelia. Still a slave to the opinions of others."

With an exasperated sigh, she said, "This is what I was talking about before. You've never given your reputation a second thought, so you don't seem to grasp how critical mine is to me."

"Nell, the rumors that have got you so fretful arose because people assume you're meeting me on the sly, leading them to conclude that we're engaged in a clandestine liaison of a, shall we say, impure nature. But if I were to court you openly—"

"*Court* me?" Courtship implied the prospect of matrimony, not remotely an option for Nell, who, at sixteen, had wedded a charismatic hothead currently nine years into a thirty-year prison sentence for armed robbery and aggravated assault. Nell's marriage to Duncan Sweeney was the worst mistake of her life, as she discovered when the Church refused to annul it. Divorce would be pointless, given the certainty of excommunication should she ever remarry. Therefore Nell secretly remained the wife of a convicted felon while all of Boston, except for Will, viewed her as a pious Irish Catholic miss with an un-blemished past.

"What I meant," he said, "was if I were to *appear* to court you. We could be seen together as often as we liked, without anyone misconstruing it. Or rather," he added as Nell prepared to point out the obvious, "they'd be mis-construing it, but by our own contrivance. We could at-tend this dinner party, or any other function, without worrying about the whispers. We could be seen in public as often as we liked, with no fear for your reputation. No one would look askance if they thought I was simply pay-ing my addresses to you, openly and honorably."

"A Hewitt, openly paying addresses to *me*?" she said. "I should think a great many people would look askance at that."

"Come, now, you must have read at least one of those vapid governess novels. Doesn't the heroine always end up married off to one of her employer's sons?"

"Or to someone even richer and more important," she confirmed, having gone through a phase in her late teens when she'd devoured such novels. "But the governesses in those novels are invariably from the same background as the families they serve. They're well-born young ladies in reduced circumstances, not some poor Irish chit who just happened to stumble upon a stroke of good luck. You and I . . ." She shook her head. "People would never believe it."

There came the snap of reins, followed by hooves clattering on the granite-paved road. They both turned to watch the funeral procession wind its way down the street and around the corner. When Nell looked back at Will, she found him studying her in that quietly intense way of his.

"Of course people will believe it," he said. "You're widely admired, you know, and not just by my mother. No one thinks of you as just some poor Irish chit who got lucky."

"Your brother Harry does."

Will smiled. "He *says* he does. The truth is, he's terrified of you."

Nell let out a dubious little huff of laughter.

"Think about it," Will said. "Every time he encounters you, or someone who has your interests at heart, he ends up with at least one fresh new scar. He knows he's no match for you—not that he'll ever admit it, but he knows."

"No match for *you,* you mean." Nell had Will to thank for Harry's having let her be for the greater part of the past year. Enraged at Harry's attempt to force himself on Nell last year, Will had dealt his brother a fractured nose and black eye, promising to crush both of his arms should he ever touch her again.

"Harry will be at the Pratts' tomorrow night," she said. "I assure you I have no desire to socialize with him."

"Nor he with you, I daresay. He'll probably ignore you completely."

"Your parents will be there," she said. "I'm surprised you'd be willing to spend that much time in their company."

"I can't avoid them forever, and your being there will take some of the sting out of dealing with them."

Nell looked away for a moment, afraid he might see, on her face, a hint of the gratification she felt at knowing her presence was important to him. "I still don't understand why you're doing this," she said. "You loathe these sorts of evenings. You don't care anything about the

Pratts, you can't bear either of your parents, you've given up trying to reform Harry . . ."

"I'm quite fond of young Martin, actually."

"You could see him alone if you wanted to."

"I do. We sometimes meet for lunch in Cambridge when I'm in town."

"Then what's the point of going to this dinner party?" she asked.

"Perhaps you've convinced me that I owe it to the late Mrs. Kimball to get to the bottom of her murder."

Is that all? she wanted to ask. Was it possible he felt she needed him around for protection, given the powerful men she was going up against? Then there was this courtship ruse. On the one hand, she balked at the notion of living a lie; yet wasn't that what she'd been doing all along? At least, if she went along with this sham, Will would be free to openly associate not only with her, but with his daughter.

"I won't deceive your mother," she said on a capitulatory sigh. "Not after everything she's done for me."

"I wouldn't ask you to. You'd never get away with it, in any event. Doesn't she expect you to remain unwed while Grace is little? You'd have to reassure her on that score."

A secretly married woman, reassuring her employer that she'll remain single while carrying on a fabricated courtship with her son? Nell kneaded her forehead. "This is mad."

"Life is mad." Will smiled down at her sober black dress. "Have I ever told you about this odd attraction I have toward beautiful young ladies in mourning attire?"

"Yes, actually." Feeling heat rise up her throat, Nell lowered her gaze and fiddled with the keys, hoping the brim of her bonnet would hide her reddened face from his view.

"And the swooning was a nice touch." He laid one hand lightly over both of hers, his fingers warm even through her black silk gloves. She felt incapable of resistance when he gently hooked a finger through the key ring and extracted it from her grasp. Closing one hand around the keys and the other around her arm, he escorted her down the front steps. "Shall we?"

"Are you taking me home?" she asked as he guided her across the street toward his buggy, a compact black phaeton with the top down.

He nodded. "By way of Mount Vernon Street."

She turned to look at him. "Mrs. Kimball's house?"

Will smiled and shrugged. "Best we get there before Mr. Pratt's cleaners do."

Chapter 6

"QUITE a house for just one person," Nell said as Will unlocked the front door of Mrs. Kimball's handsome, four-story townhouse and accompanied her inside.

The entrance foyer was spacious and imposing, with a pink marble floor and coffered walls. Will set his hat on a mirrored hallstand strewn with mail and calling cards, some of which had fallen to the floor. A porcelain umbrella stand lay smashed on its side next to two frilly parasols and a gentleman's gold-handled walking stick. Straight ahead, off a long hallway, were two massive mahogany newel posts flanking a carpeted staircase.

"The bodies were found on the second floor," Nell said, "but I think I'd like to look around a bit down here first."

The hallway led to a grand double parlor, the front half

set off from the back by gilded pillars. Gilt-framed mir-
rors and paintings, most of which depicted Mrs. Kimball
costumed for various roles, stood against the walls, having evidently been taken down from their hooks. Two
couches and a number of French gilt side chairs were
overturned, their undersides slit open and gutted, tufts of
horsehair scattered about the Persian carpet. An ivory-
inlaid table cabinet lay on the floor with one door broken
off. Even the logs in the clean-swept fireplace had been
taken out and dumped onto the hearth rug.

"This is Detective Skinner's handiwork," Nell said.
"He was looking for the Red Book."

"No doubt he could name his own price if he got his
hands on it."

The rest of the first floor—dining room, kitchen,
pantry, and water closet—was similarly ransacked. On
the theory that an intruder may have broken into the
house, they checked the courtyard door, service door, and
windows, but found no evidence of a forced entry.

They climbed the stairs to the second floor and paused
in the hall, which was lined with framed ambrotypes and
cartes de visite of Virginia Kimball costumed for various
roles, as well as playbills featuring her name in oversized
type. It was sweltering upstairs, and airless. Nell caught a
gamy-sweet whiff of old blood that made her nostrils flare.

Will pointed out a series of brownish-red footprints on
the Aubusson carpet. "I assume these are from the police
tramping through the evidence."

"If there were any prints here when Skinner first arrived," Nell said, "he might not have noticed, given the
pattern on the carpet. And even if he did, he'd never admit
it now that the case is 'solved.' Why muddy the waters?"

To the right, toward the front of the house, were three open doors, leading to a library, a sitting room, and a large W.C.; they were all ravaged. The library floor was a sea of books.

There was one door to the left. It, too, stood open, revealing an enormous butter-yellow bedroom flooded with sunlight from two south-facing leaded glass windows overlooking a lush flower garden. The smell of blood grew stronger as they approached. There rose a low insect hum that made Nell's scalp prickle.

From the open doorway could be seen a huge canopied bed against the north wall, its mattress slashed. Bedclothes lay in a heap on the floor alongside mounds of clothing, white goose feathers from the mattress blanketing them like snow. The orchid-patterned carpet must have been custom-made because it fit the big room perfectly. Just inside the door, iridescent blue flies hovered over a cluster of dried bloodstains; the largest had soaked deeply into the rug, while others were little more than smears.

"That's where Mrs. Kimball died," Nell said.

Will appraised the stains gravely. "Doesn't look as if she moved from that spot after she was shot, although she may have shifted a bit."

"Mr. Thurston testified at the inquest that he found her right there in the doorway. He said he held her until she passed."

Will nodded. "She wouldn't have wanted to die alone."

"Would anybody?"

"I've always felt I would prefer it. I used to, anyway."

Nell directed a quizzical look toward Will, but he didn't meet her gaze.

He entered the room, stepping carefully over the blood, and took Nell's hand to help her do the same. More footprints formed tracks back and forth all over the carpet. The clothespress and armoire were open, their contents strewn about. Drawers had been yanked from them, as well as from the dressing table and writing desk, and emptied onto the floor.

A bed bench upholstered in yellow silk had been upended and gutted near the foot of the bed. Nearby lay a lacquered box, its lid open, revealing an empty jewelry tray lined with purple velvet. Nell lifted the tray; the compartment beneath it was empty, too. She turned the box over and felt around, looking for evidence of a secret drawer, but there was none.

"Look at this," Will said as he pulled aside the curtains on the lefthand window. The window frame on the right side had a small gouge carved out of it, and several panes of glass were shattered, letting in a little welcome air, along with street sounds from outside—wheels on cobblestones, the neighing of horses, a newsboy yelling, "Mrs. Kimball murdered by her own maid! Fiona Gannon guilty!"

Nell said, "That's where they retrieved the bullet Mrs. Kimball fired first."

"And that's where Fiona fell." Will pointed to a pool of congealed blood, thick with flies, on the floor near the west wall. Not just blood, Nell realized, but bits of what could only be Fiona Gannon's skull and brain tissue. Leaning against that wall was an enormous oil painting that had been taken down, exposing an open wall safe, its wooden shelves entirely empty. The painting was of Virginia Kimball posing as an odalisque, her nudity cloaked by a violent burst of blood mixed with specks of other matter.

"That painting was on the wall during the shooting." Nell pointed out a mist of blood on the wallpaper surrounding the pristine, rectangular section that had been shielded by the picture. She closed her eyes and drew a deep breath, but the smell of all that blood conspired with the oppressive heat to make her feel as if the world was wobbling slightly on its axis.

Will grasped her arms to steady her. "So much for being immune to swooning."

She opened her eyes to take in the ravaged bedroom. "I'm all right. I'm just . . ." She shook her head. "It doesn't make any sense."

"Murder almost never does."

"I didn't mean that. I meant it doesn't make sense that the bullet that killed Fiona Gannon could have remained in her head, as the coroner claimed it did, if the exit wound was as explosive as it appears to have been. Brady described it as a 'crater.' He said the left side of her head had been blown completely away. I thought he might have been exaggerating, and that I'd have to have a look at the body myself to be sure, but from what I can see here . . ."

"He wasn't exaggerating," Will said soberly. "A gun pressed to the head tends to do a remarkable amount of damage."

"That being the case, wouldn't the bullet have been ejected along with . . .. everything else? And wouldn't it all have landed on the same wall?"

Will smiled at Nell with that nonchalant directness that was peculiarly his. "One of the delights of your company is never having to explain the obvious. Yes, one would think the blood and fragments from such a massive exit wound would follow the path of the bullet. It's a commonsense observation that cannot, I suspect, have escaped either the coroner or Detective Skinner."

"Giving Skinner the benefit of the doubt for the moment—"

"In a peculiarly charitable mood today, are we?" Will asked.

"Perhaps he really does believe it happened the way he said it did, with Mrs. Kimball catching Fiona in the act, being shot, then shooting twice at Fiona. Perhaps Skinner searched in earnest for the second bullet, the one that passed through Fiona's head—a spent thirty-one-caliber ball he could match to the murder weapon, hard physical evidence to show off at the inquest. He took the painting down, which revealed the safe, but no bullet hole." She looked at the section of wall that had been concealed behind the painting; it appeared to be unmarked.

Will squatted down to inspect the patina of blood covering the middle of the huge painting. "And yet . . ." He pointed to a gash in the canvas that would have been immediately noticeable but for the bloody mess that surrounded it. "Almost dead center."

They both raised their gazes to the spot the bullet would have struck.

"The safe," Will said as he stood, favoring his bad leg.

Nell closed the safe's door, a slab of maroon-painted iron with the words DIEBOLD SAFELOCK CO.—CANTON OH. stenciled on it in gold leaf. Its surface was smooth and undamaged save for a dime-sized spot above the lock—not a combination lock, but the type that opened with a key—where the paint was missing. Nell touched the little blemish, which was slightly concave. "Could a thirty-one-caliber slug have left a dent like this?"

"Any bullet could have. And one can't help but think Skinner would have noticed it."

"And searched for the bullet that did it."

Will lifted the painting to look behind it, then set it back down. Hiking up his trousers, he knelt and examined the area in front of the wall with an expression of fierce concentration. He said, "The bullet must have struck the safe, bounced back through the hole in the painting, and landed somewhere on the floor, probably within a few feet of the wall."

"If it was here," Nell said, "wouldn't Skinner have found it?"

"The fact that he didn't doesn't mean it's not here. Bullets don't just vaporize on impact." Will stroked the carpet in a methodical back-and-forth pattern as he edged away from the wall. "Depending on the type of bullet and what it hits, it might fragment, or mushroom, or otherwise deform, but it won't disappear. It might even end up relatively unscathed. The bullet you found among Mrs. Kimball's effects, the one from the window frame—what did it look like?"

"Like a lump of spruce gum after it's been chewed and spat out." Nell leaned over to scrutinize the intricate pattern on the carpet; two sets of eyes were better than one.

"Then that's more or less we're looking for." He bent over to peer at the spot where Fiona's head had come to rest after she fell. The blood and various unthinkable bits had coagulated into a grisly mass that Nell, despite her strong stomach, found hard to look at.

"Those bluebottles have been busy." Will said as he

probed the gummy matter with his fingers. "There are hundreds of first stage larvae in here."

Nell swallowed hard. It didn't surprise her that Will thought nothing of poking about in such ghastly stuff. As a battle surgeon, he'd seen and touched much worse. Would Skinner have had the grit for it? She couldn't imagine it.

"It would appear the good detective simply didn't examine the evidence quite thoroughly enough," Will held something between his gore-smeared fingers, something small and dully metallic. "If he'd just been willing to soil his hands, he'd have found it. He knew it, too. He must have."

"But he just couldn't bring himself to do it," Nell said. "He could hardly admit that at the inquest, though, so he claimed the bullet never exited Fiona's head, and he got the coroner to go along with it."

Nell crouched down for a better look, taking care to tuck her skirts away from the worst of the "evidence." It was a bullet, all right, but unlike that taken from the window, it didn't remotely resemble a squished little ball. This bullet, although buckled and badly scarred, was clearly conical in shape.

"How much do you know about bullets?" Will asked as he studied the little projectile.

She shrugged. "I know there are two kinds—round balls and the cone-shaped ones, like the one you've got there. And they come in different sizes. A bullet has to be the same size as the inside of the gun barrel."

"As measured in calibers, which are hundredths of an inch. This bullet is at least forty calibers, probably larger. There's no possible way it was fired out of a thirty-one-caliber Remington pocket pistol." He rubbed his grimy thumb over the bullet, as if to shine it. "I'm going down the hall to wash this off. I'll be right back."

While he was gone, Nell sorted through the detritus from the writing desk for something to draw on. She found a blank sheet of vellum with *Mrs. Virginia Kimball* embossed in crimson ink across the top, along with a quill and a silver inkstand. Positioning the chair on the window side of the desk, affording her a view into the room, she sketched out a rough floor plan, including the positions of the two bodies.

When Will came back, his hands were clean, and he was wrapping the bullet in his pocket handkerchief. "What are you doing?" He came to look over Nell's shoulder as she pondered the drawing.

"Trying to understand what happened."

"As compared to what Detective Skinner and the coroner claim to have happened?"

Nell sighed heavily. "The official story is that Mrs. Kimball came home from shopping to find Fiona rummaging in her jewelry box. Fiona grabs the pistol from beneath the pillow, or perhaps she's thought ahead and already has it, and shoots Mrs. Kimball in the chest from across the room."

"We can be fairly certain it was from a distance," Will said. "Didn't you tell me there was a small, neat bullet hole in the bodice of Mrs. Kimball's dress, and no gunpowder residue?"

"Mightn't any residue have been hidden under all that blood?"

Now it was Will's turn to sigh. "In any event, Mrs. Kimball fell to the floor over there." He nodded toward the bloodstained doorway.

"Fiona thinks she's dead, but in fact, she's still very much alive. Mrs. Kimball somehow manages to get her hands on the gun and—"

"How?" Will asked. "The lady is lying on the floor with a sucking chest wound, in respiratory distress. Unless Fiona set the gun down on the floor very close to her, or perhaps on the edge of the bed"—he pointed to those spots on Nell's sketch—"I can't see how Mrs. Kimball could have possibly gotten hold of it. And why would Fiona have put it within reach of the person she'd just shot?"

"Unless she thought that person was dead."

"But she wasn't."

"Maybe Fiona thought she was. It's hard to tell sometimes, even if you know about the carotid pulse, and most people just check for breathing. You know how inaccurate that is."

Will didn't look convinced. Neither was Nell, by any means, but arguing the point helped to clarify things in her mind.

"Mr. Thurston did testify that he found the Remington near Mrs. Kimball's hand," Nell said, "and we know that the bullet from the window frame came from that gun. And I can assure you her glove was stained with gunpowder residue."

Will grimaced and rubbed his neck.

"I'm just walking through the official version," Nell said, "not advocating it, God knows. So Mrs. Kimball somehow gains possession of the Remington and gets off a shot, which goes astray." She drew a dotted line from the supine Mrs. Kimball's right hand to the spot where the bullet was recovered from the window frame. "She fires again. The second shot—"

"The second shot," Will said in a tone of complete exasperation, "wasn't fired from the Remington at all. It was fired—"

"From a high-caliber revolver. I know. In the official version, the bullet remains lodged in Fiona Gannon's brain. In reality, we know it passed through her skull and the painting, and ricocheted off the safe and onto the floor several feet away—onto the very spot, in fact, where Fiona's head hit a second or so later, as she fell to the floor."

"Almost certainly already dead," Will said as he sat on the edge of the writing desk to watch Nell work.

"One can only hope so."

"Head wounds like Fiona's tend to be instantaneously fatal," he said. "Chest wounds can take a while, as Mrs. Kimball's clearly did. Therefore, if they were the only two people involved . . ."

"Then Mrs. Kimball *had* to have been shot first," Nell finished, "and Fiona second."

"Which supports the official story."

"*If* they were the only two people involved."

"We already know there was more than one gun involved. Do you mind?" Will asked as he withdrew his cigarettes and matches.

"Why do you even ask? You know I always say it's all right."

"If I were a gentleman, I wouldn't even ask." He lit up, then lifted a cut-glass vanity tray off the floor to use as an ashtray. "I would simply abstain."

"Then why don't you?" she teasingly challenged. "It's a sign of respect. I *am* a lady."

"A lady who needn't rely, I should hope, on such

puerile gestures as evidence of my regard for her." There was a hint of amusement in the softspoken statement, and a hint of something else, half-hidden beneath the droll banter, the whisperlight suggestion.

Turning away from that hint, that whisper, that treacherous lure, Nell said, "Skinner wouldn't have realized there were two guns involved, given that he never found that second bullet. He probably did think it happened the way he presented it to the inquest."

"I wouldn't be so sure. May I?" Will asked as he slid Nell's drawing across the desk. "If only we could know what position Fiona actually assumed when she fell."

"I believe she fell pretty much as I've drawn her. The stains on the rug clearly indicate where her head was. Mr. Thurston testified that she was lying on her left side in an east–west direction, and Skinner didn't dispute that."

"So at the moment she was shot, she must have been standing . . ."

"Approximately where her feet are in my picture," Nell said. "In the middle of this open area in front of us. And she would have been facing the corner between the bed and the doorway."

"She was shot at close range in her right temple and fell to the left, onto her side, which means whoever shot her must have been right next to her on this side." Will pointed to a spot on the drawing just to the right of where Fiona would have been standing.

"If Mrs. Kimball had shot Fiona from the doorway, she would have fallen backward, in the direction of the window. And unless she'd been looking toward the painting for some reason, the bullet would have struck her in the forehead, not the temple."

Will said, "I've been thinking . . . what if there was an intruder of some sort—say, a jewel thief."

"In the daytime?"

"Just ruminating out loud here. Mrs. Kimball and Fiona come home and surprise him. He's already determined the famous diamond necklaces to be paste."

"Perhaps he wasn't a thief at all," Nell said. "He could have been one of the men who bribed Skinner, or even some thug hired by one of those men. It wasn't the diamonds he came for, it was the Red Book. Perhaps he found it, perhaps not. The open safe would suggest that he did."

Will crossed to the safe and tried to insert a key from the big silver ring. It didn't fit, but the next one did. "This safe could have been opened by Skinner after he'd been called to the scene," Will said. "Maybe he's the one who found the Red Book."

"Maybe."

"We're getting ahead of ourselves," Will said. "There's an intruder—either a thief or a powerful man with something to hide. He ends up shooting both women . . ."

"Why?"

"So they can't identify him. Or perhaps because Mrs. Kimball threatened him with her own gun. In any event, after shooting them, he sets it up to look as if the maid had been caught in the act."

Nell nodded slowly as she thought it over. "How did this intruder get into the house without being seen? He wouldn't have just walked up to the front door, and there was no sign of the other doors having been broken into."

Will rubbed his jaw for a minute, scowling contemplatively. "All right, then, what if things started out, well, more or less as Skinner proposed, Fiona set about stealing Mrs. Kimball's necklaces, but she had a gun with her."

"A gun that's forty calibers or higher."

"Right. Mrs. Kimball comes home, pulls out her own gun, and threatens to send Fiona to prison. Fiona panics and fires, hitting Mrs. Kimball in the chest. Horrified at what she's done, she turns her gun on herself."

"Then what happened to it?" Nell asked.

"Fiona's gun?"

"Yes. Wouldn't it have been found in her hand, or near it?"

Will frowned as he contemplated that. "Perhaps Detective Skinner took it."

"Why would he do that when it would just make it harder to prove that only Fiona and Mrs. Kimball were involved? He would have loved having that gun there."

Will conceded with a disgruntled sigh. "Speaking of Skinner, he didn't strike me as a dim-witted man. He had to have known Fiona's killer was standing right next to her, not across the room."

"And he had to know Mrs. Kimball couldn't very well have gotten up off the floor, mortally wounded, walked up to Fiona without being noticed, and put the gun to her head. He knew his version of the murder was fundamentally flawed. He must have suspected there was a third person involved. But with half the rich toffs in Boston throwing money at him . . ."

"How many, altogether?"

"Four that I know of, not including Orville Pratt. Mr. Thurston, Horace Bacon . . ."

"I know the name. His wife is a friend of my mother's."

"Then there's a banker named . . ." Nell scoured her

memory. "Swann—Weyland Swann. And a Dr. Foster from Harvard."

"Isaac Foster?"

"Yes. Do you know him?"

"I know *of* him. He's a third-generation surgeon from one of the oldest Boston families." Will looked around the room as he drew on his cigarette. "Either it was very crowded in here that afternoon, or those men are hiding sins other than murder."

"At any rate," Nell said, "Skinner took the money and fed the inquest jury a story designed to incriminate Fiona while directing attention away from his, er, benefactors."

"No wonder he was so willing to let Orville Pratt expunge this house of all evidence," Will said, smiling as he added, "God forbid it should be scrutinized by some pink-cheeked little Irish governess who can't seem to resist the temptation to meddle in homicides."

"Not to mention a certain rakish card sharp with the same curious affliction."

Will grinned as he flung his cigarette out the broken window. "You think I'm rakish?"

Nell rolled her eyes. "Let's finish up here. I need to get home to Gracie."

They searched the upper two floors of the house, finding them virtually devoid of furniture, save for a bedroom on the fourth floor that had clearly been Fiona's. It was a cozy room with a small fireplace, two lace-curtained windows and a worn but cheerful floral rug covering most of the plank floor. In another time, it would have been occupied by one of the higher-ranking servants—a housekeeper or butler. Fiona had evidently earned it by virtue of being a domestic staff of one.

Tacked onto the walls were pages torn out of magazines, scores of them, mostly from *Godey's Lady's Book*, featuring illustrations of the latest fashions in ladies' accessories. There were fans, slippers, shawls, collars, gloves, and reticules, but the majority were of hats, and of these, many had notes scrawled on them in pencil: *Need felt, velvet and moleskin for hat, one long ostrich feather and pompom for trim; Braiding and a broom feather; Rosettes and feathers, plus tulle or ribbon to fall from back.*

This room had obviously been searched, but cursorily as compared to the rest of the house. Clothes were strewn about, and an old sea chest dumped onto the floor, but the narrow bed was left untouched; clearly, Skinner had not seriously expected to find the mysterious Red Book in the maid's room.

Nell and Will sorted through the contents of the sea chest: a handful of dime novels, stacks of magazines tied with string, a notebook filled with the names and addresses of wholesale suppliers, another with instructions for trimming bonnets, and seven thick scrapbooks containing carefully pasted fashion illustrations. Judging from the dates on the magazine pages, the twenty-one-year-old Fiona had started keeping these scrapbooks when she was twelve.

Nell and Will retraced their path through the house, pausing this time to scrutinize any papers lying about—correspondence, bills, shopping lists . . . With no revelations forthcoming, and Nell already late in getting back to Colonnade Row, Will relocked the house and escorted her down the front steps.

"Will you be taking Gracie to the Public Garden this afternoon?" he asked.

"The Commons. She wants to sail her toy boat in the Frog Pond."

"Perfect. I've got a new boat for her—a Chinese junk."

Nell halted at the bottom of the steps and turned to face him. Shanghai and Hong Kong had been haunts of his at one time. Loath as she was to inquire into his travels . . . "You've been gone just a little over a month. That's not enough time to go to China and back."

Will laughed. "I should say not. It takes a hundred days or more just to get there from Boston. Half that long from San Francisco, though. Which is where I bought the junk, by the way."

"Really?" The trip from the east coast to the west had always been a lengthy one, as well, whether overland or by ship, but the Union Pacific and the Central Pacific had connected their tracks last month, to much fanfare.

He smiled. "I made it a point to be on the first train from Omaha to San Francisco. Four days from the Missouri River to the Pacific Ocean—not bad, eh?"

"Couldn't resist taking part in history?"

"Couldn't resist taking part in a high-stakes poker game I'd been invited to by some rich Californians who never know when to fold."

"Ah. Of course." Nell wished now that she had obeyed her instinct and not asked where he'd been. San Francisco was notorious for dissolution—murder, thievery, gambling, prostitution and, of course, opium. The air in the Barbary Coast was said to be thick with it; the same in the Chinese quarter. There'd been a time when Will had been helpless to resist its lure.

Her thoughts must have shown on her face, because Will said, with quiet sincerity, "I'm not the same man I was when you met me. You've . . ." He looked down, frowning as if unsure of his words. Meeting her eyes, he said, "I've changed. You do realize that."

"Yes."

He nodded thoughtfully, ran a hand through his hair. "So, um, I don't suppose you'd have any objections to my coming by the Frog Pond this afternoon?"

"Why should I mind?" she asked with a little smile, hoping to lighten the mood. "We're courting now, aren't we?"

He led her to his waiting phaeton, chuckling as he took her hand to help her up into the seat. "Rakish. I like that."

Chapter 7

" I 'VE something rather momentous to communicate,"
announced Orville Pratt halfway through the elabo-
rate dinner à la Russe he hosted the following evening, instantly silencing the ten other people seated at his
long, damask-draped dining table. There should have
been one more guest, so as to make an even dozen around
the table, half gentlemen and half ladies, but the client
Mr. Pratt had spontaneously invited two days ago had
failed to appear, leaving the chair to Nell's left awkwardly empty.

The only sound in the Pratts' sumptuous dining room
was a muted clinking as four footmen in scarlet and gold
livery cleared away the roman punch with which the diners had refreshed their palates between the roast course
and the upcoming game course: *Canvasback Duck with
Currant Jelly and Giblet Gravy, served with Madeira* according

to the neatly penned menu propped up between Nell's
gold-plated charger and that of the absent guest to her
left.

Winifred Pratt, seated at the opposite end of the table
from her husband, waved her hand to capture his attention through the forest of candelabras separating them.
"Perhaps some champagne with which to toast the excit-
ing news?"

Mr. Pratt fixed his frigid gaze on her, the bruising
around his left eye only adding to an aura of vexation
held perennially in check. He was a tall gentleman, very
fit-looking for his age, who wore his sterling-bright hair
combed straight back from a brow so expansive as to suggest a colossal skull housing a brain of monstrous propor-
tions. He and his wife might have belonged to different
species altogether.

Pratt nodded to his butler, a stocky, taciturn fellow,
who signaled the footmen, who retreated from the room,
leaving an expectant hush in their wake. Winifred looked
around the table and mimed an eager clapping of her
plump little hands. Vera Pratt—Mr. Pratt's spinster sister,
Nell had learned, who lived with her brother's family
when she wasn't serving as Emily's companion in her
travels—caught Winifred's eye and cast her a quizzical
look, prompting her sister-in-law to whisper, "Be patient,
for heaven's sake."

Winifred's gaze was slightly out of focus, her cheeks
shiny pink; she'd had at least one refill of every wine or
liqueur served so far. Her elder daughter, Emily, started
to say something to her, then just looked away with an expression of weariness.

Emily Pratt, fresh off her tour of Europe, was a brown-eyed honey blonde whose taste in clothes utterly confounded Nell. The dress she had on tonight was similar to yesterday's funeral attire in the simplicity of its design, but the plum Shantung silk from which it had been made gave it a lushly romantic air. Her unbound hair, which fell in waves just to her shoulders, formed a corona of burnished bronze around her face.

If Emily defied the current fashions, her younger sister, the blue-eyed, golden-haired Cecilia, embraced them with a passion. Cecilia's gown, a frothy construction of pink tulle festooned with ribbon embroidery, was a creation of the celebrated Parisian modiste Charles Worth, of whom, as she'd confided to Nell before dinner, she was a private client. All her evening dresses—three dozen new ones each year—came from the House of Worth. She owned fifty-eight silk shawls made by Gagelin et Opigez, also in Paris, and had just ordered a dozen more. Her mamá was forever pestering her to pass some along to Aunt Vera, but she loved just looking at them all. Her day dresses, hats, gloves, footwear, and underpinnings came mostly from Swan & Edgar and Lewis & Allenby in London.

Warming to her subject, Nell's manifest disinterest notwithstanding, Cecilia had described the care that went into her specifications when purchasing new clothing and accessories. She studied every issue of *Godey's* and paid minute attention to the newspaper descriptions of gowns worn by European royalty, especially those of that international icon of elegance, and Mr. Worth's most famous patron, the empress Eugénie. Not since Cecilia was a young girl had she permitted her mother to choose her frocks. Everything she wore, she told Nell, she ordered to her own exacting standards, except, of course, for her jewelry, such as the almond-sized diamond nestled in her cleavage, and the matching, if slightly smaller, ear bobs, which she owed to "the thoughtfulness of Mr. Hewitt."

By "Mr. Hewitt," she of course meant Harry, with whom she'd been keeping company since throwing over her Austrian nobleman a month ago, right after the formal announcement of their engagement at the Pratts' annual ball. Ah, yes, the oh-so-thoughtful Harry Hewitt, the "Beau Brummel of Boston," whose only physical imperfections—a small scar on his left eyelid and a bump on the bridge of his nose—were souvenirs of his attempt last year, while drunk on absinthe, to forcibly ravish Nell. To Nell's knowledge, Harry still swilled absinthe, seduced mill girls, and gambled away appalling sums night after night, despite his father's threats of disinheritance. How would Cecilia react, Nell wondered, if she knew everything there was to know about Harry Hewitt? Quite possibly she wouldn't care so long as he was discreet, assuming, of course, that the diamonds and rubies kept coming.

Both Nell and Will had ignored Harry completely, both before and during dinner, and he them. Will had, however, initiated a fairly cordial conversation with his parents, an effort greeted by his father with ill-cloaked disdain, but by his mother with delight. The rift between Viola Hewitt and her eldest son, for which she blamed herself, had been her cross to bear for years. The prospect of enjoying normal maternal relations with Will made her "fairly giddy with pleasure," as she'd declared this afternoon in her cultivated British accent. Nell had come to her to explain about the sham courtship, and to assure her that she had no matrimonial designs on Will or anyone else. "All I care about is that I'll get to see my son from time to time," Viola had said. "I'm just grateful that you've made that happen."

The footmen returned, bearing fresh glasses and icy bottles of Perrier-Jouët. A cut crystal champagne flute was placed in front of Nell and filled with a flourish. She felt a moment of heady intoxication as the golden liquid swirled and fizzed, not because she'd drunk more than she was used to; she had, but she'd eaten so much that she barely felt it. It was because Will, seated diagonally across the table, was looking at her again.

It was that look of slightly dazed admiration that he'd given her when he first saw her tonight, dressed not in her usual high-necked, stylishly austere manner, but in her one and only evening dress—a luxuriously feminine gown made of prismatic, greenish-purplish silk that shifted colors as she moved. It was snug enough to require tighter stays than usual, and cut so low as to reveal far more bosom than Nell was accustomed to. Viola had had it made for the dinner party Nell had reminded Mrs. Pratt about after the funeral. A lady of rank might balk at being seen twice in the same gown by the same people eighteen months apart, for the Pratts had been guests at that dinner, but Nell had no option but to wear what she owned.

Gracie, who'd "helped" Nell get dressed earlier this evening, had been effusive in her praise. Nell looked "just like a pwincess," she'd decreed. "Evwybody will say you're the pwettiest lady there."

Indeed, Nell had received many admiring remarks that evening, and one rather off-putting comment, from Cecilia, when they were first introduced. At first, Cecilia couldn't recall having met her at that dinner party—until Nell's wrap was removed. Cecilia took one hard, trenchant look at her gown and said, "Ah, yes. Now I remember you." As if unaware of the insult she'd quite deliberately dealt, she'd launched into that soliloquy on the subject of her vast and painstakingly chosen wardrobe, keeping at it until Will finally rescued Nell with a gentle tug on her elbow.

Will, crisply handsome tonight in white tie and tails, his hair lightly oiled, a sprig of lily of the valley in his lapel, had stolen glances at her all through dinner. Nell found his reaction gratifying, of course—she was still a woman, after all—but also a bit unsettling. There were boundaries to their friendship, like a wall of frosted glass, very real but also very fragile, so fragile that neither of them dare speak of what lay on the other side. By looking at her that way, Will was, whether he realized it or not, pressing his face dangerously close to the glass.

"Well, then." Mr. Pratt pushed back his chair and stood as the footmen backed away from the table. "It gives me the greatest of pleasure to . . ." His gaze shifted over the heads of his guests. "Foster! I'd all but given up hope."

All eyes turned toward the open doorway to the central hall, where a gentleman in white tie—brown-haired, fortyish, with robust good looks—stood holding a silk top hat in one hand and a pair of white kid gloves in the other. The Pratts' butler stood behind him, an evening cape draped over one arm.

"So sorry to be late." Foster's coatsleeve rode up a bit as he handed his hat and gloves to the butler, revealing a smear of what looked like fresh blood on his shirt cuff. "It's inexcusable, I know," he said as he tugged his sleeves down and straightened his lapels, "but there was a medical emergency just as I was getting ready to leave the house."

"Not at all, old man." Pratt waved the newcomer into the room. "Some champagne for our new guest," he told the nearest footman, "and a plate of whatever he's missed up till now. Some of those oysters, certainly, and one or two lamb cutlets—"

"No, don't bother, please," Foster said to the footman directly. "I'm really not very hungry. Whatever's yet to be served will more than suffice. I never turn down good champagne, though."

Addressing his guests, Pratt said, "May I present Dr. Isaac Foster, one of my newer clients, and a gentleman of no small achievement. For those of you who don't know, though I daresay you should, Dr. Foster is a professor of clinical medicine at Harvard Medical School, in addition to being one of Boston's most respected surgeons, as were his father and grandfather before him, both of whom I was proud to call my friends." There followed formal introductions and bows all around.

Nell met Will's gaze across the table in silent communication: Isaac Foster was one of the men who had visited, and presumably bribed, Detective Skinner the day before yesterday.

"What kind of medical emergency was it?" Winifred asked. "Nothing serious, I hope."

"The patient was a dog that got in the way of a horse car," Foster said as he took his seat next to Nell.

"A *dog*?" Vera pressed a hand to her gaunt chest. "Oh, my word. Poor little thing."

Foster smiled. "Quite a sizable thing, actually, part

bear, I think, hauled to my front door in a tipcart by a fourteen-year-old boy in an apoplexy of tears. What was I to do?"

"Will he be all right? The dog, I mean." Vera Pratt had the high, thready voice of a younger lady, although, on close acquaintance, she wasn't as old as Nell had originally thought—fifty, perhaps. There were but a few strands of gray in her reddish-blond hair, but she had an underfed, drawn look about her, accentuated by her ill-fitting green satin gown, that aged her beyond her years. Vera had merely picked at the dishes served thus far, and drunk nothing but water; she'd covered her wine glass every time a bottle was brought around.

"The beast is a *she,* ma'am," Foster told her. "And I believe she'll pull out of it just fine, although I doubt she'll get off without a limp."

"My son William is a surgeon," Viola offered. "He earned his degree from the University of Edinburgh."

"Yes?" Foster asked, clearly impressed; Edinburgh was the world's premier medical school. "Do you have a practice in Boston, Dr. Hewitt?"

"I do not," Will said. "I've led a rather nomadic existence of late."

Dr. Foster looked as if there might have been something more he wanted to say to Will, or ask him, but instead, he turned to Mr. Pratt and said, "Sir, I believe I interrupted you in mid-toast."

"Thank you, Foster." Pratt cleared his throat. "It gives me great pleasure to inform you all that young Harry"— he nodded toward Harry Hewitt—"came to me this afternoon seeking permission to ask my lovely daughter Cecilia for her hand in marriage."

Winifred burst into jubilant applause. The Hewitts murmured expressions of surprise. Vera gasped; this was obviously news to her. Emily stared unblinkingly at her sister.

Will looked from Harry, flushed and grinning, to the smugly triumphant Cecilia, to Nell.

She met his gaze with a rueful little smile.

Pratt said, "Need I tell you I granted said permission, whereupon the proposal was made and duly accepted."

Spoken like a true limb of the bar, Nell thought. This would be Cecilia Pratt's third engagement, and she was barely twenty.

Pratt raised his glass high; his guests followed suit. "To Cecilia and Harry."

Everyone congratulated the newly betrothed couple— except for Will and Nell, but no one seemed to notice that in all the excitement.

"How perfect to have your whole family here for the announcement," Winifred told Harry. She gestured expansively, knocking over a lit candelabra. Vera grabbed it just in time; her tipsy sister-in-law did not appear to notice. "I'm so pleased we ran into William at the funeral yesterday."

"Did you know Mrs. Kimball well?" Will inquired of his hostess.

"Me? Oh. No. No. Not at all. She was Mr. Pratt's client, you see."

"Oh, so you'd never met her?" Will asked.

"Well . . . once. She, er . . ." Winifred let out a jittery little laugh. "She showed up at our annual ball at the end of April. Yes. Well." She shrugged and spread her hands, laughed again and lifted her champagne glass, but it was empty. She turned toward a footman, but he was already crossing to her, bottle tilted and ready to pour.

" 'Showed up?' " Will asked. "I'm afraid I don't quite understand."

"She crashed the party," Emily said. "She and that old Betty of a playwright. Really livened things up."

"How can you joke about it?" demanded Cecilia with quaking outrage.

"Girls . . ." Mr. Pratt glanced meaningfully at their guests.

"I think she must have been"—Winifred lowered her voice to a thick-tongued whisper—"drinking."

Pratt said, "My dear, I'm quite sure our guests aren't interested in—"

"Oh, come now, Orville," she said, "people could talk of nothing else after those two left, and for days afterward. You even thought she'd stolen that precious gun of yours, remember?"

Orville Pratt pinned his wife with a look that oozed venom.

"Not your Stonewall Jackson gun?" August Hewitt, the most dignified gentleman Nell knew, was gaping at his friend.

"Stonewall Jackson gun?" Will asked.

"My husband collects weapons," Winifred explained. "Edged weapons—knives and swords and whatnot. But last winter he bought this fancy French gun that had belonged to General Jackson."

Will said, "I'm impressed, Mr. Pratt. That's quite a famous revolver."

"It must be," Cecilia said. "He paid a fortune for it."

Pratt looked sharply at his daughter, clearly irked that

she'd brought up money in polite conversation. "My dear, we really needn't—"

"Twelve thousand dollars," Cecilia declared.

A stunned silence greeted this pronouncement.

"It went missing from his study the night of the ball," Winifred said.

"I'm sorry to hear that, Pratt," said Dr. Foster. "It's a beautiful weapon. I remember you passing it around that night."

"Did you report the theft to the police?" Mr. Hewitt asked.

Mr. Pratt shook his head; his bruises had taken on a livid bloodred cast. "It wouldn't have done to let the constabulary interrogate my guests as if they were common sneak thieves. And I blamed myself for showing off the gun so indiscriminately and leaving it unlocked."

"But never fear," Winifred said, "for our little tragedy had a happy ending after all. Yesterday, after we came home from the funeral, I walked into Mr. Pratt's study. He was sitting at his desk, and what do you suppose he was holding in his hand?"

"The Jackson gun?" Mr. Hewitt asked. "By Jove, you don't say."

"I suppose I must have . . . been in my cups during the ball," Pratt said, "and simply forgotten which drawer I'd locked it up in. You can imagine my chagrin when I stumbled upon it yesterday, looking for my favorite cigars."

"And after all that ranting about how Mrs. Kimball must have stolen it," his wife said. "You should have heard him after the ball, the things he called—"

Pratt said, "Winifred," in a soft, leonine growl.

"I know, I know, she's a client. Was." Winifred finished off her champagne and held her glass up for a refill.

"Merritt, where the devil is the next course?" Pratt asked his butler.

The butler gestured to the footmen, who stumbled over each other leaving the room. An agonizing silence descended over the table. Winifred was the first to surrender to it. "So!" she chirped. "You Hewitts will be making your annual pilgrimage to Cape Cod again this year, I presume?"

"Yes, of course," Viola said. "I live for those summers at Falconwood."

"When will you be leaving?"

"Mid-July, as usual," Viola said.

Winifred nodded. Viola smiled.

Everyone looked at each other.

Will's brother Martin, ever the diplomat, punctured the tension by speaking up for the first time since taking his seat. "Emily, I haven't seen you since you went overseas. I must say, your travels seem to have agreed with you. You look very well."

"Thank you."

Winifred followed the exchange with bright, doll-like eyes and a self-satisfied little smile.

"What was it, four years altogether that you were gone?" Martin asked.

"Almost. I left—*we* left, Aunt Vera and I—in May of sixty-five, right after the war ended. We came back this past February, when Father cut off our—"

"Emily," Pratt said quietly. "Don't bore our guests with details."

Martin looked from Pratt to his eldest daughter with placid blue eyes that saw everything. Although the youngest of the Hewitts' three remaining sons, Martin was, in many ways, the wisest. He was also the fairest, resembling the flaxen-haired August, just as Will, with his inky hair and rangy limbs, took after Viola.

The footmen returned with gold-rimmed plates of sliced duck and bottles of Madeira, which they served all around. Emily declined the duck. "Honestly, dear," her mother inveigled. "Not even a little?"

With strained patience, Emily said, "Mother, you know I don't eat meat."

"But it's not meat," Winifred said. "It's duck."

"You're a vegetarian?" asked Dr. Foster as he waved away his own plate. "So am I."

Emily seemed to notice him for the first time. "Really?"

"Perhaps it's all those years of surgery," Foster said, "but I've gotten to where I can't bear the thought of eating flesh."

Winifred's elation seemed only to increase as she looked back and forth between Emily and Foster, from which Nell concluded that the wellborn surgeon was a bachelor. How thrilled she must have been to have not one, but two gentlemen of breeding chatting up her marriageable daughter at the same dinner.

"Four years," Martin said, bringing the conversation back around to Emily's tour. "That's a long time to spend traveling."

"It was to have been a year-long tour," Emily said. "London and the Continent."

"I love London," said Martin as he spooned currant jelly onto his plate.

"I loathed it." With a glance at Vera, Emily amended that to, "*We* loathed it."

"Terribly gray." Vera rubbed her arms, shivering delicately. "Terribly damp. Perhaps it was just that particular spring, but—"

"It wasn't the weather," Emily said.

"No, of course not," her aunt quickly responded. "I didn't mean—"

"It was those stuffy English prigs and their absurd caste system. No offense intended, Mrs. Hewitt."

"No, I quite agree," replied Viola, who'd been, and remained, for the most part, as much of a free spirit in her own way as Emily. "I couldn't wait to get away from there myself."

Emily propped her elbows on the table, her glass of Madeira cupped lightly in one hand. It was the sort of posture all well-bred girls were exhorted to avoid, yet far from looking vulgar, Emily exuded an aura of graceful insouciance. "We escaped to Italy as soon as we could. Aunt Vera met this Russian lady there who traveled quite a bit, and we more or less threw our lot in with her."

"Madame Blavatsky." Vera might have said, "The Holy Mother," so reverent was her tone. "A marvelous lady with marvelous gifts. She's fairly young, actually, not yet forty, but so wise and enlightened, you might think she's lived for hundreds of years. Perhaps she has," Vera added with a private little smile. "It was a remarkable experience, traveling with her."

"Remarkable," Emily muttered into her Madeira. As she lowered the glass, Nell saw her biting back a smile.

"What kinds of . . . gifts does she possess?" Viola asked.

Vera looked around the table, a hectic red stain crawling up her throat.

"Go ahead, Auntie," Emily urged. "They can't be any

ruder about it than I am, and they'll probably be a good deal kinder. Most people are."

"H.P.B.'s gifts are—"

"H.P.B.?" Viola asked.

"Helena Petrovna Blavatsky," Vera said in her thin, warbly voice. "It . . . it's what we call her, those of us who travel with her. Her gifts are of a . . . spiritual nature, profoundly spiritual.

"Ah," Viola said after absorbing that for a moment. "By *spiritual,* do you mean . . . ?"

"She performs séances," Emily said.

Vera's blush spread over her face. "Well, yes, there's that, but—"

"Real séances?" Harry sat forward, his grin widening. "With people sitting 'round a circle and ghosts rapping on the table? Does she speak to the dead?" Harry had on one of his signature garish scarves tonight, a swath of Chinese-patterned red-and-gold silk draped with studied negligence over the shoulders of his tailcoat.

Vera hesitated, her gaze on the plate in front of her, her mouth working as if she couldn't quite find the words to express what she wanted to say. It seemed to Nell that she wasn't accustomed to being the center of attention, wasn't at all comfortable with it, but that she felt an obligation to enlighten her fellow diners on the subject at hand. "H.P.B. does have an . . . an aura that enables her to commune with, and even possess, the spirits of those who have passed into the dimension we call death. But as an esotericist, she—"

"Have you seen her talk to the dead?" Harry asked.

Vera sat back, still staring at her plate. "Yes. And . . . and she can move objects just by staring at them, and make letters from departed souls appear out of thin air. I've seen her make a piano play music."

"Good heavens, even I can do that," Cecilia said with a piercing little giggle.

"I'll wager the dead can do it better," Emily muttered into her glass.

"I meant w-without . . ." Vera stammered, "I meant without anyone actually sitting down at—"

"She knows what you meant," Emily said. "She thinks she's being hilarious. H.P.B. believes in . . . What is it?" she asked Vera. "There's something she calls it."

"Theosophy," Vera said.

Emily nodded. "It's this sort of religion she made up."

"She didn't make it up," Martin said as he dipped a bite of duck into the currant jelly and lifted it to his mouth.

Everyone turned to watch him as he chewed and swallowed.

"She didn't make up the *word*," Martin said. "I learned it in my divinity curriculum at Harvard. Theosophy, it's . . . well, it's sort of when you apply Eastern teachings to Western theological—"

"Yes," Vera said. "Yes! The ancient wisdom, the mystical insight. Karma, the rebirth of the soul into a new human form . . ."

"Reincarnation?" Martin asked. "Do you really believe in that?"

Vera stammered painfully until Emily said, "H.P.B. does. She believes in all that mystic hocus-pocus. Reincarnation, ghostly visitations, communion with the spirit world . . . Aunt Vera, being more of less a . . . follower of hers . . ."

"Disciple," Vera corrected.

Attention refocused on Vera.

"You . . . you'd understand if you'd ever met her." Vera still seemed unable to look her listeners in the eye; her face was a blotchy red now. "She's an amazing lady who has experienced things you and I could never conceive of. She's been known to awaken and find herself . . . well, someone else entirely. A different person, with a completely different voice, different mannerisms . . . And she wouldn't become herself again until someone called her by her real name. I'd never heard of such a phenomenon. She's truly a gifted soul."

Will sat forward. "She displayed two personalities?"

Vera said, "Yes, but the other one wasn't really her. It was a departed spirit looking for an earthly shell to inhabit—a human host, if you will. They do that, you know. They miss having bodies, being able to do all the things living people do."

Will sat back, ruminating on this.

Dr. Foster met Will's gaze with a discerning look, his smile so mild it was almost imperceptible.

Will smiled back.

"How extraordinary, Miss Pratt," said Nell, breaking her silence at last. "Did you and Emily spend the rest of those four years traveling with this Madame Blavatsky?"

"Yes. Oh, yes. It was the most fantastic adventure." Vera's smile was rapturous. "We went everywhere with her. All through the Balkans, Greece, Egypt, Syria, Russia, India, Tibet . . ."

"Tibet?" Will said. "It's devilishly hard to get into Tibet. I know—I've tried."

Most of Will's fellow diners, including his parents and brothers, turned to stare at him.

"We wore disguises," Vera said. "We were guests in the home of Master Koot Hoomi, and we saw and learned things . . . well, things I'll never forget. I'll never be the same, and I have H.P.B. to thank for it."

Winifred, probably bored with the Madame Blavatsky conversation, said, "Emily kept a travel diary. There are notes and sketches from everywhere she visited—churches, galleries . . . She drew the local flora and fauna, the way people dressed and spoke, the music they played, their bizarre heathen traditions . . . You should bring it down and show it around later, Emily."

"Mother, please," Emily said.

"I'd like to see those sketches," said Viola. "I'm sure Miss Sweeney would, too. She's quite an accomplished artist in her own right."

"Really?" Emily said.

"Of course," Winnie said, "what I really wish is that Emily would set aside her sketchbook and her wanderings and start thinking about settling down. And perhaps relearn how to dress." Winnie let out an edgy little giggle. "She's spent just a bit too much time among uncivilized peoples, I think."

Dr. Foster said, "Oh, I don't know about that, ma'am. She looks rather appealingly comfortable, if you ask me, and I shouldn't think there's anything particularly uncivilized in that."

Nell, whose snugly laced corset felt as if it were all but pinching her in two, would have given anything at that moment to be clad in loosely draped silk.

Winnie emitted another little burst of laughter in response to Dr. Foster's chivalric defense of her daughter. Nell wanted to throw something at her head.

"I quite agree," Will said. "Say, Foster, was it you who wrote that article on pulmonary obstruction in the *New England Journal of Medicine* a couple of months ago?"

"It was."

"Excellent research," Will praised, "very well presented. There was a similar piece in *The Lancet* not too long ago, but I felt you made your points with greater clarity."

"You're too kind."

Will, a professional gambler for some five years, still read the medical journals? Judging from his mother's nonplussed expression, she found this news as remarkable as did Nell. The two women exchanged incredulous little smiles.

"I was particularly interested in what you had to say about diagnosing drownings during post-mortems," Will said. "I autopsied a young lady last autumn whose body had been found in a field, but not only were her lungs water-logged, they were clogged with bits of algae and water weeds and the like."

"Any mucous froth?" Foster asked.

"Quite a bit," Will said as he cut into his duck. "The lungs had gone spongy, of course, and "

Viola cleared her throat. Will looked her way. She said softly, "Perhaps this is a conversation for another time?"

Will looked around the table as if it had slipped his mind that he was at a formal dinner party, which it probably had. "My apologies if I've ruined anyone's appetite."

"You haven't ruined mine," Emily said. "I was finding it quite interesting."

"You were probably alone in that sentiment," Will said. "Some other time, old man," he told Foster.

"Looking forward to it."

"I'm representing Dr. Foster on the sale of his house," said Mr. Pratt as he dabbed his mouth with his napkin, having polished off all of his duck save the requisite last bite. "It's right here on Beacon Hill, just a couple of blocks away. Charming little place, four stories with a verandah and a private garden, brand new kitchen and, er, comfort rooms. If anyone knows of someone looking to buy a home in a lovely neighborhood—"

"Well," Winifred said, "it *is* Acorn Street."

Pratt glared at her down the length of the table.

"I'm just saying people should know that right up front," Winifred said. "Because Acorn, well . . . you know . . . You'd be living next door to shopkeepers and the like."

Mr. Pratt sighed and motioned to the butler, who had the footmen clear away the duck course.

"I find Acorn Street quite delightful, actually," said Viola. "That narrow little cobblestone lane with the lovely brick houses on one side and the garden walls on the other . . . Reminds me of some of the quainter parts of London."

Dr. Foster said, "I like it, too. I wouldn't be moving if I didn't need more room for my surgical practice. I've built a larger place in the Back Bay. The entire first floor is set aside for examining patients and performing operations."

"Whatever the reason, it's wise of you to trade up to a bigger house in a better neighborhood," Winifred told Foster. "You'll attract the more desirable young ladies that way." She looked toward Emily, who pointedly looked away.

The footmen returned with the next course—ham mousse and green salad—and the subject under discussion turned to the current Boston real estate market and whether up-to-the-minute amenities made houses that much more attractive. Someone brought up the elevator August Hewitt had installed for his wife, permanently crippled from a bout of infantile paralysis before the war, thus redirecting the conversation to the advantages and disadvantages of modern innovations. Mr. Hewitt was, for the most part, opposed to them, especially in the home; he never would have considered an elevator had not Will pressed the issue. Will's having cared enough about his mother's well being, despite their estrangement, to broach the idea, and Mr. Hewitt's having actually taken his advice, boded well, Nell thought, for their future as a family.

THE subject of conversation among the ladies, once they'd retired to Winifred's pink and lavender sitting room to allow the gentlemen their cigars and brandy, swiftly homed in on Emily Pratt's eccentric taste in clothes. Emily's presence in the room did not deter her mother from characterizing her style of dress as "frumpy," "ugly," and "guaranteed to send gentlemen running in the opposite direction."

Cecilia, unsurprisingly, took her mother's side. Viola, familiar with so-called "aesthetic dress" movement because of her interest in art and things European, came to Emily's defense. Nell, who remained quietly neutral, wasn't entirely sure of Vera's position on the matter, since she couldn't seem to get a word in edgewise.

Vera's poorly fitted satin gown had a ruffle of a slightly different green attached to the bottom, suggesting that it had been restructured, perhaps by Vera herself, to accommodate her height. Recalling what Cecilia had said earlier about her mother wanting her to pass some shawls on to Vera, Nell wondered if the poorly altered gown had at one time been Winifred's.

"The thing I really can't fathom," Cecilia told her sister as she freshened up her sherry, "is how you can bring yourself to leave the house without a corset. I'd just as soon walk outside stark naked."

"Darling, really," Winifred huffed as she plucked two chocolate bonbons from the tray in front of her. Her inebriation was embarrassingly obvious now, her false teeth only exacerbating her slurred speech.

"Oh, Mamá, don't be such a priss," Cecilia chided. "You know what I mean, and you agree with me. Just yesterday you were telling me how proud you were that I'd gotten my waist down to nineteen inches. I'm aiming for seventeen by the wedding," she told the assembled ladies.

"Have you and Harry set a date?" Viola asked.

"We'll do that as soon as I figure out how long it will take me to lose those two inches," Cecilia said.

"Long engagements are best, anyway," Winifred decreed.

Vera nodded in agreement. "A year at—"

"Two," Winifred said. "A year isn't enough time for young people to really get acquainted, Vera. You'd know that if you'd ever had a beau."

"In two years," Cecilia mused, "I could get it down to sixteen, maybe less."

"Are you sure that's such a good idea?" Viola asked. I've heard about livers being damaged from tight-lacing."

"Oh, the liver." Winifred said with a flippant little

wave. "It doesn't really do anything. I mean, just look at it the next time you have a piece of it on your plate. It's just this *lump*."

"Tight-lacing is beneficial to the constitution," Cecilia said. "It promotes proper posture and stirs the circulation. And no male can resist a tiny waist. No normal male. Frankly, I wouldn't want anything to do with a gentleman who was drawn to *that*." She cocked her head toward her sister's gown. "I'd wonder if he was, you know . . . one of them."

Emily, who'd fallen silent a while back, pushed herself to her feet with a groan and lifted her glass of sherry. "If you ladies will excuse me," she said as she turned away, "my intact liver and I are going out back for a smoke."

Chapter 8

A FTER Emily left, Winifred tsk-tsked about her
elder daughter's shocking new habit, for which
she blamed Vera. "Where were you when she
started smoking *cigarettes*? I tell you, she's going to die
an old maid, and there doesn't seem to be a thing I can do
about it. She was always a hopeless bluestocking, even
when she was little. Bookish, solitary . . ."

"Well, yes," Vera began hesitantly, "but don't you
think she—"

"I think she'd better smarten up and start following
her sister's example before she's completely unmarriage-
able. One spinster is quite enough for any family to have
to support, I should think."

Vera sat back and looked at her lap, her lips tight,
color rushing up her throat like a fast-rising tide.

"We tried to do right by her," Winifred lamented while

gathering up a fat little handful of bonbons. "She had lessons in dancing and comportment, but none of it seemed to take. When she left for Europe, I thought, 'Thank God. She'll be in London for the spring social season. She might find a husband, maybe even someone with a title.' But then she and Vera embarked on this absurd odyssey of theirs, and . . ."

She shrugged and popped another lump of chocolate into her mouth, chewed it once or twice and swallowed it down, evidently nearly whole. "Now she's back, even worse than before. Those God-awful dresses, if one can even call them that. And she won't go calling with me, or make friends with the better class of young ladies. Do you know whom she befriended while she was still here, working for us? That Fiona Gannon. A chambermaid, and not just any chambermaid—a thief and murderess!"

Nell shook her head in commiseration, then leaned toward Winifred and whispered, "I say, Mrs. Pratt, would you mind telling me where I might find the necessary?"

L UCKILY, the bathroom was located at the rear of the house, so Nell didn't attract any suspicion when she headed in that direction. Instead of going into it, however, she located a pair of French doors and went outside.

The sun had set while they'd eaten dinner, and there wasn't much of a moon, so the Pratts' private courtyard was lit only by a haze of yellow lamplight glowing through the windows and French doors. Emily was lounging in a chair surrounded by potted trees, her bare feet crossed on an ottoman, her glass of sherry in one hand, a cigarette in the other. She raised it to her mouth, its orange-hot tip glowing brighter as she drew on it. On a stream of smoke, she asked, "Are you really a governess?"

"Yes."

Emily gestured toward a nearby chair, cast iron with striped cushions, and scraped the ottoman over so they could share it. Nell sat, kicked off her beaded evening slippers and put her feet up, waving away the silver cigarette case Emily flipped open.

"Do you like it?" Emily asked. "Being a governess?"

"I do. I love Gracie as if she were my own. And I'm very fond of Mrs. Hewitt."

"I've always liked her." Emily laid her head back, her eyes half-closed, her smile wistful. "When I was little, I used to imagine that she was my mother."

Unsure how to ease into the subject, Nell simply said, "After you left, your mother mentioned that you'd been friendly with that maid who's supposed to have murdered Mrs. Kimball."

Emily turned her head to look at Nell. "Supposed to have?"

"An inquest isn't a trial. I don't really consider her convicted. She was the niece of a friend of mine, you see, and—"

"Brady? The Hewitts' driver?"

"Yes."

"She spoke of him often. God knows what he must be feeling right now."

"He's incredibly distraught. He speaks of her as if she were just this sweet young girl, but the newspapers paint her as a monster."

"I know." Emily handed Nell her glass of sherry; Nell took a sip and gave it back. "All I can say is I . . . took to her. She wasn't afraid to let her personality show, which set her apart from most domestic servants, especially my parents', and she had ambition. Did you know she wanted to open a notions shop?"

"Brady mentioned that."

"We got along," Emily said as she swirled the sherry in its glass. "We confided in each other. I was just so grateful to have someone in this house I could talk to."

"You'll forgive me if it seems a little strange that a lady of your station would befriend a chambermaid."

" 'A lady of my station,' " Emily chuckled. "Ah, yes, I'm such an exalted creature." She fell silent for a minute. "One thing I learned from my travels is that we're all very much alike under the skin, and that those systems that divide us and keep us separate are entirely artificial. I've learned to trust my instincts above all. And my instincts told me that Fiona Gannon was worthy of my friendship." More gravely, she added, "Perhaps my instincts misled me, but I still don't regret having followed them. The one thing I liked about H.P.B., the only thing, really, was her egalitarianism. She told us about having made friends with a servant's child when she was young. So had I—the daughter of our cook."

"How did your parents react to that?" Nell asked.

"They fired the cook." Emily sipped her sherry and handed it back to Nell. "Do you wonder why I couldn't wait to get away from here? The moment the war was over, it was all I could think about."

"If you thought so little of Madame Blavatsky," Nell asked, "why did you travel with her?"

"It all came back to Aunt Vera. My parents had insisted on an older companion, of course, although I would have much preferred to be on my own. But they were paying for the trip—a yearlong tour of Europe isn't cheap—so I had no choice but to play by their rules. And I'd always gotten along better with Vera than anyone else in the family. But she was the worst traveling companion imaginable. She hated foreign cities, she hated foreign food, she hated foreigners. She got sick on ships, she got sick on trains . . . She wanted to come home. She whined, she begged, she wept. She was on the verge of cabling my parents and asking to cut the trip short when we went to Italy and met H.P.B."

"Ah."

"Vera fell under her spell within minutes of meeting her—swallowed all that theosophy humbug without question. But that's how Vera is, you know—meek, impressionable . . . utterly in the thrall of stronger personalities. She arranged for us to travel with H.P.B. and her various hangers-on, and she talked Father into paying for it. It's hard to believe those two are brother and sister, they're so different, but somehow, she always seems to know what to say to him."

"She must have been very persuasive, to have convinced him to let you travel so far, for such a long time."

"She was highly motivated," Emily said. "Aunt Vera revered H.P.B., even after she told us about the boy she killed."

Nell just stared at Emily, not sure she'd heard right.

Emily leaned toward Nell, eyes glinting as if she were about to impart a succulent bit of gossip. "It happened when H.P.B. was a child in Russia. She was rich and spoiled, and apparently quite the handful. Her parents had her exorcised regularly."

"Exorcised?"

"The family servants swore that she wielded a special power over the russalki. Those are Russian river nymphs—the spirits of young women who've drowned. H.P.B. told us over dinner one evening that when she was four years old, she took a dislike to a serf boy who'd been pestering her. She ordered the russalki to tickle him to death."

"And you believed that?"

"Oh, heavens no, I thought it was just another of her tall tales, until we went to her hometown in Russia. I asked around and discovered that a boy was found drowned in the river on her family's estate when she was four, and that everyone knew she was responsible. But her father was a man of influence, and Helena was already widely feared, so she got away with it. What she told us was that she felt invincible after killing that boy. She said others could learn to harness the powers of the spirits and demons, but that it took a great deal of faith and discipline—and that the word *disciple* came from the word *discipline*. I gave her a wide berth after that, but Vera didn't seem at all put off. Of course, she worshipped H.P.B. She probably convinced herself it wasn't true, that her idol could never have done something like that."

Nell said, "I'm surprised you were willing to travel with this lady after that."

"It was the only way I could remain overseas." Emily expelled a plume of fragrant smoke, which drifted off into the night. "So that's how I got to spend four years traveling the world. It was . . . indescribable. I felt so free, so . . . challenged."

"But then your father stopped sending money last February," Nell said.

"They'd hoped I'd find a husband overseas, someone with a pedigree who'd be willing to put up with the likes of me so long as he could get his hands on a chunk of the Pratt fortune. After four years, they finally figured out that wasn't going to happen, and that's when they cut off the purse strings. Coming home was like entering a prison. Vera, bless her biddable little heart, is the only person in this entire house I can talk to. An odd stick she may be, but she's a good listener." Emily glanced at the house and lowered her voice. "The joke's on my parents, though, because I'm taking ship at the end of the month."

"You are?"

"I've booked passage with Cunard to Liverpool. I sail on the twenty-sixth."

"Your parents don't know?"

Emily shook her head as she stubbed her cigarette out on the empty candy dish in her lap. "I'll tell them at the last minute. That way, they can't scheme to keep me home."

"Will your Aunt Vera be coming with you?"

"No, and believe me . . ." Emily frowned, looked away pensively. "No. She won't be coming. I've had enough of H.P.B. to last a lifetime—several lifetimes."

Nell was trying to figure out how to ask the indelicate question of where the money for this voyage was coming from, when Emily said, "How old do you suppose Dr. Foster is?"

It took Nell took a moment to react to the conversational detour. "No more than forty, I should think. Perhaps as young as thirty-five. Why do you ask?"

Emily shrugged as she slid another cigarette from the case.

"Your mother seemed pleased by his interest in you," Nell said. "His and Martin's."

Emily snorted with amusement as she lit her cigarette. "I grew up with Martin. We're the same age, and we always had lots to talk about. But can you honestly picture me as the wife of a minister?"

"No, I suppose not." Nell smiled. "But what about Isaac Foster?"

"If I were willing to marry and give away all my rights and freedom and money, I suppose he'd be as likely a candidate as anyone. But I'm not like Cecilia. All I can think about is traveling and writing about traveling—and perhaps even getting some of my pieces published. All Cecilia can think about is pretty baubles. She'd barter away her very soul for a rock if it glittered brightly enough. She's got diamonds and rubies from Harry, baroque pearls from Jack Thorpe—he was her first fiancé, the one who died—and sapphires from the second one, Felix Brudermann."

"The Austrian?"

Emily nodded. "A lady is supposed to give the jewels back when the engagement ends, but Cecilia held on to all of it, even those sapphires, which had been in Felix's family for generations. He'd spent every penny he had putting them into new settings for her."

"Every penny? I'd heard he was a nobleman."

Emily reached over to take the glass of sherry back from Nell. "There's nobility and then there's nobility. We Americans tend to assume that anyone with a title is rich and powerful and refined, but if you spend a little time in Europe, you realize that's just not so. Take Felix. His full name is Felix Jaeger Ritter von Brudermann. Sounds impressive, but the truth is, he's just the penniless youngest son of a . . . well, it's the Austrian equivalent of a knight or a baronet. He has nothing—no land, no education, no trade, and not the remotest hint of a personality. He's handsome as sin—that's about all he's got going for him."

"It didn't bother Cecilia that he was poor?" Nell asked.

"Why should it? When she marries, whomever she marries, she's to receive a ridiculously huge dowry, a lavish trousseau, a five-thousand-dollar wedding gown from Worth, a chateau in the Back Bay, complete with furnishings and staff, a landau with horses, a six-month European honeymoon . . . All of which, including Cecilia herself, will be under the legal control of her husband upon her marriage. Felix was nothing more than a gold digger. My father knew it—he's no fool. It took over a year for him to agree to the marriage, which he only did because he couldn't take Cecilia's screaming and weeping any longer."

"It sounds as if Felix would have come out way ahead on the deal," Nell said.

"Not by Cecilia's standards. When she was preparing to announce her engagement, she informed everyone that, after her marriage, she was to be referred to as Lady Brudermann, in the British tradition."

"But she was marrying an Austrian."

"A niggling detail. She insisted she was going to be a baronetess, which is actually a lady who holds a baronetcy in her own right, but she had no interest in hearing that. Oh, and Felix was to be called *Sir Felix*."

"Good Lord."

"She had the Brudermann coat of arms put on rings, brooches, writing paper, wax seals, sheets, towels, handkerchiefs . . . let's see . . . tablecloths, napkins, sterling flatware . . . oh, and four dozen place settings of custom Meissen china. The day she broke it off with Felix, she came out here with the china and a sledgehammer and smashed it all to bits."

"Why?" Nell asked. "I mean, why did she break it off?"

"Because even a grasping, shallow creature like Cecilia has her pride. Once it came out about Felix and Mrs. Kimball, she was fit to be—"

"Felix and Mrs. Kimball?" Nell sat upright. "When did this happen?"

"The affair?" Emily shrugged. "I gather it had been ongoing for some time. The rather dramatic, or shall I say melodramatic, disclosure of it to all of Boston society occurred the evening of my parents' annual ball, not half an hour after the official announcement of Cecilia and Felix's engagement."

"That's when Mrs. Kimball showed up, I take it."

"Oh, you should have been there. How deliciously scandalous. She strutted in wearing the most ostentatious gown you've ever seen and swept through the ballroom like the belle of the plantation. I had no idea who she was at first. Half the men were trying to squirm out of her line of vision lest she greet them a bit too familiarly, especially the married men. Thurston was with her. I understand they were hardly ever seen apart."

"Were they lovers?" Nell asked.

Emily looked at her for a moment, then burst out laughing. "Oh, my dear, no. He's a Molly-boy—a real flamer."

It took Nell a moment. "Oh, you mean . . . a sheelah." It was what Duncan had called them.

"I never heard that one."

"I think it might be Irish."

"Sheelah . . . hm . . ." Emily puffed contemplatively on her cigarette. "I really did admire her panache. And her nerve. And the fact that she didn't care one little tiny bit what any of those stuffy goldfinches thought of her. She'd set out to create an uproar, and that's just what she did. Cecilia was upset because she'd gotten lavished with congratulations and so forth after the engagement announcement, and then suddenly no one was paying attention to her anymore—it was all about Virginia Kimball. That was bad enough, but then Mrs. Kimball walked right up to Felix, never mind that Cecilia and I and a number of other people were all standing 'round, and said something like . . ." Emily cleared her throat and, in a rather poor attempt at a southern accent, said, " 'Felix, dear boy. You left your pocket watch on my dressing table the other day. I would have brought it if I'd known I was going to see you.' "

"She didn't."

"She most assuredly did. The whispers began immediately. It was like this . . . hiss of insects floating in a wave from one end of the ballroom to the other. Cecilia was apoplectic, of course. Felix denied and denied and denied, but his face was purple, and you just knew he was lying. I never laughed so hard in my life."

Emily handed the glass back to Nell, but it was empty. Nell took it and set it on a little iron table between the two chairs.

"Cecilia broke it off with Felix right after that. I don't think she would have really minded so much about him and Mrs. Kimball if he'd only kept it under wraps, but being humiliated like that in front the whole world—well, *her* whole world . . . It was more than she could bear. She was screaming, weeping . . . Harry comforted her. He must have done a workmanlike job of it because from that moment on, they were an item."

"How did Felix take it?" Nell asked.

"He was inconsolable for a couple of weeks. He'd wasted fifteen months, and the family sapphires, wooing an heiress, and her father, only to have it all blow up in his face, thanks to the bit of goods he'd been riding on the side. He came 'round to the house quite a bit at first, still denying and denying, but Cecilia held firm, and finally he seemed to get the picture. But the past two nights, he's shown up here raving about how Cecilia should take him back now that Mrs. Kimball is dead."

"He actually said that?"

"Did I mention he's something of a mutton-head? He seems to think her death has wiped the slate clean. Cecilia, needless to say, begs to differ. The footmen throw him out, but it takes three or four of them." Emily crushed out her cigarette.

"Brady told me that Fiona went to work for Mrs. Kimball around the beginning of May," Nell said. "He said you got her that job."

Emily closed her eyes, seeming to sink into the chair. "Did you ever do something with such devastating repercussions that you would have given anything—a year of your life, ten years—if only you could take it back?"

"Yes," Nell said, thinking of her marriage to Duncan.

"I did suggest to Fiona that she go to work for Mrs. Kimball, and I wrote a letter of reference for her. I'm as responsible for that lady's death as if it had been I who'd pulled the trigger and not Fiona."

Leaving aside for the moment the question of Fiona's guilt, Nell asked, "How did it come about, your recommending her?"

"Virginia Kimball's maid had quit suddenly, so . . ." Emily shrugged, her expression distracted.

"Did she place an advertisement?"

"Hm?"

"Mrs. Kimball, did she advertise for a new maid? I'm just curious as to how you happened to find out that she needed one."

"Oh." Emily lifted the glass of sherry and, finding it empty, set it back down. "I'm not sure," she said as she withdrew her cigarette case from her pocket again "I can't recall."

Nell let the silence grow heavy as Emily lit the cigarette and flicked out the match. It was Detective Cook's old trick: Ask a leading question and keep your mouth shut.

Finally Emily said, "Someone must have mentioned it to me," through a blossom of smoke.

Nell nodded, waited.

"Or I overheard something. You know . . . idle chatter." Emily looked away as she drew on the cigarette.

"I suppose you thought Fiona would be happier working for Mrs. Kimball?" Nell asked.

"God, yes." Emily met Nell's eyes at last. "She hated it here. My parents can be so stuffy and demanding. Virginia Kimball was many things, but she wasn't stuffy. I knew Fiona would have to work hard, given that she'd be the only maid, but she'd also be able to be herself. And she'd make more money and have her own room."

"Weren't you worried about your parents' reaction when they found out you'd deprived them of one of their staff?"

"I anticipated it," Emily said. "With relish—my father's reaction, especially. To him, the notion of losing a maid to the likes of Virginia Kimball . . . well, I knew it would rankle him terribly, and it did. I was pretty amused by it all, pretty smug, until I read about the murder. I'd sent Fiona to Mrs. Kimball. What happened there is ultimately my . . ." She trailed off, her gaze on the house.

Nell turned to see the figure of a man silhouetted in the open French doors—obviously Will, from his height and that characteristic hip-shot stance.

"Ah, there you are, Nell. Miss Pratt," he said, with a slight bow in Emily's direction. "I didn't mean to interrupt."

"I was just going back in." Emily rose from her chair and slipped into her shoes with a smile that suggested she knew Will had come seeking a few precious minutes alone with the object of his affections. From the doorway, she said, "I enjoyed chatting with you, Miss Sweeney. I hope we can do it again soon."

Will closed the door after Emily had passed through it, and crossed to Nell. Still reclining with her legs stretched out on the cushioned ottoman, she drew her knees up and rearranged her skirts so as to not make a display of her stockinged feet.

Will sat not on the other chair, but on the ottoman, reached beneath her skirts, seized her feet by the ankles, and laid them on his lap. "I never realized what substantial feet you have."

"Substantial!" She tried to yank them out of his grasp, but he held on tight.

"Doesn't bother me," he said, his hands sliding downward, warm and a little rough through her white silk stockings. "I've never been a fan of tiny feet. Large ones look ever so much more capable."

He kneaded her feet through the lubricious silk, his fingers so strong and deft that Nell melted into the chair, head back, arms limp. A sigh escaped her, so deep it came out sounding more like a long, breathy moan.

"A secret voluptuary, are you?" Will murmured, his voice humming all along her nerve endings. "What an intriguing revelation."

"Do you never tire of teasing me?" Nell tried once again to wrest her feet free of his grip, but it was a half-hearted effort; he was good at what he was doing, indecently good.

"I tease much less than you think, Cornelia."

She opened her eyes, but Will wasn't looking at her. He was leaning down to pick up one of her evening slippers, which he snugged onto her left foot. The right followed, but instead of withdrawing his hands, he wrapped them over her insteps, his thumbs massaging her through the silk.

"A few minutes ago," Will said, "while we gentlemen were savoring our manly brandy and cigars—noxious combination, by the way, don't ever try it—my brother Martin asked Mr. Pratt how he'd gotten that black eye, to which Pratt replied that he tripped on his front steps the other day and fell face-first into the iron railing."

Nell sat up, suddenly alert. "But didn't Mrs. Pratt tell us—"

"That he fell victim to a basher a few doors down from their house? Why, yes, she did."

"Why would he tell his wife one thing and his friends another?" Nell asked.

"Watch those wanton assumptions, Cornelia. Perhaps it wasn't Pratt who told his wife the basher story. It could have been someone else."

"Which doesn't explain why there are conflicting accounts being bandied about."

"No, it does not," Will said. "But to be honest, what's of more pressing interest to me right now is the mysterious disappearance and reappearance of the Stonewall Jackson gun. General Jackson carried a Lefaucheux Brevete pinfire revolver, twelve millimeters, which translates to roughly forty-five calibers. If we're to believe Orville Pratt, it was in his possession until the night of the ball, when it vanished from his study."

"He apparently thought Mrs. Kimball stole it."

"He would have been furious at her that night for crashing his ball. That may be the only reason he suspected her. What intrigues me is the gun's fortuitous reappearance just two days after Mrs. Kimball was killed by a high-caliber revolver. Come." Will stood and held his hand out.

"Where are we going?" Nell asked as he raised her to her feet.

"To Mr. Pratt's study. It's right in there." He pointed to two dark, curtained windows at the rear of the house.

"I don't know, Will . . ."

"Afraid to be alone with me?" he asked with a smile.

"I was once," she said, thinking of the bitter and dissipated man he'd been when they first met. "Not anymore."

He regarded her for a thoughtful moment. "I may yet give you reason to feel that way again." With a gentle tug on her hand, he said, "Let's do this."

"YOU'D think he would have learned," Nell said when she saw the big revolver lying right out in the open on top of Orville Pratt's desk. The massive ebony writing table—ormolu-encrusted, ivory-inlaid, and topped with a thick sheet of red marble—was the centerpiece of Mr. Pratt's elegantly masculine study. The walls were of carved oak paneling, the mantel red marble, the paintings age-crackled Old Masters. Hanging above and to either side of the imposing fireplace were racks and racks of swords and knives, shimmering malevolently in the dark: cutlasses, sabers, machetes, broadswords, daggers, knives, even a few spears and battle axes. Many of the weapons looked Oriental; several were clearly of ancient or medieval provenance.

They had closed the door, of course, and lit just one small oil lamp on the desk, but Nell still agonized over the consequences, especially as regarded her position with the Hewitts, should someone discover them poking about in Orville Pratt's private study.

Will lifted the gun, turned it over in his hand. "This is a Lefaucheux Brevete, all right." He held it in the light of the oil lamp and pointed to a trio of tiny initials carved in the upper part of the gun's grip: *TJJ*.

"Thomas Jonathan Jackson," Nell said.

Will looked at her and smiled, as if pleasantly surprised that she knew that. "Yes." He swung the gun's cylinder aside, revealing six empty chambers, and snapped it shut. "Have you ever loaded a revolver?"

"I've seen it done. The bullets go in the chambers . . . no, first the powder, then the bullets, then sometimes a little dab of lard or wax on top of each bullet, and then the firing cap last, for safety. Oh, and I've seen it where the bullet and the powder are wrapped up together in a piece of paper soaked in something . . ."

"Potassium nitrate," Will said, "to make it more flammable. Those are called cartridges. They can be made of metal, too."

"Metal doesn't burn."

"They work very well, nonetheless. They appeared shortly before the war, but they're just now catching on. There's a tubular metal casing that houses the bullet, the gunpowder, and the cap. When you pull the trigger, the hammer strikes the cap, which ignites the powder, which shoots the bullet. *Eh voilà!*"

"What happens to the casing?"

"With a revolver, it stays inside the gun. Of course, it

has to be a gun especially designed for that type of cartridge."

Handing Nell the gun, which was remarkably heavy, Will lifted the lamp and started tugging, one by one, on the desk's many drawers. Those few that were unlocked received a swift but thorough search before he moved on to the next one. "Eureka." He produced a rattling tin box, which he set on the desk and opened. It was about half full of bullets, each encased in a copper cartridge. A white label on the inside of the lid read:

50

LEFAUCHEUX PINFIRE CARTRIDGES

12 mm

Warranted best quality.

Will plucked out one of the bullets and held it in the lamplight. "See this little projection here on the bottom of the cartridge? With a pinfire gun, the hammer strikes the pin and drives it into the cap. Except for that little peculiarity, this is pretty much what a metallic cartridge looks like."

Nell set down the gun and took the cartridge from him. The conical tip of the grayish lead bullet extended beyond the little copper tube. "Do you suppose if we were to compare this bullet to the one you found on the floor of Mrs. Kimball's bedroom, we might be able to figure out whether they came from the same gun?"

"I don't know, Nell. A spent bullet gets pretty distorted. I doubt we'd even be able to tell if they were the same caliber."

"I'll bet Samuel Watts could tell."

"Who?"

"He's the gunsmith who testified at the inquest. Detective Cook had nothing but praise for him."

Will took the bullet and tucked it into his inside coat pocket, closed the box, and put it back in the drawer. "Tomorrow's Saturday, your day off. Why don't we pay a little call on Mr. Watts?"

She nodded. "I'd like to talk to Maximilian Thurston, too. And Detective Skinner if we have time."

"We can visit them, as well. But first we have an eight o'clock appointment to tour Isaac Foster's house on Acorn Street."

"We do?"

"Given that he's one of the men who bribed Skinner—"

"Presumably bribed—"

"Presumably bribed Skinner, I thought he'd be worth talking to. I told him I was looking for a permanent home in Boston, and that his house sounded like just the thing."

"And I'm coming along because . . . ?"

Will fumbled a bit for words. "He seems to think we're . . . not engaged, but . . . Well, the presumption is that we have an . . . understanding."

"Ah. Not yet formally engaged, but looking for a house together, which is as good as if I were wearing a diamond—"

There came a metallic snick as the doorknob turned; hinges squeaked.

Nell's heart kicked.

Will shoved her against the desk and pressed himself close to her, his back to the door.

"Will!" she rasped as the door creaked open, revealing a sliver of light, a shadowy form.

Will grabbed her arms and wrapped them around him, cradled her head against his chest. "Be still," he whispered.

Chapter 9

NELL closed her eyes and pressed her face to the smooth, cool fabric of Will's evening coat, inhaling new wool and Bay Rum, her arms banded around him, heart drumming against her stays.

He bent his head to hers, whispering "Shh, don't worry," as he stroked her hair.

"William? Is that you?" It was Orville Pratt's voice.

St. Dismas, please, Nell silently prayed, *please let nothing come of this. Please let me keep my job.*

"Oh," Pratt said as he took in the scene.

Will, still cupping Nell's head to his chest, turned to look over his shoulder. "Sir, I'm—"

"Not at all, not at all." Pratt sounded amused, indulgent. "I was young once, too."

Nell opened her eyes to see the band of light from the hallway shrink and then wink out as the door click-closed.

She slumped against him, shuddering with nervous laughter.

Will chuckled; she felt it more than heard it, a comforting vibration from deep inside his chest. "You're shivering."

He chafed her back and arms, then just held her tight, his breath warm and ticklish on her hair, his heart thumping against her ear. She closed her eyes, relishing the sensation, all too rare for her, of being enfolded in a pair of strong arms, sheltered, cared for.

His heartbeat gathered speed, and his breathing with it. Nell felt the quickening rise and fall of his chest.

She opened her eyes and saw the room around them, saw them standing here crushed together like lovers, wrapped in each others' arms, hearts drumming in unison. She loosened her embrace, looked up at Will.

He met her gaze, his eyes shadowed by that strong brow, his expression indecipherable. He kept his hands on her waist as he stepped back from her. When he released her, she felt bereft.

She busied herself plucking at her skirt and tidying her hair. "We should probably, um . . ."

"Yes, they'll be wondering what's become of us."

"Not Mr. Pratt," she said. "He knows. Or, or thinks he does."

"Better he thinks that than suspects the truth. There's only one problem."

Nell glanced up to find Will appraising her as if she were a statue in a museum.

"You don't look at all like a lady who's just been kissed," he said.

With feigned nonchalance, she asked, "What do ladies look like after you've kissed them?"

"The blood tends to rise to the surface here . . ." He reached out to brush his fingertips over one cheek and down along her jawline to her throat. "And here." His touch on her throat and upper chest—lingering, airy—made Nell feel as if she'd just drunk an entire bottle of wine all by herself.

"And the lips, of course." He stroked her bottom lip with his thumb just once, making it tingle. "They might even swell a bit . . . as I recall. It's been a number of years."

"You haven't kissed anyone in years?"

"That surprises you."

"Well . . . yes. I just assumed you . . ." How did one express such a thing? "I mean, I, I realize that, during those years you were smoking opium and taking morphine, you were . . ." They had discussed this, but in vague terms and quite some time ago.

"Lacking in fleshly desires," he said.

She nodded. "I suppose I . . . just assumed, once you were no longer addicted to opiates, that your . . . natural inclinations would return."

"Oh, they returned, all right," he said with an acerbic little laugh. "They came roaring back. 'Exploding' would not be too strong a word. It's as if that part of me had been dead for five years, and now it's come back to life, but the process leaves me in a continual state of . . . how did you put it? Inclination? From time to time it becomes . . . all but unendurable."

"Yet you haven't even kissed anyone in all this time? It's been what . . . nine months?"

Will looked down, his brow furrowed, as if composing his response. "I confess, from time to time I've been desperate enough to seek out . . . a certain type of female. But these are not women who expect to be kissed. They're solely interested in the contents of my wallet." He raised his gaze to hers again. "What lies in my heart remains quite untouched."

Nell had that slightly swimmy feeling she sometimes got upon looking into Will's eyes, as if she were about to careen into space. His gaze shifted to her mouth. She saw his throat move. He might have dipped his head just slightly, or perhaps that was the vertigo playing tricks on her.

She parted her lips to speak, but the words she needed to say, had no choice but to say, refused to come.

"Let go of me!" It was a man's voice, young and European-accented, from the front of the house.

Something crashed; there came shouting and the sounds of a struggle, but the young man's furious screams rose above it all. "Get your hands off me, you bastahds! Cecilia! Make them let me go!"

"That's got to be Felix Brudermann." Nell lifted her skirts to sprint across the room.

"Felix who?" Will beat her to the door and held her back protectively as he opened it.

"He's the fiancé Cecilia threw over for Harry after she found out he was, er, associating with Mrs. Kimball."

"I've obviously got some catching up to do," Will said as he peered down the central hallway at the ongoing melee.

Even standing on tiptoes, Nell couldn't see over his shoulder. "Your chivalry is commendable but unnecessary," she said as she darted around him. "Brudermann has no quarrel with me."

She strode down the hall toward the chandelier-lit foyer, in which a clutch of men—Isaac Foster, Martin Hewitt, and two of the red-clad footmen—held the flailing intruder pinned against the front door. Harry, the two older gentlemen, and the ladies watched from several yards away. A French Provençal console table lay on its side nearby, its delicate giltwood legs splintered, the attached mirror in shards on the marble floor.

"Stubborn wench." Will closed a hand over Nell's arm, just a bit too firmly. "Keep your distance from him. That kind of anger knows no reason."

Emily, swirling a brandy snifter as she leaned against the archway that led from the hall to the foyer, turned and smiled as they approached. "Act three."

"*Cecilia!* She's dead, for Christ's sake. It vas never anything." Felix Jaeger Ritter von Brudermann was a brawny young man of remarkable Teutonic beauty. Even red-faced and howling, his golden hair unkempt, his clothing in disarray, one could see why Cecilia, with her love of all things gorgeous, had been drawn to him.

"Why can't you just go away?" Cecilia shrieked, her hands fisted in her foamy pink gown, her face contorted in rage and bewilderment. "Go away! What's the matter with you? Why do you keep coming back?"

"I luf you! I vant to marry you!" Felix wailed as he grappled with the men restraining him.

Harry, holding the biggest cigar Nell had ever seen, answered for her. "Well, she doesn't love you, so why don't you just salvage your pride and—"

"You shut your mouth!" Felix aimed jerky if impotent punches in Harry's direction. "I know you, I know vhat you're about. You're trying to steal her from me."

"It's a fait accompli, old man." Harry took a puff, blew it out. "She's just accepted my proposal of marriage."

"*Vhat?*"

"With Mr. Pratt's blessing. So you'd best just turn 'round and—"

"You lying dog!" Felix redoubled his efforts to free himself.

"It's true," Cecilia spat out. "You see? You're wasting your time, Felix. Nobody wants you here."

"Then give me back my sapphires!"

"*No!* You gave them to me. They're mine."

Felix, spittle flying, limbs thrashing, spewed a vituperative stream of German mixed with English. The only phrase Nell caught was "greedy American bitch."

With a huffy indignation reminiscent of his father, Harry said, "How dare you call my fiancée—"

"I'll kill you, Hewitt!" Felix screamed hoarsely, then came a rather long-winded battery of German.

Will chuckled; Emily snorted with laughter.

"Do you two understand what he's saying?" Nell asked them.

Will gestured toward Emily as if to give her the floor. "He's describing various old Germanic techniques he might employ in doing away with Harry," Emily said. "Some of them . . ." She snickered as she raised the snifter to her mouth "Well, they're novel, to say the least."

Felix caught one of the footmen in the nose with his fist, the other in the throat. They stumbled backward, groaning and gagging. Seizing upon the commotion, the Austrian kicked and punched his way free of his captors and launched himself, snarling and wild-eyed, at Harry.

Harry dropped his cigar and turned to run, but he wasn't quite quick enough. Felix snatched his coat by its tails and yanked, whipping Harry's feet out from under him. Harry covered his face as he fell. "Don't!" Felix aimed a foot at Harry's groin, and when Harry reached down to shield it, kicked him in the head instead.

Foster and Martin both tried to get hold of Felix, but it was like trying to capture a rabid boar with one's bare hands. They aimed punches, but Felix just shrugged them off as he circled the writhing, moaning Harry, scouting for another place to kick.

Will strolled up to the Austrian. "*Gutenabend*, Herr Brudermann."

Felix looked up.

Will punched him in the head. He dropped like a marionette with its strings cut.

"THERE'S something I don't understand about what happened back there at the Pratts, with Felix," Nell said as Will's phaeton drew up in front of Palazzo Hewitt.

Will reined in his horses and turned to look at her. It was around midnight, but mild and dry, so he had the top down. The meager moonlight pointed up the sharp planes of his face—the straight-carved nose and lofty cheekbones, that jaw that managed to look both powerful and delicate at the same time.

"You could have stepped in sooner in your brother's defense," she said. "A few seconds might have saved Harry from a boot to the head." Harry, who'd suffered a gash to the forehead, had sniveled like a schoolgirl afterward, insisting that the constables be summoned to deal with Felix, which they were.

"Perhaps I thought another scar or two might improve his character," Will said.

Nell looked down at her gloved hands, then back at Will. "If he'd never . . . done what he did to me, would you have reacted faster?"

He hesitated. She sensed he had some typically droll response on the tip of his tongue, but he simply looked her in the eye and said, "Yes."

Nell nodded, looked away. The section of Tremont Street known as Colonnade Row looked so serene this time of night, with the windows of the mansions and townhouses almost completely dark and Boston Common deserted. It was even more beautiful in the winter, with snow glittering beneath the street lamps.

She'd grown to love living here. She loved Boston, and Viola, and her job, but most of all she loved Gracie.

Any whiff of scandal, and everything Nell most valued in the world, everything that made her life worth living, could be snatched away in a heartbeat. A bogus "understanding" with a gentleman was one thing, a love affair—a real love affair, furtive, clandestine—was quite another.

Nell turned toward Will, formulating in her mind what she wanted to say—or rather, didn't want to say, but must. As she was groping for words, Will pulled the glove off his right hand. He lifted her left hand, unbuttoned her glove, and slid it off as well.

He took her hand in his much larger one and held it, nestled in her billowing skirts, warm flesh against flesh. And then he smiled at her. It was a very quiet smile.

There was something melancholy about it, but something reassuring, too—deliberately so, Nell knew.

What he was telling her, without using ungainly words to do so, was *We needn't speak of it. We shall go on as we have been.*

Will tugged his glove back on, stepped down from the buggy, and came around to hand Nell down. He walked her to the Hewitts' front door, bid her good night, returned to his phaeton, and drove away.

Chapter 10

"AND this is the garden," said Isaac Foster as he guided Nell and Will out the back door of his Acorn Street house the next morning, all three of them shielding their eyes against the sun.

A charming little place, Orville Pratt had called it. It was charming, all right, a forty-year-old, well-kept red-brick row house on a mossy cobblestone lane. But to Nell, who'd been born in a two-room hovel, the notion of a twelve-room townhouse being considered "little" was nothing less than bizarre.

The garden was a cozy niche walled in ivy-covered brick, its air perfumed by the flowering perennials planted around its perimeter. "Those are medicinal herbs, most of them," Foster said. "A special interest of mine. It tends to be very quiet out here, very relaxing, especially in the evening."

"I can imagine," Nell said.

"Beacon Hill is the ideal location for a surgeon," Foster said. "Massachusetts General and Harvard Medical School are just a few blocks north of here."

"I suppose, if I were practicing surgery, that might be a consideration." Will pulled a tin of Bull Durhams out of his coat pocket and offered one to Foster.

"God, no," Foster said. "Those things will kill you."

"Come now," Will said as he lit up. "They're not as bad as all that."

"You read my piece on pulmonary obstruction. I discussed the effects of tobacco on the lungs."

Nell said, "There was an article about smoking in *Harper's Weekly* a couple of years ago, but I didn't know how much to believe."

"No, it's all true, about the cancer and heart disease," Foster said. "I consulted on that article."

"I'm afraid I'm still a bit skeptical," Will said.

"That's because you're a nicotine addict, and addicts believe what they want to believe."

Will didn't like hearing that; Nell could tell by his expression. After having conquered his dependence on opium and morphine, it had to sting to still be characterized as an addict.

With an amused glance at Nell, Foster said, "If you won't quit for the good of your health, you might consider it for the sake of your future marital happiness. No lady likes to be kissed by a man whose mouth tastes like an unswept hearth. Am I right, Miss Sweeney?"

When she hesitated, he said, "Forgive me. That was presumptuous."

"No, actually, you're quite right," she said. "Or so I've heard."

Foster slapped Will on the back. "If you know what's good for you, you'll quit before the wedding."

"I'll take it under advisement," Will said with a sardonic little look in Nell's direction.

"So, Hewitt, if it's not too forward of me to inquire . . ." Foster began. "You'd mentioned being a nomad last night, yet here you are looking at houses and"—he darted a glance toward Nell—"thinking about settling down. Yet you have no plans to resume your medical career?"

Will took a thoughtful draw on his cigarette. "The war pretty much sapped my interest in surgery, if you must know. There are just so many limbs a man can hack off before he never wants to see another bonesaw."

"Yet you performed an autopsy just last autumn," Foster said.

"Ah, yes—Bridie Sullivan," Will said. "That was an unusual circumstance. My mother had asked Miss Sweeney to look into the disappearance of a young lady, who, as it turned out, had been murdered. Determining the cause of death was a bit thorny, but I rather enjoyed the challenge. The forensic applications of medicine have fascinated me since Edinburgh."

"There's a renowned expert on that subject who teaches there," Foster said. "Gavin Cuthbert. His articles in the journals are riveting. You didn't, by any chance, study under him?"

"Extensively. In fact, I assisted him in his research on determining time of death, and he helped me to get an article on medical jurisprudence published in *The Lancet*."

"I read that article," Foster said. "Well done, old man. Quite engrossing, really. Were you planning to teach or practice medicine, or both?"

"Both, but it was the teaching I was most interested in, because affiliation with a medical school would have afforded me more opportunities for research. Of course, my plans got sidetracked when the war broke out. I couldn't shake the research habit, though. I took hundreds of pages of notes on the conditions of battlefield casualties. I was going to send the notebook to Dr. Cuthbert, but it was confiscated when the Rebs took me prisoner."

"Where were you held?"

"Andersonville."

Foster grimaced. Everyone knew about Andersonville; they'd all seen the shocking photographs of malnourished prisoners with their hollow eyes and skeletal bodies, and the appalling outdoor pen in which they'd been crammed.

"Is it true that General Grant called you the finest battle surgeon in the Union Army?" Foster asked.

Will blew out a stream of smoke. "Where did you hear that?"

"Your mother told me last night."

"It's true," Nell said.

"Seems a pity for such talent to go to waste," Foster said.

"I'm sure there are more than enough promising young men in your clinical medicine classes, so that I won't be missed."

"There are a few with real promise," Foster conceded,

"but unfortunately, even Harvard has its limitations in terms of curriculum. For instance, we don't offer a single course in your particular area of expertise."

"Medical jurisprudence?"

Foster scratched his chin, smiling. "Did I happen to mention I'm being considered for the position of assistant dean of the medical school?"

Will squinted at Foster through a haze of smoke as he held his cigarette to his lips.

"If I were to be granted that position," Foster said, "and if I were to happen upon a qualified candidate to teach such a course, I would make him a very attractive offer. He'd start out as just an adjunct professor, of course, same as I did, but it goes without saying he'd have access to research facilities, assistants . . ."

"I wish you luck in finding someone," Will said.

"Hewitt . . ." Foster began. "Will . . ."

"Say, didn't Virginia Kimball live around here?" Will asked. In fact, he and Nell already knew exactly where Mrs. Kimball had lived in relation to Dr. Foster.

Foster paused for a moment, as if thrown not just by the change in subject, but by the question itself. "Why, yes, as a matter of fact. Her house is on Mount Vernon, but it backs up to Acorn."

"You mean, one of those garden walls on the other side of the street is hers?" Nell asked. "Which one?"

"The, uh, the one directly across from me, actually."

"With the red door?" The brick wall in question had an unmarked, crimson-painted door in it.

"Yes, that's right. That's . . . that's actually how I knew it was her house, because she'd leave it open occasionally when she was working in her garden."

Will stared up at the house as he smoked. "Darling," he said to Nell, "do you think you ought to take another look at that big third-floor bedroom? I was thinking it might make a good nursery, but you'd be the best judge of that."

"Oh. Yes. Of course," Nell said as she retreated back inside the house. On the way here, Will had suggested that Isaac Foster might be more candid about his relationship, if any, with Virginia Kimball out of earshot of Nell.

Instead of heading upstairs, Nell ducked into a pleasantly masculine little library at the rear of the house with windows that looked out onto the garden. Hugging the bookcase-lined wall to avoid being seen from outside, the wide-open windows being curtained only with hanging plants, Nell positioned herself so that she could hear every word the two men said to each other.

Will was explaining to Foster why he'd broached the subject of Mrs. Kimball. "It was years ago. I was young and . . . easily incited to passion. And Mrs. Kimball . . ."

"You needn't tell *me,* old man."

The two men let out chuckly little groans that communicated better than words the extent of Virginia Kimball's sexual magnetism.

"I fancied myself in love with her," Will said. "I would have given anything if she'd favored me—anything. But there was this Italian count . . ."

"He was still alive? It *must* have been a long time ago."

"Thirteen years ago. I made a fool of myself, as men that age are wont to do. For some time afterward, I wished I'd never met her. But then I came to realize that she really wasn't such a bad sort, just looking after her own interests. In a way, I grew to admire her for it."

"I know exactly what you mean," Foster said. "She

had her faults, but she was self-reliant, fearless—not qualities one normally associates with feminine allure, yet I must admit they only added to her . . ." He paused as if foraging for words. "She was . . ."

Will knew enough not to fill the silence with words.

"Virginia and I . . ." Foster trailed off. Nell wished she could see him.

"So I gathered," Will said.

"She used to tie a ribbon around the knob on her garden door when she wanted me to come calling," Foster said. "I knew there were other men she . . . entertained. I would see them at night, sometimes, going into her garden, or coming out. It never really troubled me. I mean . . . one uses a French letter, of course."

"Of course."

"I didn't love her," Foster said, "I just loved . . . well . . ."

"Yes," Will said knowingly, "I think I—"

"No, it wasn't just because she was free with her favors. It was the way in which she was free. She was . . . utterly abandoned in that respect. Her appetites were as consuming as any man's, and she gave full rein to them. It was never boring, being with her."

"No, I don't imagine it was."

Nell felt an absurd stab of jealousy, knowing what was transpiring in Will's mind.

"And she expected nothing from you?" Will asked. "No declarations of love, no promise of marriage?"

"She expected gifts," Foster said. "That was understood. She preferred jewelry. At some point, I noticed she never wore any of the things I'd given her. I assumed she was pawning them."

"Really?" Will was wise to keep his responses brief, Nell thought. Foster obviously felt a rapport with him, and was in a mood to unburden himself. It was best just to listen.

"I suspected she was in embarrassed circumstances, but too proud to let on. After I broke it off—"

"It was you who broke it off," Will asked, "not she?"

"I'd started calling on a young lady," Foster said, "It began to feel sordid, continuing that sort of relationship with Virginia while I was seeing Louise. I told Virginia the truth, that things seemed to be getting serious with Louise, and that was why I couldn't see her anymore. About a month later, I found a note slid under my door. It was from Virginia, demanding eight hundred dollars, or she'd show the Red Book to Louise and the dean of the medical school."

"The Red Book?"

At last, Nell thought.

"It's this thick journal bound in red snakeskin. She uses it—used it—to write about her encounters with men. And believe me, she spared no detail. She used to like to read to me from it, omitting the real names of the men, of course. It's the most ribald stuff I've ever encountered. I could only imagine what she'd written about me. We'd done things . . . Let's just say she brought out a certain side of me."

Mrs. Kimball's former lovers would be ruined, Nell realized, socially and professionally, should the Red Book come to light. Perhaps one of them had come to her home looking for the book, either to protect himself or to use the information in it to his advantage, only to have the situation get out of hand. Or perhaps he'd come there intending to kill Mrs. Kimball, thereby ensuring that she could never expose their affair, or because he was enraged over the blackmail, or jealous of her other lovers. There were, it seemed to Nell, far too many reasons for Mrs. Kimball's gentlemen friends to have wanted her dead.

"Funny thing was," Foster continued, "Louise and I had parted ways just a few days before I got Virginia's note. Of course, Virginia had no way of knowing that. As for the dean, he and I were actually close friends, had been for years. I was privy to every detail of his own liaisons, so I had no fear that my little dalliance with Virginia would come back to haunt me. At least I was a bachelor, which was more than he could say."

"So you didn't pay the eight hundred?" Will asked.

"No, I did."

There came a pause. "I don't understand," Will said. "If she had nothing to hold over your head . . ."

"Virginia was a proud lady. Her situation must have been terribly dire for her to stoop to blackmail. I had the money. I didn't begrudge it."

Nell stood there in Isaac Foster's library with her mouth hanging open. From Will's silence, she gathered he was as astounded as she by Foster's largesse

Finally Will said, "Why didn't you just give her the money outright?"

"Oh, she would have been mortified. She never would have taken it. You see, the blackmail was her way of squeezing money out of her former conquests—I can't have been the only one she tapped—without giving away the true extent of her hardship. If you'd read her notes, you'd understand. She'd make it seem as if it were all a game to her, as if she were doing it as a perverse form of amusement rather than out of actual need."

"Notes?" Will asked. "Did you receive more than one?"

"Oh, yes, she'd come rattling my piggy bank every few months."

Will fell silent for a moment, and then he said, "You felt something for her, obviously. Her murder must have shocked you."

After a long pause, Foster said, "I was walking home from the medical school that afternoon after delivering a three-hour lecture on clinical surgery. At the corner of Mt. Vernon, I noticed a crowd gathering around Virginia's house, so I went down there and asked a boy what had transpired. He said an actress had been shot."

"Had it just happened," Will asked, "or . . ."

"About an hour before, I suppose. The lecture had ended at a quarter to five, and the paper said she was killed around four."

That was a good question on Will's part. Assuming Foster really had been lecturing on clinical surgery when Mrs. Kimball and Fiona were shot, there was no way he could have done it.

"There were constables milling around," Foster said, "just about every constable in the city, it looked like. I told one of them I was a physician, and asked if I could be of any help, but he said it was too late, that the lady who lived there was dead, and her maid, too. They brought out two bodies on stretchers. I pulled back the sheets. The first one was the maid, but I could only tell that because of the hair color. Her face . . . well . . . As for Virginia, her eyes were wide open, but so . . . blank. She'd always had this . . . spark in her eyes, you know, this crackle."

"Yes," Will said. "Yes, I know what you mean."

"Max Thurston was there—the playwright? He and Virginia were very close. He lived just across Mount Vernon from her, in one of those Louisburg Square townhouses that look exactly alike, except that his has bright blue window shutters and a lime green front door. Every afternoon at exactly four o'clock, he walked over to Virginia's for cocktails and gossip."

"Cocktails? I thought it was tea."

"So Max has been claiming, but I happen to know it was Martinez cocktails, and plenty of them. It was an entirely platonic relationship of long standing. He's quite the Lizzie. Not a bad sort, though, quite likable in his own way. You may not credit it, given his . . . inclinations, but—"

"Believe me," Will said in an amused tone, "after eighteen years in British boarding schools and universities, where one can go a very long time without glimpsing a female, I've long since learned not to make assumptions about a fellow based on what he does with whom when the lights are out."

"Max was inconsolable," Foster said. "Weeping, clawing at his head. His clothes were covered with blood, his hair sticking out at all angles—I don't know what had happened to his hat. I remember thinking how sad it was to see him like that—he's quite the dandy, always so well turned out. He'd cornered the detective in charge, fellow named Skinner, and wouldn't let him go. He kept saying he knew who'd killed Virginia, and that it wasn't Fiona Gannon—that's what the maid was called."

"Really?"

"He said it was an important man, very wealthy and powerful, but that he was afraid to name him out loud with so many strangers about. He said he'd come to the

Detectives' Bureau in City Hall the next morning, and tell him then. After he left, Skinner made some crude remarks to some of the constables—you know, about Max being a weepy old cot-betty, and how the local matrons shouldn't meddle in murder cases, that sort of thing. They were roaring with laughter when I left. I went home and poured myself a whiskey and then a few more. I don't even remember going to bed that night, but when I woke up in the morning, I realized I had a problem."

"Yes?" Will said when Foster didn't continue.

"I don't know why I'm telling you all this."

"Because I understand why you cared about Virginia Kimball. It the same reason I cared about her."

Presently Foster said, "My old friend is no longer dean of the medical school. The new fellow, Calvin Ellis—it's well known that he's a man of strong ethics and principles. He's considering me for assistant dean, which is something I've wanted for a very long time. When I woke up that morning, I realized how damaging it could be if the Red Book were to be made public at this particular juncture."

"What did you do?" Will asked, although of course he already knew.

"I bribed the detective handling the case to bury that damned book as deep as he can—or preferably, burn it— if it should ever come to light."

"I suppose I can't really blame you."

"So now that I've told you all my darkest secrets," Foster said in an amused tone, "you owe it to me to buy my house."

"All right."

Foster chuckled. "Seriously, think about it and—"

"I *have* thought about it. Nine thousand, you said?"

"Um . . ."

Nell was as stunned as Isaac Foster—more so.

"A whole house for less than it takes to buy a second-hand gun," Will said. "That sounds like a bargain to me."

"YOU'RE buying the house?" Nell asked incredulously as they strolled back up Acorn after their visit to Foster; they were on foot today.

"Don't you like it?"

"Well, yes, but what does a single man—a single man who's away from home most of the time—need with such a big house?"

"Perhaps I'm trying to attract the more desirable young ladies," he said, mimicking Winifred Pratt's advice.

"Hewitt!" They turned to see Isaac Foster leaning out of a second floor window, his hands cupped around his mouth. "This Madame Blavatsky character . . .?"

"A gibbering madwoman," Will called back. "No doubt about it."

Foster grinned as if a colleague had just confirmed his diagnosis. "Have your lawyer contact Pratt about the house. I've just got one stipulation. The sale is dependent upon your applying to teach medical jurisprudence at Harvard."

"*What?*"

"Just make an appointment with the dean and propose the course. You don't have to accept the position, even if he offers it. You just have to apply for it."

"Now, wait a—"

"Within the week." Foster waved good-bye and shut the window.

"MISS Nell Sweeney and Dr. William Hewitt to see Mr. Thurston." Will handed his card to the handsome young valet who'd opened the lime green door.

The valet, clad in a martially inspired blue uniform with fringed epaulettes and lots of gold braid, gestured them into a palatial entry hall. Lifting a silver salver from the hallstand, he placed Will's card in it and disappeared down the hall.

He returned a minute later and invited them to follow him back down the hall to a solarium so bursting with potted trees, bushes, ferns, and vines that it looked as if a tropical forest had erupted right up through the slate floor. In the middle of the room stood a green wicker table with Will's calling card on it. Maximilian Thurston, a spotless linen apron tied over his lounging jacket, stood with his back to them, one hand gripping his antler-head cane while the other tilted a watering can over a tub of philodendrons.

Without pausing in his task or even looking over his shoulder at them, Thurston asked, "Do I know you, Dr. Hewitt?"

"We met in passing some years ago." Will's resonant British drawl made Thurston's ersatz accent seem rather inane by comparison. "I doubt you'd remember me."

Only when the philodendrons were thoroughly watered did Thurston slowly straighten up and turn to face them. He looked sallow in the dappled sunlight filtering through his indoor jungle, and a bit stooped—older than on the day of Virginia Kimball's funeral. His grooming, however, was

impeccable, from the top of his slickly combed head to the
toes of his tasseled slippers. The slippers and jacket were
precisely the same cobalt blue as the design on his floral
neck scarf.

Thurston squinted at Will from across the room, then
at Nell. "Some coffee, please, Christopher," he told the
footman, who bowed and left.

Will stepped forward and laid his hat on the table.
"Sir, Miss Sweeney and I are making inquiries into the
death of Virginia Kimball on behalf of Fiona Gannon's
uncle. He believes her to be innocent, and he'd like to
see her exonerated."

Thurston laughed shortly. "Good luck to him."

Nell said, "We've just come from the home of Dr. Isaac
Foster. He told us you have your own theory as to who was
responsible. Do you mind if we ask you some questions?"

"It won't do you any good," Thurston turned and began watering an India rubber plant so huge that it curved
back on itself at the ceiling. "I've already tried to get the
authorities to listen to reason. I went to that little weasel
of a detective. He patted me on the head, then had his
bully-boys escort me from the building. He simply did
not want to hear it."

"Hear what?" Nell asked.

"That Orville Pratt killed Virginia," Thurston said
without turning around. "Fiona, too, but that's just because she happened to be there. It was Virginia he'd come
gunning for."

Chapter 11

CHRISTOPHER returned with a tray set out with three cups of coffee, a plate of pastel-hued petits fours, a bowl of sugar, a pitcher of cream, and a decanter of amber liquid. He arranged these things on the table, bowed, and left.

"What reason would Orville Pratt have had for wanting to kill Mrs. Kimball?" Nell asked.

"Let's just say he and Virginia had a little falling out." Crossing stiffly to the table, Thurston set down the watering can and pulled the glass stopper out of the carafe. "Courvoisier," he said as he poured a splash into a cup of coffee. "Exquisite. You must try it."

"A falling out?" Nell stirred a generous dollop of cream into her coffee; she would pass on the cognac, given that it was only midmorning. "That can't be the only reason you suspect him."

"The day before the murder, he showed up at her house and threatened to kill her." Thurston blew on his coffee, took a sip, and closed his eyes to savor it.

"Why?" Will asked.

"He was furious at her."

"What about?"

"That's not the important bit," Thurston said. "The important bit is the threat. I heard it with my own ears."

"Is that what you told Detective Skinner?" Will asked. "That Mr. Pratt threatened Mrs. Kimball during a row, the substance of which you refused to relate, and on that basis Pratt should be arrested and tried for murder?"

No wonder Skinner hadn't taken him seriously. Here was this presumably harmless old "cot-betty" who claimed that Orville Pratt was the murderer, but wouldn't offer any real proof. Meanwhile, some of the wealthiest and most powerful men in Boston, possibly including Pratt himself, were paying Skinner to resolve the case without mentioning their names or letting the Red Book come to light.

"I heard it with my own ears," Thurston enunciated, as if he might hammer it through their impenetrable skulls if only he said it clearly enough.

Nell and Will exchanged a look.

"Why didn't you speak out at the inquest?" Nell asked.

"I tried to, but Skinner cut me off. He turned to the coroner and said, 'Isn't he only supposed to answer direct questions?' And the coroner said that was right, and that he was done questioning me, and that the clerk should strike out my 'extraneous comments.'"

"If you'd been permitted to speak," Nell asked, "what would you have told them?"

"About Pratt coming to Virginia's house the day before the murder and threatening to kill her," Thurston said testily, as if he were being forced to reiterate something he'd already made abundantly plain.

"Not what they'd been arguing about?" Will asked. "Or what their falling out was about, or—"

"Voltaire said the secret to being a bore is to tell everything." Thurston set down his cup, took up the watering can, and hobbled back over to his plants.

Will came to stand next to Thurston. Gently he said, "I know you want to protect Mrs. Kimball. The last thing you want is for all of Boston to find out . . . certain things about her, things that might reflect poorly on her. But you also want her murderer brought to justice. You can't achieve one goal without sacrificing the other, so you're in a quandary. Am I right?"

Thurston, who'd stood utterly still, his watering can poised over a bamboo palm as Will delivered that little speech, turned to look at him.

"We already know about the Red Book," Will said, "and the blackmail."

Thurston closed his eyes; he seemed to deflate. "How'd you find out? Foster?"

"He knew we could keep a confidence," Will said. "And you need to know that, too. All we care about is finding out who really pulled the trigger that day so that we can clear Fiona Gannon's name. I swear to you, as one gentleman to another, that I'll do everything within my power to protect Virginia Kimball's reputation. I knew Mrs. Kimball. I liked her. At one point, years ago, I even thought I loved her."

Thurston studied Will with eyes that shone like blue

marbles. "I remember you," he said in a low, raw voice. "You're the one who brought all those beautiful white roses to the Boston Theatre that day. She called you Doc for some reason."

"Because I'm a . . . I *was* a physician," Will said.

"She gave them to me, the roses, because, well, that Federici bastard was—" He dipped his head toward Nell. "I beg your pardon, Miss . . . Sweeney, is it?"

"Yes. It's perfectly all right."

"She'd received a cable that morning from *il conte,* saying he'd just arrived in New York, and to expect him in Boston that evening. Naturally she couldn't let him find roses from another man in the house he'd bought her, so she asked me to take them home. They were absolutely superb, so fresh, half of them not even open yet. Six dozen—I counted them. This house never smelled so lovely."

The playwright smiled reflectively as he turned to inspect a group of flowering plants—African violets, dwarf gardenias, quite a few varieties of orchids. Will looked at Nell as if to ask, *How can I get through to him?* but apparently he already had, because Thurston said, "Virginia was faithful to Federici while he was alive. She had no choice—he had his spies. But once he was dead . . ."

He shrugged and moved on to a banana tree, testing its soil with a knobby finger. "She had appetites, and she wasn't afraid to indulge them. That doesn't mean she was immoral. Frankly, I always thought she was rather brave."

"What kinds of gentlemen did she . . . associate with?" Nell asked.

"She was attracted to confidence, power, success . . ."

"Gentlemen with the means to express their gratitude?" Will ventured.

Thurston shot him a look. "Why shouldn't they have been grateful? This was Virginia Kimball, for pity's sake, not some two-dollar strumpet."

"I meant no disrespect," Will said with a little bow.

"Yes, they gave her gifts," Thurston said. "That doesn't mean she sold herself. There's a difference."

"Of course there is."

"And it's not as if all of them had the means to lavish her with jewels and the like. There were younger ones from time to time—her 'Pretty Paupers,' she called them. Beautiful young men who made her feel young. All she expected from them was, well . . ."

"Their youthful enthusiasm?" Will said.

Thurston gave him a droll look. Nell wondered to what extent Mr. Thurston had lived vicariously through Mrs. Kimball's amorous escapades.

"Forgive me, Mr. Thurston," Nell said, "but did the neighbors not complain of seeing gentlemen coming and going from Mrs. Kimball's home at all hours?"

"They used the garden entrance on Acorn." Thurston checked the soil in his hanging plants—Boston ferns, pothos, English ivy—watering some, bypassing others. "They were less likely to be noticed on such a secluded little lane, and even if they were, well, Acorn people don't generally move in the same circles as Mount Vernon people—except, of course, for Dr. Foster. Virginia kept her garden entrance and courtyard door unlocked for the convenience of her callers. I thought that most unwise, and I told her so on more than one occasion. She said she had her Remington for protection." Sadly he added, "She thought she was invincible."

"When did she take up blackmail?" Will asked.

"When it all started falling apart for her, poor thing." Thurston shook the watering can to expel its last drops onto a spider plant, then limped back to the table, dragged out a chair, and sat, grimacing. Will pulled out a chair for Nell, then took a seat himself.

"With Federici dead," Thurston said, "and nothing much in the way of savings, she had to rely on her acting income—which was adequate for a few years because she was very well paid. But the older she got, the fewer roles she was offered, never mind that she was the most brilliant actress—and the most beautiful—in this city, in the whole country, probably. She began to feel the pinch. She was forced to sell off some land she owned outside the city, then her furniture, her jewelry . . . even those diamond necklaces she loved so much. That broke my heart, when I found out she'd parted with those. She had paste replicas made up, but it just wasn't the same."

"She wouldn't take anything from you?" Nell asked, although she knew the answer.

Thurston shook his head morosely. He noticed his cognac-spiked coffee as if for the first time, and took a healthy swallow. "She had her pride. She told me she'd figured a way out of her predicament. Of course, I was appalled when she told me what she had planned. I tried to talk her out of it, but . . . that Virgina, she was a stubborn one."

"Did she blackmail all her ex-lovers?" Nell asked.

Thurston nodded automatically as he chose a petit four, then shook his head. "Well, no, not the Pretty Paupers, of course, but the rest of them would get a little note within a few weeks of the final farewell. Once I got over my initial reluctance, I used to help her write them. She liked to include excerpts from the Red Book—really humiliating bits guaranteed to make the fellow pay up."

"How long had she been keeping that book?" Will asked.

"Oh, years and years. Sometimes she'd read aloud from it over a Martinez or two in the afternoon. Oh, how we'd laugh," Thurston said with a sad little smile. "She wrote about you, you know," he told Will.

Will looked surprised. "I can't imagine what she found to write about."

"Oh, it wasn't the sort of thing she wrote about the others. It was just a few reflections, some observations . . . quite poignant, really. She actually had quite a flair for writing, but then she was remarkably intelligent. Most people don't know that about her."

"Do you have the Red Book, Mr. Thurston?" Nell asked.

He gave her a baleful look. "No, Miss Sweeney, I do not. I dearly wish I did. It would almost be like having Virginia back again, or at least her spirit, to be able to reread some of those entries. And after all, that book represented years of her life, and it wasn't *all* about, well . . . the sport of love. I'd pay anything to have it. But no, I have no idea where it is, unless perhaps Pratt made off with it. She kept it in her bedroom safe, which was open and empty when I got there."

Nell said, "She must have targeted quite a few men, to have supported herself for what, several years?"

"I've no intention of naming names, if that's what you're after," Thurston sniffed. "As far as I'm concerned, they have a right to their privacy. They paid enough for it, God knows."

"We know about Horace Bacon and Weyland Swann," Will said. "And, of course, Isaac Foster."

"Foster was one of the better ones. I quite liked him. He was good to Virginia. He treated her like a lover, not a . . ." Thurston glanced at Nell over the rim of his cup. "Not like some of the others did. She was quite forlorn when he ended it. Of course, he was also a good deal younger and handsomer than most of them."

"Except for the Pretty Paupers," Nell said.

"Well, yes, obviously."

"Was Felix Brudermann one of them?" Will asked.

Thurston lowered his cup with an expression of disgust, but Nell knew it wasn't the coffee and cognac that had turned his stomach. "Odious, kraut-munching ape. No class, no finesse, and not a mark to his name. She took up with him around Christmastime. I detested him at first sight, and told her so. I said, 'He's a mindless brute, Virginia.' She said, 'I know. Isn't it marvelous?' She said a little dose of brutishness was just what she needed after all those old men. She got what she asked for, and then some. Felix had a rather . . . aggressive approach to *l'amour*."

Will looked up from unstoppering the decanter. "How aggressive?"

Thurston sighed, sipped his coffee. "At first she liked it, more or less. But Felix just didn't know where to draw the line. He got too rough, so she told him it was time for him to leave. He did, but not before backhanding her into the bedpost."

Will muttered something under his breath.

"The bruise took two weeks to heal," Thurston said. "She covered it with makeup, but you could still tell it was there."

"When was this," Nell asked, "that he hit her?"

"February fourteenth. That black eye was his Valentine's Day gift to her. That was the last time she saw him until the Pratts' annual ball at the end of April."

"But at the ball," Nell asked, "didn't she tell Felix that he'd left his watch on her dressing table 'the other day'?"

Thurston nodded, cackling. "She'd heard his engagement was to be announced that night, and she told me she couldn't just stand by and watch any girl, even a ninny like Cecilia Pratt, bind herself in matrimony to 'that vicious Hun.' She knew she'd be widely reviled for saying what she said—in front of witnesses, no less—but she felt it was the only way to make a real impression on such a silly little squab. And, of course, the best way to punish Felix. As far as saying it was 'the other day,' her reasoning was . . . How did she put it? 'A lady's capacity for forgiveness tends to be in inverse proportion to the freshness of the transgression.'"

"Was that why she crashed the ball?" Nell asked. "To get back at Felix by warning Cecilia off him?"

"Oh, good heavens, no. That was just a little side mission. Virginia's true purpose was to light a fire under Orville Pratt. He'd been ignoring her little notes, you see, even though what she was asking was mere loose change to someone of his means. His lawyerly arrogance, you know—despicable snipe."

"Wait," Nell said. "She was blackmailing Mr. Pratt?"

"Attempting to."

"So she and Mr. Pratt . . . ?"

"Oh, yes," Thurston said. "For about three years, ever since he took her on as a client to sell that land for her. She kept him on retainer, in a manner of speaking. I believe he'd waived his fees in light of their . . . personal relationship. But then, a few months ago, he took on a new mistress, also an actress, but much younger, and he lost all interest in Virginia."

"Who's the new one?" Will asked.

"Daisy Newland. Nineteen years old, and an abysmal actress. I'd die before I'd let her be cast in one of my plays. She does, however, have certain . . . compensatory assets that appeal to some directors . . . and patrons. Pratt rents her a suite in the Tremont House, just down the street from the family manse. He's a man who likes to keep his leisure pursuits as convenient as possible. I always thought part of Virginia's appeal for him was that she lived so close. Did you know he's trying to relocate the Somerset Club from the corner of Somerset and Beacon to David Sears' house, now that Sears has retired to his country home?"

"Well, the Sears place is much bigger than what they've got now."

"It's closer to Pratt's house," Thurston said. "That's all he cares about. Orville Pratt doesn't go in search of his pleasures. His pleasures come to him."

"How did he react when Mrs. Kimball showed up at the ball?" Nell asked.

"He went so white I thought he might keel right over.

He let Virginia spirit him off to a quiet corner, where she produced the Red Book and had him read her accounts of what they'd done together." The playwright grinned impishly. "And what he'd worn while they were doing it."

"Worn?" Nell asked.

"Let's just say some of Virginia's prettier underpinnings were always a bit stretched out of shape after Mr. Pratt's visits."

Nell stared at him in disbelief as she battled to keep certain mental images at bay. Will smiled and sipped his cognac-laced coffee.

"Pratt knuckled under," Thurston said. "He agreed to send his valet to meet her maid the next evening—her former maid, Clara. It was Clara who delivered the notes and collected the payoffs. She'd meet the gentleman—or, more often, his man—in some relatively isolated location at night. He'd hand her an envelope, she'd bring it back, and Virginia would give her five dollars out of it for her efforts. Clara probably doubled or tripled her pay that way."

Mr. Thurston swallowed the last of his coffee and rose from the table with the help of his cane. He crossed to a little copse of ficus trees, which he inspected with a critical eye, pushing aside branches, probing the soil. "I was enjoying a few drinks with Virginia the next evening when Clara came in wet and shivering—it was pouring rain that night. She was *quite* put out. She's a Swedish spinster and a born malcontent, always carping about something, so one doesn't normally pay much mind. But on this particular evening, it turned out that Pratt's

valet never showed up with the money. Clara had waited
on the designated street corner for half an hour in the rain
before giving up."

"He promised to pay but didn't?" Will asked. "What
did Mrs. Kimball do?"

"She and I were actually debating that very question
when who should barge through the front door, soaking
wet, three sheets to the wind, and brandishing the biggest,
nastiest dagger I've ever seen?"

Will sat up straighter. "Pratt?"

"He was drunk?" Nell asked.

"Pickled to the bone," Thurston said as he plucked
dried leaves off the trees. "Staggering, raving . . . and he
wasn't alone. He thought he was, but he'd been followed
there by that dreary sister of his, and the daughter. Not
Cecilia, the other one, the one who wears those pecu-
liar . . ."

"Emily," Nell said. "The sister is Vera."

"Yes, well, they came in behind him, but he was so
soused, he didn't notice at first. He started screaming
about that precious gun of his, which had apparently
gone missing. He said he knew Virginia had stolen it,
which of course she hadn't. She told him to report it to
the police if he was so upset about it, but he said, 'You'd
like that, wouldn't you?' He said they'd be sure to question Virginia because of her showing up at the ball unin-
vited, and that she'd tell them about her and Pratt.
Virginia stood up to him, literally, despite the dagger.
She ordered him out of her house, with a warning that if
he didn't pay up the next day, she'd have his section of
the Red Book made into a pamphlet and passed out on
street corners."

Will laughed appreciatively. "I must admit, that would have been entertaining."

Thurston deposited a handful of crackly leaves on the table and proceeded to pick some more off the plant. "Pratt went wild when he heard that. He screamed that she'd get her money when he got his gun. He called her a . . . a vulgar name for a certain kind of female, and a thief. He said he knew he wasn't the only man to slip through her garden door, nor was he the only one she was shaking down, and that the things she'd written in the Red Book just proved she was a born . . . well . . . You get the idea."

"Quite," Nell said.

"Clara was present for this tirade," Thurston said. "It was the last straw for her. She started shrieking about how she'd had enough, she couldn't take another day under Virginia's roof, the extra money wasn't worth it, and so on. She said she was leaving that night—she didn't care about references. And all the while, Pratt was still bellowing and waving that dagger around. I'd begun to worry that he might try to use it, when the sister—Vera? She stepped forward and told him it was time to go home."

"He quieted down then?" Will asked.

"It was like pulling a switch. He hadn't realized they were there—not just the sister, but his daughter as well—listening to him rant about his affair with Virginia. He looked quite abashed. Vera took the dagger from him, and apologized to us for his behavior, then they shepherded him out of the house."

"But that wasn't the end of it," said Nell, thinking of his supposed threat the day before the murder.

"For a while, it seemed to be," Thurston said as he withdrew a large, utilitarian-looking atomizer from a cabinet. He brought it over to a corner sink tucked away amid the foliage, and filled its glass jar with water. "He didn't pay, but there was nothing Virginia could really do at that point."

"No street-corner pamphlets?" Will asked.

"That was just a bluff." Tucking the glass jar under the arm that held the cane, Thurston pumped the bulb, dispensing a fine mist over his hanging plants. "She couldn't afford to have pamphlets printed up, and Pratt knew it. A month went by, then, on the last day of May, he came here again, sans kinfolk and even more furious than before."

"You were there?" Nell asked.

"I was almost always there in the evenings," Thurston said. "Afternoon cocktails usually lasted till about eight o'clock, then we'd have a little light supper and some postprandial liqueurs. It was about eleven when Pratt showed up. His rage . . ." Thurston shook his head. "I'd never seen anything like it. The fact that he seemed to be stone cold sober only made him that much more fearsome. He was roaring about that bloody gun. He said, 'I paid you, now where's my gun?' Except that wasn't quite how he put it, but I wouldn't repeat his language in front of a lady."

Will said, "Wait a minute. Had he and Mrs. Kimball made some sort of arrangement to exchange the gun for payment?"

"Absolutely not," Thurston said as he shuffled around the room, misting his plants. "There'd been no communication at all between them since his last unwelcome visit a month before. Virginia and I were completely baffled by what he was saying, but he seemed to think we were just being coy, and that only enraged him further. He kept insisting that he'd paid what she'd demanded, and now he wanted his gun. He said he'd personally handed over five thousand dollars to Fiona Virginia had hired her right after Clara quit—in return for which Virginia had supposedly promised to give back the gun and keep her mouth shut permanently about their past together."

"Fiona had taken over bagwoman duty from Clara?" Will asked.

"Oh, yes, she'd made it clear when Virginia first interviewed her that she was prepared to assume all of Clara's old duties—*all* of them—for what she'd been paying Clara."

"Two dollars a week plus five for every payoff she handled?" Nell asked.

"That's right. Virginia had asked her how she knew about that, and she said she'd heard about it from the daughter."

Nell nodded as she thought it through "Emily and Fiona were friendly. She must have told her about following her father to Mrs. Kimball's the night after the ball and seeing Clara quit."

"She wrote Fiona a reference," Thurston said. "Virginia took to the girl immediately, hired her on the spot."

"Was Fiona there during Pratt's second visit?" Will asked.

"Oh, yes. She denied having taken any money from Pratt. He accused her of lying, and said Virginia must have put her up to it. Virginia told him to leave or she'd summon the constables. That really sent him over the edge. He went absolutely purple, and his eyes . . . they were like a wolf's eyes, almost colorless and utterly predatory. He turned on Virginia. He said, 'I'll kill you, you deceitful . . .' Well, suffice it to say the name he called her was one I'd never, ever thought to hear from the mouth of a gentleman. Virginia slapped his face. He slapped her back."

"He *struck* her?" Will asked. Even when he'd been a dissolute opium addict, William Hewitt had exhibited a touching protectiveness toward women.

"What did she do?" Nell asked.

"She didn't do anything. Pratt was already out cold before she'd had time to react." Thurston smiled at his listeners' reactions. "Once upon a time I was, believe it or not, Harvard's bare-knuckled boxing champion. They called me "Thunderfist Thurston" for my right hook. I must admit, it was gratifying, after all these years, to find that I could still put a fellow down with one swing."

"I know the feeling," Will said. "I boxed when I was in university back in England."

"Cambridge?" Thurston asked.

"Oxford—an unofficial club."

Nell said, "Dr. Hewitt got the chance to practice his own right hook on Felix Brudermann last night."

"Good show!" Thurston exclaimed. "Did you knock him out?"

"He was conscious, more or less," Will said, "but not happy about it."

"Pratt was a rag doll, but a heavy one," Thurston said.

"It took all three of us—Virginia, Fiona, and myself—to haul him outside and wrestle him into a hackney. If I'd known then what I know now, I would have tied a paving stone 'round his neck and dumped him in the Charles River. Virginia might still be alive then."

"But you'd be a murderer," Nell said. "It wouldn't have been worth it."

Thurston looked at her as if she'd said something absurd. "Of course it would, if it meant Virginia would have lived."

"Even if you'd ended up hanging?" Will asked.

"I loved Virginia," Thurston said. "I would have done anything for her, sacrificed anything."

Will said, "Yes, but—"

"Have you ever loved anyone, Dr. Hewitt?" Thurston asked. "Not your mother, I mean, and not Virginia— you've already admitted you merely thought you'd loved her. I mean real, all-consuming, helpless-in-the-face-of-it love."

Will stared at Thurston for several long seconds, then lowered his gaze to his coffee cup, his jaw tight. He took a sip, swallowed it. "I believe so."

"Would you give your life for this person?"

"Yes."

"Then you know how I felt about Virginia. The fact that we were never lovers doesn't alter the devotion I felt toward her. Yes, I would have gone to the gallows for her. And what's more, I think she would have done the same for me."

Will nodded mutely. He seemed to be avoiding Nell's eyes.

"Poor Virginia." Thurston set the atomizer on the table and lowered himself with difficulty into a chair. "She lost another maid that night."

"Fiona quit?" Nell asked.

"Yes, she was most apologetic about it, but she said it had been a mistake, her coming to work for Virginia. She said she'd gotten in over her head, and that she was going to open that notions shop she always used to talk about."

Will said, "With what money?"

"That's what Virginia asked her. The girl claimed she had enough saved up, but how could she have, on a maid's salary? Virginia tried to talk her out of it. She was quite soft-hearted, deep down. She was worried about the girl, you know, biting off more than she could chew and ending up on the streets or hooking out of some North End bagnio. But Fiona stood her ground. She did give a week's notice, which was more than Clara did."

"If she hadn't," Nell said, "she would probably be alive now."

Thurston nodded. "Pratt came back the next day and killed them both, then set it up to look as if it were Fiona's doing."

"You're saying he killed them out of simple anger?" Will asked.

"If you'd seen him that evening, sputtering and ranting, you'd know how unhinged he'd become. Virginia was the real target, although I'm sure he was put out with Fiona after she'd essentially called him a liar in front of us. I think he became so utterly enraged that he had no real control over his actions. Or, who knows? Perhaps he'd been planning it for some time."

Will said, "I'd like to know when he really found that gun."

"All I know is he killed my Virginia," Thurston said, "and I promised her, as I stood over her coffin, that I would see him hang for it."

"I was wondering about that coffin and how she was . . . laid out," Nell said.

"I'm sure a great many people have been wondering about it," Thurston said with a mordant little smile. "She'd planned every detail herself—circled the coffin in a catalogue, described her hair and makeup, and how the flowers were to be arranged on her. The gown was a costume she'd kept from a production of *Hamlet* some years ago. And she was most explicit about being buried as quickly as possible. She'd never been one to drag out the ending of a scene. 'One should exit swiftly,' she always used to say, 'even with a bit of unseeming haste. Far better to leave them wanting a bit more of you than a bit less.' Speaking of which . . ." The playwright rose to his feet, taking most of his weight on the cane. "I do hate to be rude, but I must dress for a read-through with the cast of my new play, so . . ."

Will pulled Nell's chair out for her, then gestured toward Thurston's cane. "I say, is that what I think it is?"

"Like it?" The playwright handed it over, leaning on the table for support. "It's Belgian. I bought it in the early fifties, when they were all the rage."

"Air?" Will held the cane at eye level and sighted down its wooden shaft, as if down the barrel of a rifle, which was when Nell realized that was precisely what it was.

"Percussion," Thurston said. "Breech-loader. A far sight more powerful than those puny cane guns Remington is coming out with now. Takes a forty-four caliber bullet. The trigger folds up into that silver ring."

Will met Nell's gaze for a split second. "Mind if I take a look at the action?" he asked.

"Be my guest. But do take care—I keep it loaded."

Will twisted the handle and pulled it out, exposing the exotic weapon's inner workings. "That's odd. You bought this in the early fifties, you say?"

"You're wondering about the metal cartridge. I had it converted last year to fire those."

"That explains it, then." Will shoved the action back in, twisted it closed, and returned the device to its owner. "A fine weapon, beautifully kept. Thanks for letting me take a peek."

Thurston walked his visitors to the front door, his gait laborious. Their visit had tired him, it seemed.

Thurston appeared lost in thought as he shook Will's hand. "Virginia adored you, you know."

Clearly taken aback, Will said, "I . . . I'm afraid you're misremembering, sir—or possibly trying to be kind. My affection for Mrs. Kimball was entirely unreciprocated. The very afternoon I gave her those roses, she dismissed me from her life in no uncertain terms."

Still clutching Will's hand, Thurston smiled. "Oh, how she used to rhapsodize about you—your handsomeness, your keen mind, the . . . let's see, how did she put it in her book . . . Ah, yes, 'the white-hot passion simmering beneath that cool facade.' She was mad for you, you know. But . . ." Thurston lifted his shoulders on a sigh. "*Il conte* was coming. He provided for her, kept her like a princess. She needed to get you out of the way, and quickly."

"Perhaps if she'd simply explained the situation," Will said, "and asked me to leave of my own accord . . ."

"Would you have gone away peacefully, or would you have stuck around and tried to fight for her?"

Will's expression, as he pondered that, was telling.

Thurston chuckled. "As I say, most people never realized how smart she was, how . . . complicated. But I did. I always knew."

Chapter 12

FROM Louisburg Square, Nell and Will strolled down to the Pratt "family manse" at 82 Beacon Street and asked to see Orville Pratt, but he wasn't there. He was at his club, Mrs. Pratt told them, lunching with friends, as was his custom on Saturdays.

Upon their arrival at the Somerset Club, the doorman informed them that Mr. Pratt hadn't been there that day, and wasn't expected. "I've never known him to show up here before suppertime on a Saturday," the doorman said.

The Tremont House, where Orville Pratt kept his new mistress, was virtually across the street from the Somerset Club. "How terribly convenient," Nell said as they headed there.

It was the first time she'd ever been inside the luxurious hotel, and it took all her willpower to keep from gaping at its architectural splendor. "Miss Newland?" The desk clerk didn't even have to look it up. "She's on the second floor, suite two-oh-two."

Will's first knock went unanswered, as did his second. As he raised his fist a third time, a girlish female voice called, "Who is it, fer Chrissake?" through the door.

"I'm William Hewitt, an acquaintance of Mr. Pratt's," he said. "I'm here with Miss Nell Sweeney. It's imperative that we see him right away."

"He ain't here." After a brief pause, she said, "And I don't know any Mr. Pratt."

Mr. Thurston had been right; Daisy Newland was an abysmal actress.

Will said, "Kindly tell him that it's a matter having to do with Mrs. Kimball and the Stonewall Jackson gun. If he can't see us right now, perhaps we'll call on Mrs. Pratt and see if she can be of some help."

About half a minute ticked by, and then the door was opened by a blonde in a lacy dressing gown with its bodice half-unbuttoned, putting her "compensatory assets" on audacious display. Her hair was loose and tangled, her skin creamy, her lips a vivid cherry red. She was softly pretty in that down-stuffed way some girls have, but for a pair of black-limned, dully sullen eyes.

Daisy didn't greet them, merely turned and sauntered away across the fussily decorated sitting room, trailing a miasma of saccharine perfume. Rapping on a closed door, she said, "You ready yet?"

There came a muffled male response that Nell couldn't make out. The girl crossed to a cocktail cabinet, emptied the last few ounces of whiskey from a decanter into her glass, and stretched out onto a velvet fainting couch to sip it. The skirt of her wrapper parted, revealing her legs from the knees down; if she realized it, she didn't seem to mind. She stared at Will over the rim of her glass, which made Nell feel as if all the little hairs on the back of her neck were quivering on end.

Orville Pratt emerged several long minutes later, perfectly attired in a fine black frock coat and bow tie. He looked every inch the quintessential Brahmin businessman—save for his black eye, which was turning greenish, and his faintly ruddy lips. It looked as if he'd tried to wipe them off, but the more vivid shades of lip rouge tended to leave a stubborn stain. Nell assumed he'd kissed off some of Daisy's rouge—until she realized that his lips were smudged not with cherry red, but with a warmer, more orangish vermilion.

Pratt glowered at his unwanted callers, his gaze settling on Will. "What's the meaning of this, Hewitt?"

"Fiona Gannon's uncle has asked Miss Sweeney to look into Virginia Kimball's murder," Will said. "We have reason to believe that your Lefaucheux may have been involved."

Pratt frowned as if he hadn't quite heard right. "Fiona Gannon committed that murder, using Mrs. Kimball's own gun. That's been well established. For you to barge in on me like this, with utter disregard for my privacy or the dictates of common civility, only proves what your father's been saying about you all these years. No gentleman would have done such a thing, and if you have a shred of common decency, you will leave this instant and apologize to Miss Sweeney for having brought her here. In return, I'm prepared to overlook your appalling judgment and go on as if none of this had transpired."

"Well done, sir," Will said. "I could never have composed that speech on such short notice. The reason we're here is that it's come to our attention that you threatened to kill Mrs. Kimball the day before she was, in fact, killed. You can see how that might pique our interest."

"Perhaps I didn't make myself clear," Pratt said. "I expect you to take Miss Sweeney and—"

"No, I'm afraid it's I who haven't been clear," Will said. "Miss Gannon's guilt has not, in fact, been well established, and there's every reason to expect this case to be reopened. When it is, your name will top the list of suspects."

"Just because some dotty old poofter of a playwright claims he heard me make a threat?"

Nell said, "You're referring to Mr. Thurston, I assume. What makes you think he's the one who told us what you said?"

"What I'm *alleged* to have said." The lawyer stalked over to the cocktail cabinet and shook the empty decanter. "Jesus, Daisy, this was full just three days ago."

"There's some gin," she said as she raised the glass to her bright red mouth.

Pratt poured himself a generous helping of gin and took a gulp, his face screwed up in revulsion.

"We know about your affair with Mrs. Kimball," Will said.

"Preposterous!" Pratt's ears were a red-hot crimson. "Who told you that? Thurston? He's hated me ever since I took on Mrs. Kimball as a client. He was jealous of everyone she knew."

Nell said, "We know she blackmailed you after you ended it."

"She *blackmailed* you?" Daisy said with gleeful astonishment.

"I wouldn't get any ideas," Will advised her. "It's not a pastime for amateurs."

"You were too proud to pay up, though," Nell said, "so Mrs. Kimball lit a fire under you by crashing your annual ball, which seemed to work, until you, uh, misplaced your Lefaucheux. You drank yourself into a rage, grabbed one of your daggers, and went to her house to accuse her of stealing it."

Daisy barked with laughter.

"An amusing story." A vein crawled across Pratt's vast, pink brow like a worm burrowing just under the skin. "But I daresay it's as far-fetched as those idiotic little farces of Thurston's."

Will said, "It gets more dramatic."

"Mrs. Kimball demanded her money," Nell said. "You demanded your gun. Eventually Vera and Emily took you home. But a month later you were back, with some tall tale about having given Fiona Gannon five thousand dollars in exchange for your—"

"*Tall tale?*" Pratt wheeled to face Nell, half his drinking sloshing onto the rug. "That lying little bogtrotter! I handed her that money myself, and she stood there and denied ever having—" He shut his eyes and growled something under his breath.

Will smiled at Nell as if impressed that she'd smoked this much of an admission out of Pratt. "So," he said, "you admit that Mrs. Kimball made you an offer—the gun for five thousand dollars."

"I admit nothing to you," Pratt said with seething contempt. "Who do you think you are, either of you, seeking me out here, of all places, and—"

"If you'd prefer," Will said, "I'd be happy to send a

police detective over, and you can talk to him. Of course, you've handled enough criminal cases to know that if you do that, certain unsavory details will become public knowledge sooner or later. Even if you're found innocent of any wrongdoing toward Virginia Kimball, all of Boston, including your wife and your clients, will know some very interesting things about you. If, instead, you talk candidly to us, we'll reveal only as much as is necessary to see justice done."

Will paused to let that sink in. Pratt dropped into a chair and stared at the Persian rug. Daisy regarded him with frank but mild interest, as if he were an actor in a play and not the man who'd been sharing her bed for the past few months.

"The gun for five thousand . . ." Nell said. "Did Mrs. Kimball put this in a note?"

Pratt shook his head without looking up. "She didn't want to admit to grand larceny in writing. She had Fiona come and lay it all out. I hand over five grand, and the next day the gun is delivered to my house—and the shakedown ends."

"Why the next day?" Nell asked. "I would think you would have demanded that the gun be returned to you when you handed over the money."

Pratt let out a humorless little grunt of laughter. "Yes, well, as it was explained to me, Virginia didn't think Fiona would be able to fight me off if I were of a mind to take the gun without paying up. In any event, the conditions were non-negotiable. One thing I've learned as an attorney is if the other party flat out refuses to compromise, there's not a great deal one can do but go along or walk away from the deal."

"You were that desperate to get that gun back?" Will asked.

Pratt sighed and drained his gin.

"So you paid up," Will said, "but the gun was never delivered."

"Did it never occur to you that she might not even have had it?" Nell asked. "After all, she'd been denying it for some time. And then, when she said she had to get the money before she'd give up the gun . . ."

Pratt rubbed his gigantic forehead with an unsteady hand, as if trying to smooth away that vein.

Nell said, "So you let a couple of days go by, and then you went to Mrs. Kimball's and threatened to kill her."

"Manhandling her in the process," Will said, "whereupon Mr. Thurston proved he's got what it takes in the ring."

"That punch came out of nowhere!" Pratt sprang to his feet, his face so red—from mortification, evidently, at having been bested by the likes of Maximilian Thurston—that it looked as if it were about to burst. "He sneaked it in. It was completely unsportsmanlike, not that one would expect otherwise from one of them. Had it been a fair fight, I would have—"

"A gentleman deserves a fair fight," Will said evenly. "The kind of vermin who would strike a lady deserves whatever he gets."

"*Lady?*" A frantic little burst of laughter erupted from Pratt. "How can you even think to call a whoring bit of baggage like that—"

Will whipped a fist across Pratt's face, sending him flying back into his chair. Pratt cursed like a stevedore. Daisy's startled shriek degenerated into a flurry of giggles.

"My word, Will," Nell said. "You've been doing that an awful lot lately. Aren't you afraid of damaging your hand?"

"I used my left this time. It's not as strong as the right, but this way he gets a new black eye on the other side, and there's a certain pleasing symmetry to that."

"Clever you."

Pratt called Will a great many things, all unspeakably foul. Daisy just couldn't seem to stop laughing.

"You'll have to invent a new lie for what happened to you this time," Nell told Pratt.

"By the way," Will said, "why did you tell your wife that you'd been robbed by a basher, and the rest of us that you'd tripped on the stairs?"

Pratt sat forward, rubbing the side of his face. "I never told my wife . . . Oh. Vera must have told her that. She can't seem to stop looking after me. Gets damnably irritating."

"So you don't deny having visited Mrs. Kimball the day before her murder and threatening her?" Nell asked.

Pratt cupped his face in his hands, muttering in evident exasperation. "Yes. *Yes!* I got fed up. Who wouldn't? She got her money, I didn't get my gun. I went there, and I . . . I probably said some things I shouldn't have, but it was just in the heat of anger. It didn't mean anything."

"Perhaps not," Will said, "but the next day, Virginia Kimball was found shot to death. You do understand why you're at the top of our list."

"All right," Pratt said. "How much to get me off that list?"

"I beg your pardon?" Nell asked.

Will said, "He's offering us money to ignore the fact that he may be a murderer."

"For God's sake, I'm not a murderer."

Will smiled. "With all due respect, that *is* what murderers tend to say."

"And to answer your question," Nell said, "there's no amount of money you could offer that would sway us. The only way you can get off the list is by convincing us you didn't do it."

"Oh, for God's sake," Pratt grumbled. "I was nowhere near Mount Vernon Street that afternoon."

"Where were you?" Nell asked.

"That's not imp—"

"Here?" Will asked.

Pratt's hesitation was telling.

"Would you swear to that in a court of law, Miss Newland?" Will asked.

"Hm? Oh, um . . ." Daisy shrugged and made a little *pfft* sound. "Sure, I guess."

"No." Pratt rose to his feet, hands outstretched as if to ward off such a prospect. "No, no, no, no, no. That can't happen. Don't you see that? My reputation, my marriage . . ."

"Even if it keeps you from hanging?" Will asked.

Pratt said, "No one could seriously think I shot those two women. This is . . . this is mad. This entire conversation is mad. Why am I standing here listening to this?"

"Mrs. Kimball and Miss Gannon were killed with a forty-four- or forty-five-caliber revolver," Will said. "Who's to say you didn't go to Mrs. Kimball's looking for your Lefaucheux the day after Thurston dealt you that black eye? You used the unlocked garden and courtyard doors to sneak into the house. You did find the gun, but then Mrs. Kimball came home. Or perhaps Fiona caught you upstairs, and—"

"This is absurd. I don't need to listen to any more of this." Pratt raised his chin and puffed out his chest in a burlesque parody of the image he liked to project. "I'm a person of substance in this city, in case it's escaped your notice. People look up to me. They listen to what I have to say. Who are you? A professional gambler—yes, Hewitt, I know how you make your living—and an Irish governess. If it should come down to your word against mine, either one of you, I have very little doubt as to who will prevail. In the meantime, I'll thank you to leave this flat immediately."

"With pleasure," Will said as he took Nell's arm and led her toward the door.

"And if you think you can gain ground by eviscerating my character," Pratt continued, "I shall not only deny your allegations, but turn them against you. I've had decades of practice playing dirty. I'll wager I'm a bit more skilled at it than you two."

Pausing in the doorway, Will said, "Ah, but it's as much about ammunition as skill. You see, we know about the Red Book, Mr. Pratt. We know what Mrs. Kimball wrote about you and your . . . proclivities."

"Speaking of which," Nell added, "a little cold cream will take that lip rouge right off."

Pratt touched his lips, the color leaching from his face, as they closed the door. Daisy's laughter pursued them down the hall.

"CITIZENS with information about a case." That was how Nell and Will announced themselves to the clerk sitting outside Detective Charles Skinner's office in City Hall.

It was midafternoon by the time they arrived there, Will having taken Nell and his daughter for a leisurely luncheon at the Revere House—to the immense joy of Gracie, who normally didn't get to see too much of her beloved "Miseeney" on Saturdays. The restaurant meal, an exhilarating novelty for the child, had left her sated and drowsy; she'd dosed in her "Uncle Will's" arms during the cab ride back to Colonnade Row. He'd carried her into the house and all the way up to the third-floor nursery, kissing her sleep-flushed cheek as Nell tucked her into bed. That kiss had made Nell's heart clench.

Skinner rose behind his desk as Nell and Will entered his office, which stank of meat and onions; a wad of greasy paper lay on the floor next to his overflowing wastebasket. He wore the cordially baffled expression of a man facing visitors whom he knew he'd met recently, but couldn't quite place.

"Mrs. Kimball's funeral," Will reminded him. "Miss Sweeney is the lady who was overcome by the heat. I'm the physician who—"

"Yes, yes, of course. Of course. Dr. Hewitt."

Skinner invited them to sit in the pair of cracked leather chairs facing his desk, then took a seat himself, his hands linked over his plaid-vested stomach. "I'm told you have some information for me?"

"Quite a bit, actually," said Nell as she unfolded her sketch of Mrs. Kimball's bedroom.

"It's about Virginia Kimball's murder," Will said.

"Ah. Yes, well . . . that's not actually an open case. It's been resolved, so I'm afraid any information you have wouldn't really be of any . . ." Skinner stared at the sketch as Nell flattened it out on his desktop, frowning as he realized what it was.

"This is the scene of the murder." Pointing to the sketch, Nell said, "Here's where Mrs. Kimball fell. Fiona fell in this direction. Here's where her killer was standing. Here's where the blood from her head wound—"

"How did you get into that house?" Skinner asked, his voice like rolled steel, all business now.

"A more pertinent question," Will said, "might be how you could have seen what we saw and still have blamed the murder on Fiona Gannon?"

With a condescending little smile, Skinner said, "I assure you, my conclusion, and the conclusion of the county coroner and the inquest jury—erudite gentlemen, all— was arrived at after a thorough consideration of the facts."

Will said, "Perhaps the inquest jury didn't have access to all the facts."

Skinner said, "Perhaps you ought to leave police work to the police."

"That might be reasonable advice," Will said, "if the police in this city would stop holding their hands out long enough to actually investigate the crimes they're supposed to be solving."

"I believe I've heard enough," Skinner said as he rose to his feet. "I'll thank you both to take your little drawings and your theories and—"

"You lied under oath during the inquest, Detective, and we have proof of it." Will made this statement as casually as if he were discussing the weather. "What's the punishment for policemen who commit perjury? Dismissal from the department?"

"Oh, I'm sure it would be dismissal plus a prison term," Nell said.

The detective sat back down with an unconvincingly blasé smirk. "And what makes you think I lied?" His bravado was belied by a telltale tightness in his speech and his restless eyes that kept looking for something new to focus on.

Will unwrapped his handkerchief from around the bullet he'd found on Mrs. Kimball's bedroom floor. "I fished this out of the blood that had soaked into the rug under Fiona's head." Holding it out so Skinner could see it, he said, "It's the bullet that killed her. As you can see, this is no thirty-one caliber lead ball."

Skinner stared at the spent slug with a rigid lack of expression. "So?"

"So you testified that Mrs. Kimball's Remington, a five-shooter, was missing three rounds when you found it at the scene. We do know that three bullets were fired in that room that afternoon—one into the window frame, one into Mrs. Kimball, which was buried with her, and one, this one"—Will held the bullet between thumb and forefinger—"into Fiona Gannon's head. The bullet from the window frame came from the Remington. This one did not, nor, it's safe to say, did the bullet that killed Mrs. Kimball. According to Maximilian Thurston, she always kept the Remington fully loaded. So if only one bullet was fired that day, how did it end up with three rounds missing?"

"Unless," Nell suggested, "you fired two yourself before handing it over to Mr. Watts for ballistic testing. Of course, you testified that you'd found it with those rounds missing, hence the perjury. The coroner perjured himself, too, undoubtedly at your behest, about the bullet having remained in Fiona's head. You knew everything all along. You saw the blood spray, you saw Fiona's wound . . ."

"You saw those powder burns on her face and cap," Will said. "You knew the direction in which she fell. You had to know her killer was standing right next to her with the gun pressed to her head. Mrs. Kimball was mortally wounded. She couldn't have gotten up and done it herself. The evidence of a third person in that room was overwhelming, yet you contrived, you and the coroner, to paint Fiona Gannon as a thief and a murderess."

"Did you suggest to Orville Pratt that he have Mrs. Kimball's house cleaned to expunge it of evidence," Nell asked, "or did he come up with that idea himself?"

In a flat, strained voice, Skinner said, "You are delusional, *Miss Sweeney*"—he sneered her name—"if you suppose I'd submit to an interrogation from the likes of you."

With quiet wrath, Will said, "You will submit to far worse than that from me, Detective, if you presume to address Miss Sweeney in that manner again."

Chapter 13

S KINNER looked away with an air of ostentatious disdain, but it was an unpersuasive performance; William Hewitt knew how to exude an aura of cold menace to which other men paid attention.

"What's your interest in this?" Skinner asked Will.

"Miss Gannon's uncle believes her to be innocent, as do Miss Sweeney and I."

"The chit's dead," Skinner said. "Does it really matter so much?"

Nell said, "You're a policeman, for God's sake. Don't you have *any* interest in bringing the real murderer to justice?"

"The real murderer—and who do you suppose that is?" the detective asked.

"I have my suspicions," she said. "How could I not, knowing that Orville Pratt and three other men bribed you to bury the Red Book and keep their names out of the investigation?"

"Did you ever find that book?" Will asked.

"If I had, do you think I'd tell you? As for these supposed bribes, I have no idea what you're—"

"You were visited the day after the murder," Nell said, "by Mr. Pratt, Isaac Foster, Weyland Swann, Horace—"

"How would you know that?" Skinner demanded. "It's that Cook bastard, isn't it? Goddamn flannel-mouth son of a—"

"Careful," Will growled.

"He's the one that told you, isn't he? You Irish are always whispering to each other, cooking up your schemes . . ."

"It wasn't he," Nell lied.

"Who, then?"

"Do you think I'd tell you?" she asked, echoing his own taunt.

"You're barking up the wrong tree, anyway," Skinner said. "Those men have all got alibis as to where they were when those two women were shot. Bacon was in court, Swann was in a board meeting, Foster was giving a lecture, and Pratt was . . . visiting a friend."

"His mistress," Nell said. "She'll testify however he wants her to, so long as he keeps paying her rent."

Skinner smiled greasily. "Now, what would a sweet little paddywhack like you know of such things?"

Will tensed as if to leap from his chair; Nell pacified him with a hand on his arm. "That doesn't sound like much of an alibi to me," she said. "And I know Mr. Thurston told you about Pratt's having threatened to kill Mrs. Kimball the day before the—"

"That sorry old nanny goat?" Skinner snorted. "Let me tell you something. Old Lady Thurston has a vivid imagination, which I suppose is good for writing plays, but it's not so good when it comes to being a credible witness. And in case you were wondering, Thurston claims he was home alone during the murder—all by his lonesome, no one to back him up on it. Just a little food for thought, there." Skinner sat back and crossed his arms. "Why'd you two come here, really? If you were fixing to have me brought up on perjury charges, you'd have gone directly to Chief Kurtz, or the D.A. You wouldn't be here."

Nell said, "You're going to tell Orville Pratt to hold off on having the house cleaned."

"Why? So you can make a case for the Gannon girl being innocent?"

"How about so we don't tell Chief Kurtz and the district attorney that you lied under oath?" Will drawled.

Skinner looked everywhere but at Nell and Will. "What excuse am I supposed to give Pratt?" he finally asked.

Will said, "That's entirely your affair. If you can manage to keep that house untouched until we're done looking into things, I promise we'll do what we can to make your deceptions and machinations look like mere bungling instead of what they really were. That should save you your job and possibly a jail term. But if that house gets scoured of its evidence before Miss Sweeney and I have wrapped things up, I guarantee you'll answer for your deceit."

Skinner was fumbling for a response when Will and Nell rose from their chairs.

"Good day, Detective," Nell said as they turned to leave.

"THERE it is." Will pointed to a green-and-gold sign hanging over a shop in Dock Square behind Faneuil Hall.

SAMUEL L. WATTS
GUNSMITH
REVOLVERS & RIFLES
BOUGHT • SOLD • REPAIRED
Custom Firearms

A bell tinkled as Will held open the door for Nell, ushering her into a dim, cluttered shop that looked as if it had been there, accumulating objects and dust, for eons. Firearms of every conceivable type were displayed in rows on the smoke-bruised brick walls, alongside racks of tools. Vises, lathes, and anvils sat on massive tables, their age-burnished surfaces strewn with drills, wrenches, hammers, polishing stones, rifle barrels, stocks, pistol grips, and innumerable other bits and pieces of guns. Coals smoldered in a hooded stone forge at the very rear of the shop.

"'Afternoon." They turned to find a man smiling up at them from a small worktable half-hidden amid the chaos, where he was cleaning a partially disassembled revolver by the light from a nearby window. He started to rise; Nell waved him back down as they approached him, sawdust and metal filings crunching underfoot.

"Mr. Watts?" Will said as he removed his hat.

"If I'm not, then I've been in the wrong place for about thirty years." Samuel Watts was a bulky, affable-looking fellow in shirtsleeves and an oil-stained leather apron, a pair of spectacles sitting low on his nose; his curly black hair and beard, the latter threaded with gray, looked long overdue for a trim.

Will made introductions, then produced the bullet taken from Mrs. Kimball's bedroom rug and the cartridge he'd swiped from Orville Pratt's study. "We were wondering if it's possible to tell whether this spent bullet might be from a pinfire cartridge like this one."

Setting down his bore brush and the pistol barrel, Watts took the bullets and peered at them over his glasses. "*Like* this one," he asked, "or *exactly* like this one?"

"Exactly," Will said. "Say, a cartridge from the same box."

"It's possible. They're both about the same caliber."

"The spent one is a forty-five?" Nell asked. "Are you sure?"

"Forty-four or forty-five," Watts said. "No smaller. I've got no way of telling if it was a pinfire, but I do know it came out of a metal cartridge."

"You're positive?" Nell asked.

The gunsmith smiled indulgently. "Miss, I've been in this business since I was a boy apprenticed to my grandpa. Yeah, I'm positive. Not that I could say for sure if it came from one of *these* cartridges—not without test-firing the fresh cartridge from the same gun that fired the spent one. You don't happen to have it handy, do you—the gun?"

Will shook his head. "I dearly wish we did."

"What kind of a gun is it?" Watts asked. "Maybe I've got one lying around."

"A Lefaucheux Brevete," Will said.

Watts looked at Will for a second, handed back the bullets. " 'Fraid I don't have one. You don't see too many of them. Only fella I know of who owns one of those is Mr. Orville Pratt." He took off his spectacles, breathed vapor onto the lenses, and wiped them with a clean rag. "Only fella in Boston, anyway. Stonewall Jackson carried one as his sidearm. I reckon that one's still down South somewhere."

Reasoning that it was hardly a secret, Pratt himself having crowed about it to all of Boston society, Nell said, "As a matter of fact, Mr. Pratt's Lefaucheux is the one that belonged to Stonewall Jackson."

"So he thought when he bought it," Watts said as he shoved the bore brush through the pistol barrel, "but I set him straight on that score. God knows how much he paid for it. Some flimflammer made a killing on that one."

Nell and Will looked at each other. "The gun's a fake?" she asked.

Will said, "When did Mr. Pratt find this out?"

Watts aimed the barrel toward the window and peered into it with one eye. "Few weeks ago. It was the end of April. I remember, 'cause she came in wet and grousing about all the rain we'd been having, and I said, 'That's April for you.' "

"She?" Nell and Will said it together.

"Pratt sent his daughter on account of him being real busy with work or some such," Watts said. "Had her bring me the gun for an appraisal, and to find out how to find a buyer, 'cause he'd decided to sell it."

"Which daughter?" Nell asked.

Watts scratched his chin with the stem of the brush. "I didn't catch the first name. She was pretty enough, but she had on some kind of funny . . ." He made a flowing gesture down his body.

"Emily," Nell said.

"She said it was Stonewall Jackson's Lefaucheux, and I said one of my customers had been talking about that gun just yesterday. He told me he'd been at some big blowout at the Pratts' the night before, and he got to hold the very gun General Jackson carried during the war. Well, she showed me the gun, and I took one look at it and said her pa might as well hang on to it, 'cause he wasn't gonna get more than eighty bucks or so. It was a good weapon, nice and clean, worked real well. But it had never belonged to Stonewall Jackson."

"You knew that for a fact?" Will asked.

Watts traded his brush for a rag, with which he wiped down the pistol barrel. "Jackson's Lefaucheux is one of the most famous guns in the world right now. I've seen pictures of it, read detailed descriptions. Pratt's gun looks nothing like it, and it's got a completely different serial number. He got the wool pulled over his eyes."

"How did Emily react to the news?" Nell asked.

"She was one unhappy young lady," Watts said as he set about reassembling the pistol. "Looked like she was fighting back tears when she left. Probably wondering how she was gonna break the news to the old man."

"Did you ever discuss the matter directly with Mr. Pratt?" Will asked.

"Yeah, just the other day. You know that actress that got killed up on Beacon Hill? Virginia Kimball? Well, me and Pratt both testified at the coroner's inquest, me 'cause I'm a ballistics expert and Pratt 'cause he was Mrs. Kimball's lawyer. I went up to Pratt during a break and introduced myself. Told him how sorry I was about the Lefaucheux being a fake, and that if he was aiming to buy any more collectible firearms, he should have me check 'em out first. I said if he was busy, he could just send his daughter with the gun, like he did last month, but it wasn't a step he could afford to skip—not unless he wanted to get bamboozled again."

Will glanced at Nell as he rubbed his neck. "How, er . . . how did he react to that?"

Watts paused in his work to consider his response. "He was real . . . I don't know. Real quiet like, in a daze almost. He just sort of stared at me, like I'd been talking Chinese or something. Then finally he kind of blinks, and thanks me in that real stiff way of his, and walks away. I put it down to him being, you know, preoccupied with the inquest. That kind of fella, big, important lawyer and all that, he's probably got stuff on his mind all the time."

"I should think," Will said, "that he had a great deal on his mind just then."

Chapter 14

"GOOD evening . . . Merritt, is it?" Will greeted as the front door of 82 Beacon Street swung open around dusk later that day.

"It is, sir." The thickset, funereally attired butler bowed as he took Will's card. "Good evening, Miss Sweeney . . . Dr. Hewitt."

"Is Miss Emily Pratt at home, by any chance?" Nell asked.

"I'm sorry, miss, but Miss Emily is out for the evening."

"Oh." Nell and Will had come up with quite a list of questions for Emily over supper, which provided a welcome respite from a long and exhausting day. It was a simple but excellent meal in a private upstairs room at Atwood & Bacon's, which Will had secured in exchange for a half eagle pressed into the palm of the headwaiter.

To get to it, they'd had to negotiate a labyrinth of creaky stairways and passages leading at last to an isolated little nook, warmly paneled and hung with century-old paintings. It had been lovely sharing a good meal all alone with Will. He'd leaned back and propped his feet up on the bench next to her, smiled at her in the candlelight, watched her in that dreamily engrossed way of his . . . She hadn't wanted it to end.

"Are the rest of the family at home?" Will asked.

Merritt shook his head. "They're visiting friends, I'm afraid. Oh, except for Miss Pratt—Miss Vera Pratt. She's, er . . . I believe she's taking the air out back in the courtyard."

"How lovely on such a mild evening," Nell said. "You don't suppose she'd mind if we went back there just to say hello?"

Merritt hesitated for some reason, then bowed again and invited them to follow him toward the rear of the house. They followed him through the French doors and into the candlelit courtyard, in which Vera Pratt stood with her eyes closed and her arms outstretched, humming tunelessly. She had on another poorly altered frock tonight, of a shade of green that accentuated her paleness.

To either side of Vera stood a round iron table ringed in candles. Strange designs had been scrawled in chalk onto the brick pavement. The largest of these was a six-pointed star about ten feet in diameter, in the center of which Vera stood. Surrounding this hexagram was a snake swallowing its tail. Other symbols included a Greek cross with its arms at right angles, another cross with a loop for an upper arm, and some kind of Oriental writing.

Vera stood absolutely unmoving, as if she didn't realize other people were standing right in front of her.

Nell looked at Will.

Will looked at Merritt.

The normally stoical butler wore an expression of resigned forbearance, from which Nell surmised that this wasn't the first time his employer's sister had conducted this particular evening ritual since returning from her travels.

Merritt cleared his throat.

Vera didn't move.

"Miss Pratt," the butler said. "You have visitors."

Vera opened her eyes, took in Nell and Will, and blinked. "Oh." She smiled, lowered her arms. "Oh, my word. How lovely to see you both again."

Nell and Will both nodded stupidly until Will finally said, "We were just, er, walking past the house, and we thought we'd drop in and say hello."

"I'm so glad you did." Vera's smile faded. "I suppose you were actually looking for the rest of them, but they're dining on the Abbots' yacht tonight. Perfect evening for it, don't you think?"

"Yes, indeed," Nell said. Pity Vera wasn't invited.

"Is that where Emily is?" Will asked.

"Oh, no, Emily can't bear that sort of thing. She's out walking with Dr. Foster."

"Isaac Foster?" Will said.

"Yes, he came calling after supper and asked if she might like to join him for a stroll in the Commons. Winnie wanted me to go with them—you know, for propriety's sake—but Emily said she wouldn't go if she had to drag along a chaperone. Winnie didn't insist. She's just so excited to have a gentleman like Dr. Foster taking a fancy to Emily. Very pleasant gentleman, I think."

"Yes, he seems like a fine fellow." Will glanced at Nell.

"Miss Pratt," Merritt said, "would you and your guests care for some coffee?"

"Oh!" Vera seemed rattled, as if unused to entertaining guests. "Yes, I suppose . . ." Turning to Nell and Will, she asked, "Would you . . . would you like . . . ?"

"That sounds delightful," Nell said.

"Well, then, yes," Vera warbled. "Thank you. Thank you, Merritt. Marvelous idea."

The butler left. Nell, Will, and Vera stood staring at each other in the candlelit courtyard. When Nell's gaze lowered to the chalk drawings, Vera said, "You're probably wondering what I'm doing."

"Er, well . . ." Nell didn't know whether to nod or shake her head.

"Yes, actually," Will said.

"I'm trying to call up a departed spirit," Vera said, as casually as if she were talking about asking a neighbor to tea. "I've seen H.P.B. do it, and she's tried to teach me how, but I'm . . . I don't know. She says I lack the mental discipline. Everyone always says I'm a little . . ." She wagged her fingers around her head. "But I'm determined to keep on trying till I've got it. Chairs?"

"I . . . beg your pardon?" Nell said.

"Would you like chairs to sit in? You would, wouldn't you, if we're to have coffee." Vera looked around, hands fluttering. "I pushed them to the side . . ."

"I've got them." Will dragged three chairs into a little circle and guided the ladies into their seats. Merritt reappeared, set up a tray table laden with coffee, port, fresh raspberries, and candied ginger, bowed, and left.

Vera poured the coffee; Will poured the port, which Vera declined. "Strong spirits sap our mental auras, thus weakening our connection with the spirit world."

"Funny they didn't mention that to me in medical school," Will said as he poured Nell and himself rather stiff ones.

"It's a pity Emily's not here," Nell said. "We'd very much wanted to talk to her."

"Yes?" Vera blew on her coffee, which she took black and sugarless.

"I don't know if she told you that Fiona Gannon's uncle is a friend of mine."

Vera gasped, her hand pressed to her chest. "The poor man! Having a murderess for a niece."

"That's the thing," Nell said. "He believes her to have been innocent, and after looking into things a bit, Dr. Hewitt and I have come to share that belief."

Vera looked back and forth between them. "If Fiona didn't do it, who did?"

"We're not sure," Will said. "But what we do know, with absolute certainty, is that there was a third person involved. Nobody who's seen the room where those women were killed could have any doubt about that. Our aim is to have the case reopened and see that Fiona Gannon is publicly exonerated."

"My word." Vera paused to digest all that. "But, er . . . what does this have to do with Emily?"

Choosing her words with care, Nell said, "Some rather curious things have come to light—things we need to discuss with her."

Vera stared at Nell, her face chalk-white in the semi-darkness. "You don't think . . ." She laughed uneasily. "You can't think Emily had anything to do with . . ."

"We're not sure," Will said. "That's why we want to talk to—"

"She's a wonderful girl," Vera said, her quavery voice rising in pitch. "Spirited, yes, but a girl of the highest moral character."

Of course Vera would want to defend her niece, Nell thought. Emily was her only friend in this house, perhaps in all the world.

"Did you know she stole her father's Lefaucheux?" Will asked.

Vera's gaze shifted away from Nell and Will. She started tidying items on the tray table. "I . . . she . . ."

"You did know," Nell said.

"N-no. No. I have no idea what you're—"

"Miss Pratt," Will said, leaning toward her. "We know for a fact she had the gun. She must have been the one who stole it."

Vera bit her lip, her eyes glimmering. "I promised Orville I would never tell anyone—"

"You're not." Nell took Vera's hand and squeezed it. "We're telling you. We already know. All you need to do is just . . . fill in some of the details, let us know why she took it. If it was just an impulsive act on her part that had nothing to do with the murder, you'll be doing her—and your brother—a favor by clearing things up."

Vera looked thoughtful for a moment; she nodded as

she sorted that out. "Yes. Perhaps . . . perhaps you're right. And I suppose it can't really hurt Emily, me telling you these things, because no matter who finds out, Orville would never press charges—about the, the gun, I mean. He wouldn't risk the scandal."

"Of course not," Nell said.

"The gun . . . That was just a girlish . . ." Vera flapped her hands as if that would help her to come up with the right word. "You know. To punish her father for cutting off the purse strings and bringing her home. Of course, it was a foolhardy thing to do, and I told her so, but she's got a mind of her own, and Orville, after all . . . You must understand, he's a good man deep down, but he can be insufferable about some things."

Will said, "Mr. Watts, the gunsmith Emily consulted, said she was trying to sell the Lefaucheux."

Vera sighed as she took a sip of coffee. "She wanted money to continue her travels. I think she considered it . . . what is the word—ironic?—using Orville's gun to pay for that."

"Did you know the gun had turned out to be a fake?" he asked.

Vera nodded miserably. "Emily was beside herself."

"The next day," Nell prompted, "you and she followed your brother to Mrs. Kimball's house on Mount Vernon Street."

"Emily had come to me, very agitated. She'd overheard her father talking to his valet in his study. Burns, the valet, was saying he needed 'the eight hundred' because it was time to go meet someone named Clara on a street corner. Orville, well, he'd been drinking all afternoon. He started ranting about Virginia Kimball, saying she had his Lefaucheux and he meant to get it back. Emily heard Burns asking Orville if he really thought he should be taking that dagger, but Orville just ignored him and left."

"So you followed him, you and Emily," Nell said.

"What else could we do? We thought he might actually kill her over that gun. Imagine how Emily felt. It was all her fault, after all, because she'd been the one to take the gun but Orville thought Mrs. Kimball had done it. We ran after him in the rain and tried to keep him from going into Mrs. Kimball's house, but he . . . well, he said some rather rude things about our . . . interference, and ordered us to go back home. We didn't go, though. I wanted to, but Emily insisted, so we . . . we followed him into the house. We came in behind him, quietly—he didn't realize we were there. The things he was saying to Mrs. Kimball, and that Thurston fellow . . . well." Vera shook her head. "I hated for Emily to hear it, to see her father like that, to know . . . those things about him."

"The next day," Nell said, "Emily tried to sell the gun, but found out it was a fake."

Vera nodded. Night had fallen, and there was very little moon; the wavering light from the candles softened her haggard features. "I told Emily it was worthless, and that she should put it back in her father's study. She said she'd been thinking about it, and maybe it wasn't so worthless after all. *She* knew it was a fake, but her father didn't."

"What did she mean by that?" Will asked.

"She didn't tell me. I don't think she fully trusted me, which hurt, but it was really for the best. I would have fretted something awful if I'd known."

Nell leaned forward. "Known what?"

"What she was up to." Vera gazed wanly at the bowl of raspberries, chose one, and put it in her mouth. She ate it with a slightly pinched expression, wiped her fingertips on a napkin. "I didn't know, though, until . . . it was about a week ago. Yes, a week ago today, last Saturday. I saw a Cunard ticket on Emily's writing desk in her room. First class aboard the RMS *Propontis,* sailing to Liverpool June twenty-sixth. I asked her how she'd gotten the money for the trip, and she told me . . ." Vera closed her eyes, slumped in her chair.

"She told you what?" Nell coaxed.

Vera opened her eyes, looking weary, drained. "You know that Fiona Gannon used to work here."

"Yes."

"It was Emily who got her the job with Virginia Kimball. I knew that, but I didn't know why—I mean the real reason. It wasn't just because Mrs. Kimball wasn't as stuffy and demanding as Orville and Winnie. It was because Clara, well, she'd been more than a maid. She'd . . . she'd delivered the notes to the gentlemen and collected the money—for extra pay. We'd heard her say that when we were there that night."

Will said, "So Emily convinced Fiona to offer Mrs. Kimball her services as bagwoman, which would vastly increase her income, thereby enabling her to buy her notions shop all the sooner."

"I believe that's the gist of it," Vera said. "So Fiona went to work for Mrs. Kimball, and about . . . oh, I suppose it was about two weeks later, maybe a little more, Emily talked her into . . . well, the plan she'd had in mind all along."

"Offering your brother his Lefaucheux back in exchange for five thousand dollars," Nell said, "but making it seem as if the offer was coming from Mrs. Kimball."

Vera nodded. "He already thought she had the gun. Fiona agreed to it, rather reluctantly, according to Emily, because of the . . . I suppose the scope of the deception, and the fact that she'd grown fond of Mrs. Kimball. But she wanted that shop, and she and Emily were to split the five thousand equally, so . . ."

"So Pratt paid up," Will said, "and Emily made plans to take ship."

"Without you," Nell said quietly.

Even in the dark, Nell could see the color rise in Vera's cheeks. "Emily . . . she . . . she's a very independent girl, very . . ." She lifted a piece of candied ginger, frowned at it, set it back down. "She's young. She needs her freedom. She explained that. And she . . . she was very kind about it. She offered me some of the money—not much, because she needed a certain amount just to get by overseas, but as much as she could. I turned it down. I knew she'd need every penny just to support herself, and I've got Orville and Winnie. I'll never lack for anything."

Except respect and decent companionship, Nell thought.

Will said, "Why didn't Emily return the gun to her father once she had the money?"

Vera looked heavenward and raised her hands, as if she'd pondered that question herself a thousand times. "To irritate him? She wouldn't discuss it with me, and that's the only reason I can come up with. If you could imagine having such a difficult relationship with your father . . ."

Nell met Will's eyes. Neither of them had to imagine such a thing. They knew all too well what it was like.

"So he assumed Virginia Kimball was holding on to the gun," Will said, "that she'd taken his money and reneged on her half of the deal.

"That's why I . . ." Vera ducked her head. "Oh, my Lord, Emily would be so put out with me if she knew what I did, but I just couldn't let Orville go on thinking that about Mrs. Kimball. Not after I saw her floating there in her coffin, so . . . sad and beautiful."

"You gave Orville back his gun?" Nell asked.

Vera nodded sheepishly. "When we got home from the funeral. I tried to keep it a secret where I'd gotten it from, but he said he knew Emily had taken it, that he'd found out the day before. I begged him not to tell her I was the one who gave it back. Emily and I . . . we've grown very close, and I'd hate for her to think I'd . . . betrayed her, or . . ."

"I understand," Nell said.

"Your brother knows the gun is a fake," Will said. "Did he tell you that?"

"Yes. He said Emily had stolen it to sell, and it served her right that it had turned out to be worthless. He said it was a good lesson to her, he just wished it hadn't cost him seventeen thousand dollars. He said I wasn't to let anyone know about the gun not being Stonewall Jackson's, nor about Emily taking it—that it would shame the family if all that were to come out. But I . . . I think he'd appreciate why I told you. I did it for Emily, so you'd understand that the gun was just a bit of youthful imprudence. It had nothing to do with Mrs. Kimball's murder."

Nell and Will both sat back in their chairs; they shared a sober look.

On a heavy sigh, Will said, "Here's the problem, Miss Pratt. Mrs. Kimball and Miss Gannon were both shot with a high caliber revolver—a forty-four or forty-five— that uses metal cartridges. There aren't too many of those around. Unfortunately, one of them is Mr. Pratt's Lefaucheux."

Vera cocked her head, frowning. "No, it was . . . wasn't it Mrs. Kimball's own gun that was the murder weapon? A Remington something . . ."

"I'm afraid not," Nell said soothingly. "It was definitely the Lefaucheux, or a gun very much like it."

"And Emily was in possession of the Lefaucheux when Mrs. Kimball and Fiona Gannon were killed," Will said.

"But . . . why?" Vera asked. "Why on earth would she have done such a thing? She had nothing against Mrs. Kimball—she admired her, in a way. And she considered Fiona a friend."

"My best guess," Nell said, "is that the five thousand had whetted her appetite, and she went to Mrs. Kimball's when she thought no one was home in search of more sources of income—the necklaces, or perhaps even the Red Book."

Vera looked puzzled. "Red Book?"

"It's . . . something from which she could potentially have extracted a good deal of money," Will said.

Nell said, "She knew how to get into the house undetected from hearing her father mention the garden entrance. So she stole upstairs, but it turned out Fiona was home, and that was when things started going wrong."

Vera stared at nothing, looking increasingly stricken. "Emily, Emily . . ." she whispered shakily. "Oh, my God."

Chapter 15

To get to Boston Common from the Pratts' house, Nell and Will had merely to walk east along Beacon Street and cross Charles, which divided the Public Garden from the Common. Nell had been in the sprawling, pastoral park hundreds of times—the Hewitt home on Colonnade Row faced it—but rarely at night. Even with the ambient light from street lamps to illuminate the tree-lined brick walkways, it often felt as if they were strolling, arm in arm, into a black abyss. Nell was very glad of Will's company.

Not eager to spend the rest of the night wandering aimlessly along these paths, Nell asked Will, "If you were to take a lady for an evening stroll in the Common, where would you go?"

"That new fountain near the Park Street wall," he said,

"the one Gardner Brewer donated. There's something about flowing water that incites a certain . . . tranquil intimacy."

The sound of running water grew louder, but not unpleasantly so, as they neared the Brewer Fountain—a monumental, triple-tiered bronze replica of one created for the Paris World's Fair. It loomed before them, its sheets of cascading water shimmering in the amber gaslight from the lamps along Park Street.

At first Nell thought there was no one else around, but then she noticed, through the veil of water, a dark form on the other side of the fountain—two forms, she realized as she and Will circled the stone pool at the fountain's base. Two dark-clad people were sitting next to each other on the edge of the pool, their backs to the water. Even in the dark, Nell could make out the lady's chapeau *chinois* of black straw. She drew in a steadying breath.

Will patted her arm as they walked up to the couple. "Good evening."

Dr. Foster, looking oddly distracted, stood and tipped his hat to Nell. "Miss Sweeney . . . Hewitt." Will bowed to Emily, who sat with her head down, a handkerchief twisted in her gloved hands.

Nell said, "Your aunt told us you'd be here, Miss Pratt. I hope you don't mind that we . . . I say, are you quite all right?"

Emily dabbed at her eyes with the handkerchief and looked up. Her eyes were a bit too bright, her nose ruddy. "I'm fine." She smiled unconvincingly. "I'm pleased to see you, Miss Sweeney. Won't you sit with?" She patted the spot next to her that Foster had just vacated.

Nell sat carefully, tucking her voluminous skirts away from the spray.

"Lovely evening for a walk." Foster said, but his smile looked forced.

"It is," Will said, "and I wish I could say that's why we came here, but unfortunately that's not the case."

Turning to Emily, Nell said, "Miss Pratt, do you remember my mentioning Fiona Gannon's uncle, Brady, and how he's convinced his niece didn't kill Virginia Kimball?"

Emily nodded, her expression guarded.

"It turns out Mrs. Kimball was killed with a high-caliber revolver that fires metal cartridges—a gun like your father's Lefaucheux."

Emily's eyes widened slightly. She looked toward Dr. Foster.

"Perhaps," Will told her, "you'd feel more comfortable discussing this with just Nell and I."

"That isn't necessary," Emily said. "I . . . I've just told Isaac . . . Dr. Foster everything. There's nothing he doesn't know." Her chin quivered; her eyes welled with tears as she lowered her face into her hands.

Foster sat next to her and rested a hand on her back. "Is this necessary? You can see how upset she is."

"I'm afraid," Will said, "that it's either us or the police. Miss Pratt, I know you're distraught, but if you tell us what happened, and why, perhaps . . . perhaps we can get you the legal help and . . . other help you might need."

"L-legal help?" she rasped.

Foster said, "Do you think it will come to that? I can't imagine her father pressing charges."

Nell and Will exchanged a look.

"Why don't you tell us what you've just told Dr. Foster, from the beginning?" Nell suggested. "How did the subject of the gun come up?"

"We . . . we'd been talking for qu-quite a while." Emily glanced at Foster, who gave her a little smile. "And I . . . I felt it only right to tell him that I'd be resuming my travels at the end of this month. He, um . . . I don't remember exactly what he said, but—"

"I said it was my understanding that her father had cut her off," Foster said, "and I wondered aloud how she proposed to fund such a trip. A rather rude inquiry, I suppose, but faced with the prospect of losing Miss Pratt's company just when I'd gotten to know her, I felt justified in making it."

"I b-blurted out the truth," Emily said. "About w-watching my father pass that gun around at the ball and, and thinking about the money he paid for it. My God, twelve thousand dollars . . . Aunt Vera and I could have spent *years* overseas with that kind of money. She told me what he's budgeted for Cecilia's wedding."

"Vera?" Nell asked.

Emily nodded, the handkerchief clutched tight in her fist. "Ten thousand dollars. Plus another five for the gown, and eighty thousand to build that grotesque château. Yet he begrudged me a few spare thousand to travel with, which meant I was left with two choices—marital enslavement to some man, or a life sentence of spinsterhood under their roof, like poor Vera."

Emily fumbled in her reticule for her cigarette case.

"Not another one," Foster sighed.

"Under the circumstances," Will said as he produced a

match and lit it, "perhaps we can save the reprimands for a more suitable time."

Watching Will lean forward to light Emily's cigarette, Nell realized she hadn't seen him smoke since that morning, in Isaac Foster's back garden.

Emily's cigarette trembled as she drew on it. "I confess, I got quite agitated, watching him show off that damned gun. Vera kept bringing me brandies to calm me down, but the tipsier I got, the more . . . reckless my thoughts became. Finally I just . . ." She shook her head helplessly. "I just did it. I got my hands on it, hid it in the folds of my dress and took it upstairs to my room. It was the queerest thing, almost as if I were watching someone else do it. I woke up at noon the next day with a deuce of a morning head, appalled at what I'd done. By then, my father was on a tirade about the missing gun. I went to him to make a full confession, but he started bellowing about me being just another problem to deal with, and why couldn't I be more like Cecilia. He'd already started drinking, and he said some things . . . called me some things . . . things he had no business calling me. So I just turned around and went back upstairs and tucked the gun away under my mattress."

Nell said, "That evening you followed him to Mrs. Kimball's."

Emily nodded as she expelled a cloud of smoke. "I felt so guilty, listening to him accuse her of taking the gun. I'd half convinced myself to give it back, but later that night, Vera and I were talking over a bottle of sherry, and she told me some things about my father . . . how he's always had mistresses, even when he and my mother were first married, and how he cheats his clients out of money, as if he needed any more! This was the same man who'd lectured me since birth about propriety and responsibility, who continues to insist that I give up everything I love to become a proper, insipid little Brahmin matron. His hypocrisy sickened me."

"So you decided to sell the gun," Nell said.

Emily nodded as she tapped her ash onto the ground. "I brought it to a master gunsmith with a good reputation. He told me it wasn't Stonewall Jackson's gun at all. It was virtually worthless. I told Aunt Vera I should give it back to him, but let everybody know it was a fake, just to embarrass him. But then she said something. She said, 'Too bad for Mrs. Kimball that she *doesn't* have the gun. Orville would pay her just to get it back, and more than a measly eight hundred, too.' She just said it in passing, but it got me thinking."

"Yes, I imagine it would," Nell murmured.

"I stayed up all night thinking about it," Emily said. "The next day, I told Fiona that Mrs. Kimball's maid had quit, and perhaps she should offer herself as a replacement. I told her about the blackmail. I said if she got the job, and if she was willing to handle that end of things, as Clara did, she could save a great deal of money for her shop."

"She didn't know at the time about your plan to sell your father back his Lefaucheux?" Nell asked. She knew the answer, but she wanted to hear it from Emily.

Emily shook her head. "I thought it would scare her off. As a matter of fact, she was fairly balky a couple of weeks later, when I suggested it, but she wanted that shop so badly that she finally agreed. I didn't want to send a note, because I wasn't sure I could duplicate Mrs. Kimball's handwriting well enough, so Fiona went directly to my father and laid out the deal. He paid up the next day. Fiona and I split the money."

"And the first thing you did," Nell said, "was book passage for Liverpool."

"That very afternoon," Emily said.

"Vera didn't mind not being included?" Nell asked.

"Mind?" Emily said on a burst of incredulous laughter. "She went mad when she ran across that ticket and realized what it meant—I mean completely out of her wits. She was shrieking, sobbing. . . . I half expected foam to come spewing out of her mouth."

Nell and Will stared at each other. This didn't sound much like Vera's account.

"I'd never seen her fly off the handle like that." Emily shook her head as she crushed her cigarette underfoot. "I didn't know she had it in her. Part of me was actually impressed. Finally, a strong human emotion from docile little Vera Pratt. But it was also pretty unnerving. She was screaming things about Fiona and me . . . things I'd never thought to hear out of her mouth. She was incensed that we were 'hogging all the money.' She said she thought we'd had an understanding."

"You offered her part of your money?" Nell asked.

"A great deal of it, actually, but she said it wasn't enough to finance her travels with H.P.B. She said she'd been forced by virtue of being a portionless spinster to live under her brother's thumb as if she were a child, and she knew we all thought she was naïve and gullible, but that she was a lot smarter than she let on. She said H.P.B. was the only one who realized that, who took her seriously and respected her as a person. I calmed her down eventually. Regardless of what she may think about herself, she's really pretty malleable."

Nell and Will mulled that over to the silvery rushing of the fountain.

"Are you all right, Emily?" Foster asked softly.

She nodded. "It's just . . . I'm not used to feeling ashamed." She sniffed, and wiped her nose with the handkerchief. "As much as I needed that money, and as justified as I felt, doing the things I did . . . it doesn't feel worth it. I used to take such pride in having principles and ideals. Now . . ."

"Now you've had a taste of humility," Foster said with a smile. "You'll be even better for it, believe me."

She gave him a watery little smile in return.

Will said, "May I ask you, Miss Pratt, why you didn't return the Lefaucheux to your father once he'd paid the five thousand?"

"I couldn't," she said. "When I went to fetch it from under my mattress the next morning, it was gone. I suspected it had been pinched by the chambermaid who does my room—I can't bear her, and the feeling is mutual—but there was no way I could question her about it without giving away the fact that I had the gun. Vera and I tore apart my room, and then the rest of the house, but it was as if it had disappeared into thin air. That day went by, and then the next, and the next. I'd never seen my father so out of sorts. I knew why, of course. He thought Mrs. Kimball had taken his five thousand dollars but kept the gun. Then he showed up with that black eye, and I just knew it had something to do with this mess."

"When did he get the gun back?" Nell said, curious as to Emily's take on it.

"The day of the funeral. But he already knew it was a fake, and that I was the one who'd taken it. The day before, he told me the gunsmith I'd spoken to had been at the inquest and told him everything. He said I'd cost him five thousand dollars, over and above the original twelve he'd spent on the gun. I pretended not to know what he was talking about—I told him I'd just taken it to vex him. Do you know what he plans to do? He's going to make back that five thousand, plus a little more for 'mental anguish,' by skimming it from Mrs. Kimball's estate. He called me a liar when I said I hadn't seen the gun for five days, but he didn't care about getting it back at that point. He said it was worthless—almost as worthless as I —" Emily's voice broke; her shoulders shook.

Foster wrapped an arm around her, whispered something in her ear. She nodded, blotting her eyes with the damp handkerchief. Will handed her a fresh one. She mumbled her thanks.

Still embracing Emily, Foster said, "This is where the tale takes a bit of a strange turn. The next day, after the funeral, Mr. Pratt showed Emily the gun and said he'd found it in her room."

"I t-told him he couldn't possibly have found it there," Emily said, "because it had disappeared from there almost a week before, but that only infuriated him. H-he said he'd found it under my mattress, but how could he have?"

"He didn't," Will said. "He got it from your aunt Vera. She told him she'd taken it from your room."

Emily gaped at him. "That's impossible. Why would she have said a thing like that?"

Nell nodded. "That's what she told us she said. She asked him not to let you know she was the one who'd returned it to him."

Emily shook her head with an expression of dazed confusion. "But *it wasn't in my room*. It *wasn't*. It hadn't been in my room for almost a week. Why would she . . . ?"

"That might be worth finding out," Will said.

"A UNT Vera?" Emily knocked a third time on the door of her aunt's bedroom; still no answer.

"She's probably still out back," Will said, "summoning the dead."

Foster grabbed Emily's hand as she reached for the doorknob. "Let the men go first."

"He's right," Will said. "Why don't you and Nell stay back till we've had a look?"

Foster cracked the door open, paused, opened it further. He and Will stepped into the room; a few seconds later, they gestured for the ladies to enter.

It was a small room, humbly furnished in relation to the rest of the house. The bed was narrow, the rug small, the walls bare. In front of the single window stood a writing desk, on which an oil lamp illuminated a scattering of books and papers. Everything had a uniform, colorless look to it, almost as if they'd entered a pencil sketch of a modest little bedroom rather than the real thing.

Nell's gaze was drawn to the only spot of color in the entire room: a thick red book lying open and facedown on the desk.

Chapter 16

" I see it," Will said as Nell extended her hand to point. He got to the desk first and lifted the book, using his thumb to mark Vera's place. It was bound in crimson snakeskin, its pages densely inked on both sides with minuscule handwriting. Some of the ink had seeped through the tissue-thin, finely ruled pages, but not badly enough to obscure what was written there. Virginia Kimball's penmanship was neat and unhurried.

Emily said, "I remember my father saying something to Mrs. Kimball about 'the Red Book.' "

"This would appear to be it," Foster said. "It's a recounting of her . . . relations with men." After a moment, he added, "She'll have written about me in there."

Emily looked at him. He held her gaze, looking not so much embarrassed as worried as to how she would take this revelation.

Presently she nodded, her expression relaxing into a near-smile. "Thank you for telling me."

Will opened the book to the place Vera had saved; Nell read along with him:

Nov. 21st, 1868

It took me half an hour to get Orville laced up into my pink satin corset this afternoon, the new one with the black lace trim. There was a ten-inch gap in back, and the front view was even more ludicrous, of course, but he didn't care. He thought he was beautiful. He always does. His self-delusion would seem pathetic if it weren't borne of such arrogance. Hell, it seems pathetic anyway. It's all I can do, once he's got on the stockings and the jewelry and the face paint, not to howl with laughter.

Skinning his rabbit when he gets himself tricked out that way takes all my self-control. I close my eyes and imagine I'm someplace else with some other man, someone who can inspire some semblance of passion from me—that simpleminded young Adonis who drives the ice cart, or Tommy Kimball in that barn loft where he took my maidenhead while begging me to marry him, or my old standby, Doc, who makes love with feverish passion and exquisite tenderness every time . . . for such is the advantage of a lover one has only ever enjoyed in one's imagination. . . .

Will closed the book, his eyes shadowed.

"I saw my father's name on that page," Emily said. "May I read it?"

Will glanced at Nell, who gave him an almost imperceptible shake of the head. "There's really no point to it, Miss Pratt," he said. "Suffice it to say she had ample ammunition for blackmail."

"And not just against your father," Nell said. There was a list of men's names on the desk, with dates and scribbled comments next to them. She turned it around so she could read it. "Your name is on here, Will, and yours, Dr. Foster, and Mr. Pratt's, and . . . oh, my. These must be the men Mrs. Kimball wrote about in the Red Book, but this isn't her handwriting."

Emily, reading over Nell's shoulder, said, "It's Aunt Vera's. She must have read the whole book and taken notes."

"Listen to this." Foster, who'd been sorting through the papers on Vera's desk, showed them a letter bearing that day's date. "It's to Helena Blavatsky. 'My dearest guru, priestess, and friend of the heart,'" he read. "'Soon, very soon, I shall be able, at last, to rejoin you in your journeys—by which I mean, of course, not just your travels around the globe, but your explorations of the mind and the spirit. The pecuniary limitations which have thwarted me thus far shall soon be vanquished. And you will be pleased to know that I am progressing in my quest to coax a departed spirit into this earthly plane. Recent events seem to have focused my abilities in this area, to the point that I feel as if I am on the verge of a glorious assimilation not unlike that which you yourself have experienced.'" Foster scanned the rest of the letter. "There's more. It's all pretty much in the same vein."

"Vera's been busy." Nell picked up a letter with *Mrs. Virginia Kimball* embossed across the top in red. It had been folded to make an envelope, and sealed with wax. "This is a blackmail letter from Mrs. Kimball to Mr. Pratt, dated March twenty-fifth. My guess is that Vera got this from her brother's study. It looks as if she was using it as an exemplar to teach herself to copy Mrs. Kimball's handwriting." Nell pointed to several sheets of paper on which Vera had practiced, over and over, Mrs. Kimball's signature and various snippets from the blackmail letter.

Finally, there was a half-finished letter Vera was composing to "Orville" on Mrs. Kimball's writing paper, and in her hand, demanding three thousand dollars within two days "or I'll share your most entertaining performances from the Red Book, complete with costume changes, with your wife, your clients, every member of the Somerset Club, your friends, your business associates, in other words, everyone in your world who matters. Do not call my bluff, as you did the first time. I swear to God, if I don't have that money in my hands the day after tomorrow, you'll be a ruined man."

"This makes no sense," Foster said. "How could Vera think Mr. Pratt would take a letter like this seriously? Virginia Kimball is dead."

"Relatively speaking." It was a female voice, throaty and seasoned with a hint of a genteel southern accent.

They turned to find Vera Pratt standing in the doorway wearing an open silk wrapper over a matching nightgown, her hair cascading over her shoulders, a stemmed cordial glass in her hand. The glass held a ruby-colored drink with a cherry in it; even from ten feet away, Nell could smell the sweet red vermouth and gin. It was a Martinez cocktail.

"Doc." Vera crossed the room in a leisurely way, hips

swaying, her gaze fixed on Will. "It's been so long." She reached up to stroke his cheek, her eyes glimmering. "There are so many things I've wanted to say to you, explain to you. . . ."

Emily stepped forward. "Aunt Ver—"

Nell grabbed her arm and shook her head.

Will glanced at Nell, then met Vera's eyes. "There's no need to explain, Mrs. Kimball."

"But I was so cruel to you."

"You had your reasons. I understand. I do, really."

Vera closed her eyes. When she opened them, they were wet with tears. "If you knew how much it means to me, hearing you say that."

Will nodded, looking slightly stunned.

Vera's gaze lit on the Red Book in Will's hand, and the letters Nell and Foster were holding. "Y'all are probably wondering what I've been up to," she said with a wicked little smile.

Nell said, "It looks to be the same thing you were up to before your . . . tragic demise."

Vera chuckled as she lifted the glass to her mouth. "It'd take more than one puny little bullet in the chest to keep Virginia Kimball from her fun."

"Yes, I can see that," Nell said. "I can't help wondering how you pulled it off, though."

"My miraculous resurrection, you mean?" With an airy wave of her hand, she said, "Nothing to it. Vera was looking for a departed spirit to 'inhabit her earthly shell,' which was actually a pretty good idea, seeing as how she has no personality of her own. I, meanwhile, took one look at the Other Side and just knew I had to get back into a nice, warm body as soon as I could. Not that I'm too

keen on this one," she said with a contemptuous glance
down at herself, "and I'm *definitely* not looking forward to
sleeping all alone in that sad little bed of hers, but I reckon
beggars can't be choosers. And there *is* a certain comic
irony in possessing the body of the person who did you in.
Max should write a play about that. It'd be a hoot."

Emily sucked in a breath; Foster wrapped an arm
around her. "So you really . . . I mean Vera . . . she really
murdered . . . ?"

"Your aunt is what you call a 'killer mouse.'" Vera
propped the bed pillow against the wall and reclined there
with her drink in her hand, looking like Cleopatra on her
barge. "She just scuttles along the walls trying not to be
noticed, squeaking and creeping, creeping and squeaking, then one day she all of a sudden goes on the attack."

"What was it that incited this particular mouse to attack?" Will leaned against the desk, arms crossed.

"We know you'd been out shopping," Nell said.

"Oh, I'd bought the prettiest little hat you ever saw,
and now I'm never going to get to wear it, thanks to Vera
Pratt, damn her. She was already there when I got home,
raising hell with poor Fee up in my room. I heard them as
soon as I walked in the front door. When I got upstairs, I
found my jewelry case open and my necklaces spilling
out. Vera had a gun in her hand, but her back was to me,
so she didn't notice me right away. She was screaming at
Fee to give her the Red Book."

"So you fetched your Remington pocket pistol from
under your pillow," Nell said.

"Yes, but Vera turned and saw me, so she grabbed Fee
by her apron sash and held the gun to her head. That's
when I realized it was Orville's precious Stonewall Jackson

gun. I said, 'So you're the one who stole it.' She told me it was actually you, Emily. She said she swiped it out from under your mattress to punish you after you made plans to take ship without her. She'd been hoping to use my necklaces to pay for her own travels, until she got a good look at them and realized they were paste. She came up with a backup plan, though."

"The Red Book," Will said.

"So she could blackmail her brother?" Nell asked.

Vera shrugged. "And maybe some of the others. Who knows how a mind like that works? Fee, bless her heart, refused to tell her where the book was. She told me not to tell her, either. She kept saying Vera could never kill her, that she didn't have it in her, but I wasn't so sure, especially when Vera cocked the hammer back."

"So it was a standoff," Will said, "you with your gun aimed at Vera, and Vera with her gun on Fiona."

"Vera swore she'd shoot Fee if I didn't give up the book. It wasn't worth gambling with Fee's life, so I told her it was in the safe behind the painting, and I tossed her the keys, along with a warning that I'd kill her if she hurt Fee. Vera told Fee to take the painting down. Fee refused. Vera screamed at her, threatened her . . . Fee tried to grab the gun. That's when . . ." Vera squeezed her eyes shut, shook her head. "It was the most horrible thing I've ever seen. There was this . . . explosion, and Fee's head just . . ." She gulped her drink with a palsied hand, tears trickling from her eyes.

"You tried to shoot Vera then?" Nell asked.

"Yes, but I missed. She fired at me, and next thing I knew, I was flat on my back, feeling like there was a hundred-pound sandbag on my chest. I opened my eyes and saw Vera gathering up the necklaces and putting them in Fee's hands. I realized she was framing her, but I couldn't move. I couldn't do anything to stop her."

Will said, "Tonight, when Miss Sweeney and I told Vera that it looked as if the case would be reopened and Fiona exonerated, she changed the scapegoat to Emily." It was odd to hear him speaking to Vera about herself in the third person, but this entire encounter had been bizarre. "She was subtle about it. She kept insisting Emily couldn't have committed the murder, yet what she told us indicated otherwise."

"Manipulation and suggestion," Vera said. "The arsenal of powerless women everywhere."

Foster said, "Perhaps I should, er, head on over to Joy Street?" He meant the Joy Street police station.

Nell shook her head. "City Hall, the Detectives' Bureau. Colin Cook will be on duty. You're best off fetching him."

"What now?" Vera asked as Foster left. "They slap me in manacles and measure me for a noose? What an igno-minious end for Vera Pratt—that's what everyone will think. They won't realize they're actually hanging the murder victim." She laughed as she tilted her glass to her mouth. "A true comedy of the absurd."

"I doubt very much that you'll hang, Miss Pratt," said Nell, deliberately using her real name in the hope of snapping her out of her delusion. "In all likelihood— assuming your lawyer's up to snuff—you'll be found not guilty by reason of insanity."

"Yes, of course," Vera mused. "They'll think I'm mad. They'll never believe it's actually me. *You* don't, and you've been talking to me all this time. Why should they? They'll assume Vera is simply insane."

Emily said, "We'll testify that we saw you this way, Aunt Vera."

"That's right," Will said. "And Dr. Foster and I are physicians. We're familiar with this sort of psychological anomaly. So when you're, well, Vera again, if there's any doubt that you had displayed another personality—"

"When I'm *Vera* again?" She sat bolt upright, laughing incredulously. "What on earth makes you think I'd ever want to be Vera again?"

"But . . ." Nell glanced at Will and Emily, who looked as befuddled as she felt. "Surely . . . eventually . . ."

"If you think I'd give up this body, sorry though it is, and go back to that dreary Other Side, then you're madder than I'll ever be. Oh, no. I'm not going anywhere, and if Vera doesn't like it, she's only got herself to blame."

She smiled as she settled back against the pillow and raised her glass to her mouth. "Seriously, though, why on earth would she ever want me to leave?"

July 1869

Roxbury, Massachusetts

"IS that Max Thurston?" Will asked as he and Nell, with Gracie snugged between them in his phaeton, drove up to the entrance gate of Forest Hills Cemetery. A majestic, gothic-inspired edifice complete with arches and turrets, it looked more like the gateway to a medieval castle than to a graveyard, however swanky.

There were several people milling about on this sunny Friday morning, Forest Hills' acres of picturesque parkland being a popular destination for strolls and picnics. One of those people was a nattily attired, goateed gentleman exiting slowly through the main arch with the aid of a cane.

"Mr. Thurston!" Nell called as Will wrapped the reins around the brake handle.

Thurston looked toward them, his free hand shading his eyes, and waved. Nell had wondered if they'd run into him. Although this was their first visit to Virginia Kimball's final resting place, Thurston was still, some six weeks after her interment, paying almost daily visits to her gravesite.

"Would you carry these for me?" Will asked Gracie as he retrieved the flowers he'd brought along from the floor of the groom's seat.

Gracie's eyes widened as she took the bouquet, which was enormous and bound with a wide crimson ribbon. "This is the pwettiest thing I've ever seen!"

They joined Thurston on the walkway leading to the gate. He tipped his silk top hat to Nell and Gracie, asking, "And who is this lovely little lady?"

"Gwace Elizabeth Lindleigh Hewitt," Gracie said.

"Hewitt, eh? A relation of yours?" Thurston asked Will.

"She's my . . ." Will hesitated, having always hated to lie, especially to people for whom he felt some measure of fondness. Thurston's friendship with Nell and Will had been cemented when they gave him the Red Book, a gesture of affection and trust that had moved him to tears. Since then, they'd spent quite a bit of time together.

"Gracie is his mother's adopted child," Nell said; the truth, if a vague and partial version of it. "I look after her."

"What an enviable vocation." Leaning down to Gracie, the playwright said, "That's quite a bouquet you've got there, Miss Hewitt."

"It's for a lady who went to heaven," Gracie said.

Thurston pressed a hand to the small of his back and straightened up slowly, smiling at the child's artless statement. "A very thoughtful gesture." To Nell and Will, he said, "The monument is up."

"Yes, we're looking forward to seeing it," Nell said. Thurston had commandeered from Orville Pratt the responsibility for commissioning a tombstone for Mrs. Kimball's grave, a duty Mr. Pratt had eagerly relinquished.

"I say, Hewitt," Thurston exclaimed. "Very sharp neck scarf you've got there—very sharp, indeed. So good to see you showing a little style."

"Er, thank you," Will said as he adjusted the swath of orange and yellow striped silk knotted around his throat.

"I made it for him," Gracie said proudly. "For his birthday. And Miseeney painted a picture of me and put it in a gold fwame and gave it to him for his new house."

"Well done," Thurston praised. "So, when was your birthday, old man, and why wasn't I told of it?"

Nell answered for him. "It was yesterday—and he didn't want a fuss made."

"So, in direct opposition to my wishes," Will said, "these two impudent wenches cooked me up a much too grand birthday dinner in my new kitchen."

"We had to bwing our own pots and pans," Gracie said, "'cause Uncle Will doesn't have any, and we ate on a blanket in the garden, 'cause there's no table in his dining room, and no chairs, neither."

"Either," Nell said.

"Either. But we put candles and flowers on the blanket, just like a table, and it was *so, so* pwetty when the sun went down." Gracie was bobbing up and down now, as she did when she got excited. "Miseeney made oyster soup and bluefish and beef with mushwooms and apple fwitters—for me, 'cause I love them—and tomato salad, but she didn't make me eat that, 'cause I hate tomatoes."

"Don't care for," Nell said softly.

"Don't care for tomatoes. *At all*. I made the powidge."

Thurston cocked his head. "Powidge?"

"With waisins and honey."

"Gracie's specialty," Nell explained.

"And we had chocolate cake for dessert, but Misseeney said thirty-four candles was too many to fit on a cake, so we just had one big one, and it dwipped all over the fwosting, but it tasted good, anyway."

"What a lovely way to end a dinner alfresco," Thurston said. "It sounds divine. Say, I've got an idea. Why don't the three of you join me tomorrow evening for a cold supper in my courtyard?"

"What a delightful invitation," Nell said, "but I'm afraid Gracie and I will be on our way to the Cape by then."

"Oh, well, that won't do at all," Thurston said with mock petulance. "When will you be back?"

"The end of August."

"Well, then, I shall have to plan some absurdly lavish dinner to celebrate your return—something really overblown and vulgar. In the meantime," he said earnestly, "I shall miss you a great deal, Miss Sweeney. I've been very blessed, indeed, to have made friends such as you and Dr. Hewitt at this . . . particular juncture of my life. When I lost Virginia . . ."

He glanced at Gracie, who was now several yards away, practicing her curtseys with the bouquet in her outstretched hand. "I was tempted, seriously tempted, to join her in oblivion. I couldn't conceive of ever feeling anything but pain. Virginia would have been appalled, of course. She would have sneered at my weakness, berated me for it. Say what you will about her, but she never gave in, never lost sight of what she really wanted in life."

"Which was?" Nell asked.

"To be magnificent." Thurston smiled. "People always assumed she was some pampered southern belle, that she'd grown up on a plantation with the best of everything, and she let them believe it. But the truth is, her father was an itinerant preacher, one of these real hellfire-and-brimstone types who believed that he could instill a sense of godliness in his offspring through frequent and vigorous beatings."

Will looked toward Gracie, his jaw tight.

"He traveled all over Tennessee and Kentucky, dragging his family with him. It was Virginia's job to collect the offerings. She told me she used to watch the basket fill up and imagine all the things she could do with her life if that money was hers to keep. She was always dreaming of something better. That was one reason she liked Fiona Gannon so much—they had that in common."

"How did she end up in Boston?" Will asked.

"There was this young man, the son of a family they were staying with, the Kimballs. He was her first love. He asked her to marry him, and she said yes. The next day, he . . ." Thurston glanced at Gracie to make sure she was out of earshot. "He fell on a . . . I can't remember what she called it. Some sort of horse-drawn farm implement with iron spikes . . ."

Nell winced. "Oh."

"She was devastated, of course. And then she realized she was with child. She reckoned her father might actually beat her to death if he found out. So, one Sunday after the collection, she emptied the basket into her purse and bought a train ticket to New York. That's where she got started in theater—well, low theater, you know, but she loved it, and she was a natural. She said listening to her father rant and rave from the pulpit had been good training for burlesque."

"What of the baby?" Nell asked.

Thurston shook his head. "Cholera took him when he was just an infant—that terrible epidemic back in thirty-two."

"Oh, how awful."

"Virginia managed to break into the legitimate theater," Thurston said. "She learned her craft, and well, too. By the time she arrived in Boston, she was the best there was."

"I wish you could have seen her act," Will told Nell. "She really was quite brilliant."

Thurston said, "I asked her to marry me once."

Nell and Will stared at him.

"She just laughed, of course, so I pretended it was in jest. But it wasn't. Virginia Kimball was the only woman I ever loved."

Nell didn't know what to say to that. From Will's nonplussed expression, neither did he.

"Miss Sweeney . . ." Thurston lifted his hat and executed a courtly bow. "I meant it when I said I'd miss you. Hewitt . . ." He offered his hand. "We're neighbors now. I shall expect to see much more of you."

"You shall."

Thurston called good-bye to Gracie, who ran up to give him a farewell hug. He returned the embrace with obvious feeling and kissed the top of her head before taking his leave.

"I don't understand," Nell said as she watched him walk toward his waiting carriage.

"About his wanting to marry Mrs. Kimball?"

"Well, yes. He's . . . I mean, men like that, aren't they just supposed to be attracted to . . . other men?"

"Love is a capricious phenomenon. It doesn't always go where it should or do what we expect it to." He took her arm to escort her through the main archway, while Gracie skipped on ahead.

Inscribed in gilded letters on the gate were the words I AM THE RESURRECTION AND THE LIFE, which made Nell think of Vera, that night they'd found the Red Book in her room, speaking of her—or rather, Virginia Kimball's— "miraculous resurrection." Since her arrest on a charge of double murder, Vera had clung stubbornly to the conviction that she was Mrs. Kimball, thus virtually guaranteeing her acquittal by reason of insanity—not that she would ever have the luxury of living freely as one of the women she had, in fact, murdered. The six weeks she'd spent at Massachusetts General were only the beginning of what would surely be a long, perhaps even lifelong, stay. However, according to Emily, who regularly visited her there, it wasn't such a bad life. This particular hospital's psychiatric department was one of the most progressive in the country. Orville Pratt had also paid for his sister to be put up in a lavish room with a private nurse, special meals, books, magazines, watercolors, a chess set, a piano . . . every amusement she desired. Having settled into her glamorous new persona, Vera Pratt ruled her wing of the hospital like a queen—a far cry from her old life "scuttling along the walls trying not to be noticed."

Nell might have found all this more galling had not Fiona Gannon been declared innocent of all wrongdoing on the front pages of the *Daily Advertiser,* the *Massachusetts Spy,* and every other paper in the city. No doubt the item would have been buried on an interior page had it not been part of a much bigger story, that of the highborn Miss Vera Pratt's descent into lunacy and murder. Fee's public exoneration didn't bring her back, Brady had said, but it did take some of the anguish out of it.

Walking through Forest Hills was like taking a stroll on an English country estate. Rolling lawns were punctuated with craggy outcroppings and patches of woods; two swans drifted by on a glassy lake. A hawk circled overhead; birds chattered. Gracie, dancing and twirling with her bouquet, looked like a fairy child celebrating summer.

"That's it, I should think." Will pointed to the tips of a pair of white wings just visible beyond a rise up ahead.

He paused, staring at the wings, and touched his frock coat over his wallet pocket. It was a familiar, if increasingly rare, gesture.

"Have one," she said.

He smiled his thanks, withdrew a tin of Salem Aleikums, and lit one. It was his first cigarette all day—perhaps in several days. He'd been on the same tin for a couple of weeks now.

"Are you smoking less because of what Isaac said?" She'd asked him when she realized he was only lighting up at times of stress.

"Yes," he'd said with a smile. That smile had gotten her thinking: Isaac Foster's warnings about the dangers of smoking had gone beyond health issues. *No lady likes to be kissed by a man whose mouth tastes like an unswept hearth.*

Perhaps it was that aesthetic drawback to tobacco that had prompted Emily to give up smoking once Isaac started courting her seriously, which was shortly before she'd been scheduled to depart for Liverpool. According to Emily, he'd pleaded with her to put off her trip. He wasn't looking to enslave her, he'd promised, nor lay claim to her property, nor strip her of her rights. All he wanted was to love her and give her everything she wanted, whether it was travel, or writing, or babies, or all three. The argument had proved compelling; Emily had cashed in her Cunard ticket.

Will finished his cigarette as they walked slowly over the rise to Virginia Kimball's gravesite. Her monument, conceived by Max Thurston and carved out of flawless white marble by a respected Boston sculptor, consisted of an angel atop a pedestal. The pedestal was tall and stately, with odd crenellations around the top edges and an inscription on the front:

VIRGINIA EVELYN KIMBALL
DEPARTED THIS LIFE
JUNE 1, 1869

Aged 48 Years

*And from her fair and unpolluted flesh
May violets spring*

There were, in fact, violets growing on the grave, a veritable blanket of them—Max Thurston's doing, obviously.

The larger-than-life angel, who was attired in a gown

very much like that in which Virginia Kimball had been buried, was executing a curtsey, hair rippling, arms outspread to display her magnificent wings. What Nell had taken for crenellations around the pedestal were, on closer inspection, sculptural representations of footlights. The angel's smile was enigmatic, and although her head was bowed, her eyes were looking forward, as if at an appreciative audience.

"That's Mrs. Kimball's face," Nell said.

Will nodded.

She re-read the inscription. "Forty-eight years . . . That doesn't make—"

"I know," Will said. "If she was forty-eight when she died, she would have been only eleven during the Asiatic cholera pandemic of thirty-two. Assuming she was sixteen when the pandemic hit New York, she would have to have been fifty-three when she died."

"I won't tell if you won't."

Will smiled at her, took her hand. He started to say something, then seemed to think better of it. He looked toward his Gracie, cavorting among the gorgeous headstones and memorial statues with her bouquet, then back to Nell.

Squeezing her hand through her glove, he said, very softly, "I'll miss you, too, you know."

Well, you'll be getting a bit of your own, because I miss you horribly when you're away, which is far more often than I'm away. That was what she wanted to say. Instead, she said, "Will you be in Boston when I come back from the Cape?"

"Yes," he said unhesitatingly. "I'll be here."

Nell held his gaze until she couldn't bear it any longer,

then looked toward Gracie and cupped a hand around her mouth. "Don't go too far, buttercup. Stay where we can see you."

"Why don't you bring me those flowers?" Will called.

Gracie sprinted back with the bouquet—such an exquisite and huge assortment of orchids that Nell suspected he'd stripped every florist in Boston of that particular flower.

Sinking to one knee, he laid the orchids at the base of the monument. "I got it right this time, Mrs. Kimball."

First in the Gilded Age mystery series
by P. B. Ryan

Still Life with Murder

0-425-19106-0

Boston 1868: The privileged are enjoying the height of the Gilded Age—but not all are so lucky. As governess to the wealthy Hewitt family, Irish immigrant Nell Sweeney is sent to discover the truth behind the rumor that the Hewitts' son—thought to be killed in the Civil War—is still alive and about to be tried for murder.

"A SKILLFULLY WRITTEN STORY OF INTRIGUE AND MURDER SET DURING BOSTON'S FAMOUS GILDED AGE. NELL SWEENEY...IS A WINNING HEROINE."
—EARLENE FOWLER

Also in the series:
Murder in a Mill Town

0-425-19715-8

Available wherever books are sold or at
www.penguin.com

KATE KINGSBURY
THE MANOR HOUSE MYSTERY SERIES

In WWII England, the quiet village of Sitting Marsh is faced with food rations and fear for loved ones. But Elizabeth Hartleigh Compton, lady of the Manor House, stubbornly insists that life must go on. Sitting Marsh residents depend on Elizabeth to make sure things go smoothly. Which means everything from sorting out gossip to solving the occasional murder.

A Bicycle Built for Murder
0-425-17856-0

Death is in the Air
0-425-18094-8

For Whom Death Tolls
0-425-18386-6

Dig Deep for Murder
0-425-18886-8

Paint by Murder
0-425-19215-6

Berried Alive
0-425-19490-6

Available wherever books are sold or at
www.penguin.com

KATE BORDEN

Welcome to
COBB'S LANDING

DEATH OF A TART

The first book in the
Peggy Turner mystery series!

As mayor of Cobb's Landing, Peggy Jean Turner is
thrilled with the idea of creating "Colonial
Williamsburg" in the bankrupt town.
All goes swimmingly, until the town tart
turns up dead—and Peggy must risk everything
to solve the crime.

0-425-19489-2

Available wherever books are sold or at
www.penguin.com

PC992